ONE MYSTERIOUS C~~~~
TWO NAKED DE~~~~

THE WHEAT FIELD

GUARDS ITS SECRETS WELL....

Explosive praise for
The Wheat Field

"Irresistible . . . will deservedly make plenty of best-of-year lists."   —*The Dallas Morning News*

"A compelling read about a turning point in American history."   —*The Washington Post*

"Thayer hypnotizes us into a trance state with his dreamy descriptions of rushing rivers and golden wheat fields and days of innocence past. But don't be fooled by the pretty scene painting. Besides being a graceful stylist, this author is also a subtle manipulator of the facts that Pennington filters through the haze of time."   —*The New York Times*

"Gripping . . . beautifully written . . . well-drawn and altogether appealing . . . a fascinating story, well worth the time and money."   —*St. Petersburg Times*

"Taut writing. . . . *The Wheat Field* has all the elements of a first-class whodunit. And unlike some of the characters, the reader is never cheated."   —*Minneapolis Star Tribune*

"Sex—explicit and longed for—is a big part of this story [and yet] Steve Thayer writes beautifully, regardless of subject matter . . . lyrical . . . accurate protrayals of the townsfolk [and] musings on Wisconsin's crime through the centuries."   —*St. Paul Pioneer Press*

"An attractive account of detection."   —*The Boston Globe*

"Gruesome, disturbing, and erotically charged. . . . Thayer has built a tight plot that draws you in deeper and deeper. . . . Read it you should."   —*Rocky Mountain News*

continued . . .

"A haunting novel of murder and obsession. . . . As the reader cuts through layer after layer of intrigue, he finds it increasingly difficult to put the book down. The ending is a surprise—but then again, almost every page in this book is a surprise. . . . This is one book that you probably ought not to miss."
—*Wisconsin State Journal*

"What really sets this novel apart from other crime stories is the voice of Pennington. He tells us from the start that he has secrets, but as his tale unfolds we suspect that they might be darker than he admits and that as a narrator he might not be entirely reliable. Thayer creates a palpable sense of time and place." —*The Arizona Republic*

"Almost epic. . . . This is a tale of flawed human beings caught in the frail web of life." —*Tulsa World*

"Thayer is a skillful storyteller. He deftly switches the action between time periods and events, and the suspenseful plot is steeped in secrets and sizzling sex. The tension will keep you on your toes until the climactic end. In *The Wheat Field*—a tale filled with treachery and lechery—our protagonist ponders the question: Can you watch people act badly and yet remain good yourself? Steve Thayer has the compelling answer." —*BookPage*

"The characters and the setting come alive and the suspense is chilling."
—*The Stuart News/Port St. Lucie News* (Stuart, FL)

"Darkly gothic. . . . Thayer's narrator—Pennington—is an original." —*Fort Worth Star-Telegram*

"Such a well-crafted example of storytelling that I couldn't put it down . . . *The Wheat Field* is a story of obsession. . . . It portrays a shrewd picture of voyeurism and penetrates the facade of small-town America, where power lust and politics will unravel secrets that would make Washington, D.C., proud. . . . Steve Thayer is undoubtedly here to stay among today's class of intrigue writers. In addition to weaving a wickedly delicious narrative, he adheres to the most important rule in mystery writing: he never gives away the ending. As a book reviewer, there are few things more refreshing than the unexpected. [I was] caught utterly off guard."
—*The News Enterprise* (Hardin County, KY)

"[An] exciting work that stars a flawed and brooding hero who captures the attention of the audience from the very first page. The historical police procedural is cleverly designed to bring out the era yet provide an exciting who-done-it investigation."
—BookBrowser

"Thayer has a knack for building tension and defining place, and his small-town sinners are all too believable . . . [a] spectacular ending."
—*Publishers Weekly*

"Tingle-inducing. . . . Thayer masterfully blends atmosphere (his description of the Wisconsin Dells before tourism is wonderful), a plot full of shocks, and deeply realized characterization. A full-throttle suspense tale."
—*Booklist*

"I don't know that I've ever been as truly surprised by an ending."
—*Deadly Pleasures*

THE
WHEAT
FIELD

STEVE THAYER

AN ONYX BOOK

ONYX
Published by New American Library, a division of
Penguin Putnam Inc., 375 Hudson Street,
New York, New York 10014, U.S.A.
Penguin Books Ltd, 80 Strand,
London WC2R 0RL, England
Penguin Books Australia Ltd, 250 Camberwell Road,
Camberwell, Victoria 3124, Australia
Penguin Books Canada Ltd, 10 Alcorn Avenue,
Toronto, Ontario, Canada M4V 3B2
Penguin Books (N.Z.) Ltd, Cnr Rosedale and Airborne Roads,
Albany, Auckland 1310, New Zealand

Penguin Books Ltd, Registered Offices:
Harmondsworth, Middlesex, England

Published by Onyx, an imprint of New American Library, a division of Penguin
Putnam Inc. This is an authorized reprint of a hardcover edition published by
G. P. Putnam's Sons. For information address G. P. Putnam's Sons, a division
of Penguin Putnam Inc., 375 Hudson, New York, NY 10014.

First Onyx Printing, March 2003
10 9 8 7 6 5 4 3 2 1

REGISTERED TRADEMARK—MARCA REGISTRADA

Printed in the United States of America

PUBLISHER'S NOTE
This is a work of fiction. Names, characters, places, and incidents either are
the product of the author's imagination or are used fictitiously, and any
resemblance to actual persons, living or dead, business establishments,
events, or locales is entirely coincidental.

BOOKS ARE AVAILABLE AT QUANTITY DISCOUNTS WHEN USED TO PROMOTE PRODUCTS
OR SERVICES. FOR INFORMATION PLEASE WRITE TO PREMIUM MARKETING DIVISION,
PENGUIN PUTNAM INC., 375 HUDSON STREET, NEW YORK, NEW YORK 10014.

FOR MAGGIE

PROLOGUE

MAGGIE

SHE WAS A witch. She was a whore. I thought that when she was dead, that when her cursed smile was literally removed from the face of the earth, that would be the end of her. But I was wrong. All those years I spent in love with a woman who wasn't in love with me. Now I am an old man in love with a ghost.

It was several years ago that I retired. Turned in my badge. Holstered my service revolver for the last time, and collected my pension. I sold my home down in Kickapoo Falls and sailed out to this north woods cabin on a remote island off an enchanting peninsula. Still in my beloved Wisconsin, but a world away from the roads and the highways on which I had spent my career. Now I sit here on the water's edge of a

Great Lake and I write about the chapters of my life. And the chapter that haunts me the most is that obsessive chapter I simply call Maggie.

She was a woman of Algonquian beauty. Dark hair. Dark skin. Dark spirit. More than once, I confess, during my long and storied career, I shouldered what Maggie called my magic rifle, and took the law into my own hands. If there is a God, and as I grow old I suspect there is, I will have to answer for the men that I have killed. And, more important, for the woman that I killed. Perhaps, if I'm lucky, writing of Maggie's death will make living with myself these final years just a little bit easier.

So let the story begin. The year was 1960. The year of the wheat field murders.

Kick-a-poo. **1.** A member of a tribe of Algonquian-speaking Indians formerly of northern Illinois and southern Wisconsin. **2.** The language of the Kickapoos. **Translation:** *Kiwegapawa*, "He who stands about."

— *The American Heritage Dictionary, New College Edition*

THE WHEAT FIELD

CHAPTER 1

DEATH IN A WHEAT FIELD

THE DELLS WERE beautiful back then. In the years after the war. Before they turned the valley into a playground. Threw it wide open to tourists. And other monsters.

I found Maggie Butler in a field of wheat. Her face was gone. A shotgun blast. Her husband of sixteen years was dead next to her. His groin was missing. Same shotgun.

A farmer named Gutterman led me to the scene.

"I was coming across the field in the combine," he told me, "when I saw the crows, and then this big open circle . . . strangest thing I've ever seen. So I climbed down to investigate. First I saw all this blood, and I thought . . .

poachers . . . that they had skinned some deer.
But then I saw that they were human bodies.''

It was a strange and horrifying sight, all right.
The sun was just up. Soft yellow in a clear August sky. Laid out before me in golden shadows,
completely naked and covered with blood, was
one of the most prominent couples in the
county.

Karl Gutterman's farm sat off Old County
Road C, south out of Kickapoo Falls. About half-
way to Devil's Lake. A mile from the farmhouse,
I left a dirt road and walked through virgin
wheat up to my waist. Acres of endless gold.
Then right in the middle of the field, in the mid-
dle of nowhere, I came to an open ring, as if the
wheat had been steamrolled into a perfect circle.
Almost like a stage in some theater in the round.
A pagan worship circle.

The ashen farmer pointed to the bodies. He
was stuttering. ''That's Michael Butler . . . and
that . . . that must be Maggie.''

Yes, it was Maggie Butler. Even in unspeakable death, her body was beautiful. She was on
her back. Naked to the sun. Her long legs were
summer tan and crossed at the knees, as if to
protect her dignity to the very end. Her breasts
were bigger than I'd always imagined. Maybe it
is sick to think sex thoughts like that at a murder scene, but I had those thoughts and more
that day. Below the neck, she remained angelic.

Almost peaceful. The shotgun that had probably killed her was next to her outstretched arm.

"You went to school with them, didn't you?"

"Yes," I muttered, surveying the scene.

"Wasn't that right before the war?"

Nearly twenty years had passed. But Maggie and Michael wouldn't make the reunion. I remember looking away. Staring up at the sky. God, what a beautiful day it was. A summer blue sky. Only a slight breeze was blowing. Not a cloud in sight. It was dog-day hot, but not unbearable. Sweat stuck to my armpits. Sweat ringed my Stetson. I could feel tears forming in my eyes. I took a deep breath. Regained my composure. Then I crouched down in that deathbed of wheat, hat in hand.

At first glance, it appeared a murder-suicide. Maggie had blown her husband's balls off. Then she turned the gun on herself. Blew her brains out. But a closer examination suggested we had a double homicide on our hands.

Michael Butler's bloody body was in a far different repose from that of his wife. He died scared. Where Maggie's beautiful face was gone, Michael's face was frozen in terror. His eyes were still open. Flies swarmed about his mouth and nostrils. He hadn't died fast, like Maggie. Most likely his wounds had sent him into shock. Then he slowly bled to death through the openings where his organs should have been.

"Deputy Pennington?"

"What is it?"

Gutterman pointed to a white stub atop the crushed wheat, a few yards from the bodies, but equal distance to them both. It was a cigarette butt. A Lucky Strike. Somebody had smoked and watched. There were also holes pressed into the wheat. Three holes. Perfect little circles that might have been made by a cane, or maybe somebody leaning on the barrel of a gun.

Gutterman shuffled around the circle of death like a chicken. There were two bloody bodies on his property. He was looking for answers. I was searching for clues. Gutterman was a fifty-five-year-old farmer with six kids. He'd probably never been out of Wisconsin. In his wheat field that day, he seemed stupefied. Flustered. I guess I should have felt sorry for the dumb bastard, but I remember his agitated presence was pissing me off. I wanted to be alone with Maggie. "Where are their clothes?" he demanded to know. "And their shoes?"

"The killer took them."

"But why . . . I mean, who would do something like this?"

"Well, in a homicide case, we always start with the nearest and dearest. That's usually the spouse. Maybe Maggie did this, but I don't think so. Next on our list of suspects is the person who discovered the bodies. That would be you, Mr. Gutterman."

He stared at me in disbelief. "I don't think that's funny, Mr. Pennington."

"That's because I'm not joking."

There aren't many men in Kickapoo County that I tower over, but I towered over farmer Gutterman. He hadn't served in the war: He was married with children. He was too old. He was needed on the farm. Excuse, excuse, excuse. I looked down at him. No, I didn't believe for a second that Gutterman, a simple farmer, was a murderer. But I couldn't help be curious about the secret showcase in the middle of his wheat field. So I threw the fear of God into the little son of a bitch. Or at least, the fear of the county sheriff. "One way or another, you're going to have to explain to Sheriff Fats how this circle got on your property."

"Deputy, you've got no business accusing me of sordid things. I'm a hardworking, God-fearing Presbyterian. I pray to God it was some monster from Chicago did this. I hate to think it could have been one of our own."

He was wearing a pair of dirty bib overalls with a NIXON button incongruously pinned to one of the breast pockets. On the other pocket he had a SPRAGUE FOR SENATE button. I was in uniform. Our summer khakis. Otherwise, I'd've been wearing my KENNEDY button. The young senator from Massachusetts had given me the campaign button right after I shook his hand. Mostly, I wore it to antagonize people. There were times back then when I thought I was the only Catholic in Kickapoo County—and one of the few Democrats. The presidential election was still two months off. By today's muddy standards, it is considered a pretty civil affair. But I remember the contest of 1960 as bitter and divisive. I also remember being told to solve the wheat field murders before election day.

CHAPTER 2

SEX ALONG THE ROAD:
PART ONE

I REMEMBER THE first time it happened to me. They were tearing up the bed of a Ford pickup. Never before had I watched two people having sex.

This was years before the wheat field murders. Though a combat veteran, I was still quite young. Remember this about the war—a lot of us enlisted when we were only seventeen and eighteen years old. It sometimes seems in the movies that most soldiers spent World War II falling in and out of love. That wasn't the case. We spent four years at war and then we came home. We just didn't know that much about women. I'd venture to say that a lot of the boys killed in the war didn't live long enough to kiss a girl.

Anyway, I'd only been with the sheriff's department a short time. I remember it was warm. Probably midsummer. A lot of tourists were in town. It was dogwatch and I was cruising the River Road, north on the Upper Dells. There was a big, bright moon hanging over the cliffs. You could read a book by it. I passed a pickup truck off to the side of the road. It was parked above the river, facing the western bluffs. It seemed suspicious. The area was not a common site for necking. The kids usually stayed closer to town. I doubled back with my lights off. Rolled to a stop about fifty yards away and cut the engine. I stepped from the squad, my trusty flashlight in hand. It was one of those heavy steel five-battery suckers. In those days our flashlights doubled as nightsticks. I never felt comfortable drawing my gun, but day or night, I always felt good with that flashlight in my hand.

I kept the powerful light turned off. Just listened. Find them with your ears. Spot them with your eyes. Shoot them with your scope.

My suspicions proved dead-on. As soon as I stepped from the squad, I heard a woman screaming. I was about halfway to the truck when I realized what kind of screaming it was. That's probably why he brought her so far out. She was a screamer. In fact, it wasn't until I got close enough to see into the back of the truck that I was sure somebody was back there with her.

The moonlight threw deep shadows, and I moved into one. I could see but not be seen. One good thing about war, it does teach you how to sneak up on people in the dark. A good thing to know in combat. Or police work. And a good thing to know if you're into . . .

The laws were different back then. If we caught them necking, we'd give them a verbal warning and send them on their way. If any of her clothes were off, we'd bring her in. Call her parents. Not his parents. Just hers. And if we caught them actually fucking, we were supposed to jail them both; most of us just chose to watch.

This was a young couple. Almost too young. The truck was black. Their bodies were white. They both had long, athletic legs. I couldn't see their faces, but I pictured her as dark-haired and pretty, while he remained anonymous. What struck me the most was the needy way she clung to him. Naked. Uninhibited. Almost desperate. She had her legs wrapped around his waist, with her arms around his neck. She was pulling him into her. No, she was forcing him into her. At first I wondered if it was possible that he was really inside of her. Remember, I'd never seen such a thing. Then I watched as he extended his arms, like a pushup, so that he could stare between their legs and watch himself penetrating her. When he did this, she arched her back and I could see the nipples on her breasts. Beautifully rounded breasts, with thick, dark nipples.

The three of us were in the middle of the woods in the middle of the night. Still, I kept glancing over my shoulder, afraid someone would see me seeing them. It wasn't what I saw that night that I remember as much as what I was feeling. I was the little altar boy committing the big sin. But is it a sin to watch? Or is it just a sin to enjoy watching? Hell, I felt cheated. Like I'd missed the beginning of a great movie. I wanted them to start over. I wanted to see him strip her. To drop her bra. To slip his hands beneath her ass and pull her panties off those long, gorgeous legs. I wanted to see the expression on her face when he first entered her.

Her screams were reaching the point of ecstasy. I closed my eyes, because the sounds were more erotic than the sights. I sat on the ground. Imagined myself deep inside of her. Her tongue, deep inside my mouth. I was sweating. I brought my knees up to my chest. Wrapped my arms around my legs. Then I bowed my head and listened to the illicit lovemaking of this beautiful pair of strangers. I remember it as one of the most erotic nights of my life, and they didn't even know I was there.

In the moonlight that summer night so many years ago, even my most jealous and murderous thoughts seemed sexual. Oh, how easily I could have killed that seductive young couple. Penetrated them with bullets. Walked up behind them with a spare revolver and executed them for fornicating in the back of a truck. In my county. On my shift. Two shots for him, right in the back. Then, as she scrambled to escape the dead lover on top of her, I'd shine my flashlight on her. Bang. Bang. One to her heart and one to her face. Some early morning farmer would find their bodies. Then I, their judge, their jury, and their executioner, would be the first police officer on the scene. Raising me above suspicion.

Yes sirree, I had those sick thoughts and more as I sat crumpled on the ground that night. Never will I forget how my first act of sex left me feeling like an abandoned child, even though my participation in that act was secretive and from a distance.

The young woman let out one last scream that I was sure could be heard throughout the valley. Years later, pornographers would refer to this as the cumshot. Then they were through. I pictured them lying together in the bed of the truck, their

arms and legs intertwined. There were sounds
of human whispers, of night owls and crickets,
and of small creatures moving mysteriously
through the woods. All of this beneath a full
summer moon above the Wisconsin River.

I watched them dress. Got a good look at their
faces. She was as pretty as I had imagined. And
just as young. I made a note of the spot. And
the truck. In fact, I took down the license plate
number. Our three paths would cross again. I
watched them drive away.

CHAPTER 3

CLUES
IN A WHEAT FIELD

LOOKING BACK, I find it hard to believe I almost lost my life that year—that for all of the combat I saw in Europe, it was the people of Kickapoo Falls who almost did me in. Standing in the wheat field that sunny morning, I would not have believed that the law would turn on me. That the town would turn on me. That I would throw a senate election into turmoil. That my soul would be ripped from my chest. And that in the end, I would sail back to the land of my ancestors, where I would, upon my return, cut out the heart of the only thing that I ever loved.

Maggie always wore two rings. Her wedding ring on her left hand. Her class ring on her right hand. KICKAPOO FALLS HIGH 1942. When she married in '44, her wedding ring was the talk of the town. Michael had forked out a thousand dollars for the gem at Marshall Field's in Chicago. Sixteen years later, I was numb as I stood staring down at that ring, subtly reflecting the sun and the wheat. Yes, the wedding ring was still on her finger, but the class ring was like her face. Missing. Why would someone leave behind a precious diamond and steal what was, essentially, a worthless stone?

Possibility number 1: Maggie hadn't been wearing the class ring when murdered.

Possibility number 2: Our killer didn't appreciate the difference between a valuable diamond and a worthless stone. Some kind of simpleton? A child? A drunk?

Possibility number 3: The class ring had sentimental value.

All morning long I watched as people moved slowly through the hard red spring wheat, then emerged into the circle, like ghosts coming through a wall. Stepping into the mysterious orb, their summer-tanned faces faded instantly to ash white. Their mouths dropped open, but no sound poured fourth. Two more deputies arrived that way, Bergstrom and Hess. Then a state trooper, Russ Hoffmeyer. We closed Old County C, north and south. It's a back road, and I asked deputies to record the plate numbers of any approaching vehicles. Killers like to watch. They have a nasty habit of returning to the scene. Enjoying the hell they've wrought.

In about an hour, Sheriff Fats made his way through the standing wheat, a movie camera strapped over his shoulder like a weapon. He was a father figure to me. The wise old mentor who was grooming me to take over his job. I don't recall his surname. It was one of those long Polish names, or maybe Fats was Czech. Doesn't matter. For as long as he was Sheriff of Kickapoo County, and that was a long, long time, he was called "Fats." A legend among Wisconsin cops. Another God-fearing Presbyterian. A church deacon. A man who believed in the Bible and the rifle, which may be why he took me under his wing. I was good with a rifle.

"I swear," he whispered, taking in the scene, "this once-great country of ours is going straight to hell in a handbasket."

He was actually more big than fat. A soft-spoken man. The kind of cop who thought it advantageous to hide his intellect, as well as his dark side. He was near retirement. Claimed this was his last election. He was running unopposed. Again. Before the murders, I was rumored to be the candidate to replace him. Even then I thought I'd make a good sheriff.

In 1960, I was an unmarried man still south of forty. I liked Patsy Cline records and Gene

Tierney movies. After the war, I'd gone down
to the university in Madison for a year on the
G.I. Bill, but I wasn't cut out for college. If I
have the time to think, I'm the smartest man I
know. But college is a different kind of smart. I
wouldn't have made a good officer, for instance.
In combat, life and death decisions have to be
made in a split second. But investigative work
is different. I have the time to reason away what
other fools believe. Which may be why the
wheat field murders haunt me so.

"Have you ever seen anything like this,
Deputy?"

"No," I told him, "not even in the war."

"And you were the first one here?"

"Yes. Karl Gutterman led me in."

Fats glanced up at the forlorn farmer on the
edge of the circle. "Is he clean?"

"He looks clean."

"Any clues?"

"Some little round holes indented in the
wheat . . . might be from a gun barrel. And a
cigarette butt. A Lucky Strike."

"You used to smoke Luckys, didn't you?"

After Madison, I spent a year at a seminary
school in St. Paul. But I didn't have the courage
it takes to be a priest. So I came home. Applied
to the sheriff's department. I was a veteran, and
Sheriff Fats, himself a veteran of the First World
War, always made room for our kind.

There was one other person in the wheat field that sunny morning. He arrived with Fats, as usual. Detective Dickerson. Or "Dickhead," for short. We deputies never quite understood the hiring of Dickerson. Fats had wanted a full-time detective, so he hired this little Dickhead all the way from Texas. Found him through friends at the Gunn Club. Dickerson was a mousy little man with a sharp intellect who tried hard to be the perfect cop. Too hard. He crossed all the *t*'s and he dotted all his *i*'s, but it still wasn't enough. Police work is people work. I was never the most sociable person in the world, but about town I was well liked. Dickerson never was. Fats gave him a desk and called him Detective, but mostly he ran errands. The real investigations were given to me.

"Looks like another black eye for Wisconsin." That remark came from Dickerson. He was in his usual costume. A shiny black suit, with a cheap white shirt and a narrow black tie. Black-rimmed eyeglasses. "Unless, of course," he added, softening the blow, "this is the work of someone who was just passing through."

"No, this took some planning," I told him, stating the obvious. "I think we're looking for locals."

Fats winced when I said that. "Well, we've got two locals lying right in front of us here, Deputy. So let's not rule out a murder, and then a suicide . . . not just yet." The first time the old sheriff suggested the murder-suicide scenario, I wrote it off as foolish pride. Fats was proud of Kickapoo County. He was proud of the people who made it their home. Now he leaned into my ear, almost so that Dickerson could not hear the bit of advice he had for me. "When you're sheriff, you'll want to close a case like this fast. Don't let it linger."

"It appears to me there's some kind of sexual element here." That, too, came from Dickerson, and I didn't know whether to laugh or to shoot the bastard.

It was hard to put a finger on my hostility for Dickerson. I hated him from the start. It wasn't just the fact that he'd come up from Texas, or that he was trying to play detective. Simply out of his element. It was more than all that. I sensed something inherently evil in Dickerson. Not really a mouse among men. More like a rat.

"There's a lot more going on here than sex, Detective."

"What do you mean?" Dickerson asked.

"Maggie's body," I told him. "After she was shot, somebody crossed her legs."

"Why would a killer do such a thing?"

"Because he loved her."

One last thing about that morning in the wheat field. Cameras. There were two of them. Dickerson carried in an old Brownie for shooting stills, but Fats had a movie camera. In fact, Fats drew his movie camera faster than most cops draw their guns. Several people around town had movie cameras that shot silent 8-millimeter film, but the big, bulky camera Fats owned was 16 millimeter, capable of recording sound. If I remember right, his children had given it to him for his sixtieth birthday. A 16-millimeter movie camera was expensive, as was the film and the projector needed to show the film. He was supposed to film his family, his grandchildren mostly, but Fats took to filming everything. It got so bad that when he used the word "shoot" or "shooting," we couldn't tell if he was talking about his gun or his camera. We started calling him Sheriff DeMille. He got a big kick out of that. But now he was filming a murder scene, and I didn't like it.

"Is that necessary?" I asked him. "Stills would be better."

"Oh, we'll have our stills, Deputy, but this here is the future. Someday all murder scenes will be filmed."

By the time Michael and Maggie Butler got around to having their pictures taken, the summer day was heating up. Honeybees now swarmed about Michael's mouth and nostrils, searching for the eggs that blowflies like to lay in the body's dark cavities. A murder of crows appeared overhead. Then, one by one, the cops who showed up in the wheat field that morning began to vanish. Slipped back into the golden stalks, shaking their heads in disbelief. Finally, I was left alone with the remains, waiting for the coroner to arrive from Madison. The beautiful face that had haunted me for so many years was gone now. Blown away in an instant. Her long, black hair was a river of blood. I had come home from the war and waited for Maggie Butler to have babies and grow old. While at the same time, I stayed young. Slim and trim in my tailored uniform. Gun on my hip. Badge on my chest. But Maggie never had children. And she never grew old. Not in my eyes. I wanted to kill her. Isn't that funny? For years I'd dreamed of seeing Maggie Butler naked. Now I had.

CHAPTER 4

MURDER
IN THE VALLEY

WISCONSIN IS AN Indian word. It means land of dark rushing waters. For some inexplicable reason, Wisconsin murder makes great headlines. Land of the bizarre.

Fats kept a lid on the newspapers by implying it was a murder-suicide. He made no mention of the unearthly circle in the middle of the wheat field. That didn't stop rumors from spreading through the valley like a plague of locusts—wild rumors about everything from satanic sacrifices to witchcraft to flying saucers. The summer of 1960 brought us reports of zigzagging orange globes, roaring black cones, silent silvery disks, and disembodied humming noises that knocked birds right out of the sky.

It was also the summer farmers began reporting animal mutilations. A cow, a lamb, or maybe an old horse would be found dead in a field with its entrails missing. Seemed every aggrieved farmer in Kickapoo County was convinced that somehow their mysterious loss was tied to the wheat field mystery. The sheriff covered his ass by reminding everybody the investigation was still wide open.

"Should have a final report in just a couple weeks, boys."

That was his standard line. The local *Republic* printed whatever Fats told them, usually without question. It was the Chicago papers he was worried about, and Milwaukee, and St. Paul. The last thing anybody wanted was big-city reporters snooping around Kickapoo Falls for all the wrong reasons. I thought back to some of the words that were muttered in the wheat field that morning.

"I pray to God it was some monster from Chicago did this. I hate to think it could have been one of our own."

Only three years earlier, a diminutive farmer named Ed Gein was arrested for grave robbing up in Plainfield, just north of the valley. Police conducting a search of his cobweb-filled farmhouse found human heads preserved in plastic bags. There were lampshades and chairs made out of human skin. The headless body of a missing woman was found hanging in the summer kitchen, eviscerated like a deer. Body parts were found preserved in jars in the kitchen cupboards, pickled for eating. The cannibalistic monster was found incompetent to stand trial. So they locked him up in a nut house and threw away the key. For years afterward, Ed Gein stories and Ed Gein jokes were endless, and beyond tasteless.

"Looks like another black eye for Wisconsin."

On a hillside at the Spring Green bend in the Wisconsin River sits Taliesin—Frank Lloyd Wright's architectural masterpiece. It was in August of 1914 that Wright's mistress and her two small children sat down to lunch with a work crew at the magnificent home on the hill. Wright was in Chicago. They were served their lunch by a white-coated servant from Barbados, who had only been at the house for a few weeks. Once everybody was eating, this servant excused himself. He bolted the doors and windows. Then he poured gasoline on the rugs. Now, with Taliesin in flames, he roamed the house with a hatchet, burying it in one skull after another. Of the nine people who sat down to lunch that warm summer day, seven died of head wounds and burns, including the two children. Like Ed Gein, the hatchet murderer in Spring Green never stood trial. He starved himself to death in the county jail.

In 1934, John Dillinger shot it out with the FBI at the Little Bohemia Lodge up in Rhinelander, Wisconsin, leaving two people dead. Dillinger escaped.

That same year, Baby Face Nelson went on a shooting spree down where the Fox River crosses the Wisconsin border into northern Illinois—leaving two FBI agents dead. Next day, Nelson's naked and bullet-riddled body was found in a ditch alongside the road.

Even Al Capone kept a summer lodge in Wisconsin.

In fact, if you want to go way back, in 1901, congressional investigators traced the wanderings of an anarchist named Leon Czolgosz to a homestead in Kickapoo County. But he failed the land, as they say here, and he moved to Buffalo, New York—where a year later he assassinated William McKinley, twenty-fifth president of the United States.

That's the thing about Wisconsin. There is no escaping the irony. I don't know much about California, or Cape Cod, or the coast of Maine, but I do know that summer through autumn, it would be difficult to find a more beautiful place in America than southern Wisconsin—from the Kickapoo River just east of the Mississippi to the popular Dells on the Wisconsin River. It's river bluff country. It's dairy farm country. Corn and alfalfa country. And wheat. The soil is rich and dark. If there's more fertile farmland in America, I can't imagine where it would be. With some luck, our location in the Midwest grew to be damn near ideal. By car, Chicago and Milwaukee were only two hours to the east. St. Paul and Minneapolis, three hours to the west. The University of Wisconsin was just down the road in Madison. And yes, we had a good county hospital, but the Mayo Clinic was only a stone's throw away.

According to the 1960 census, there were 4 million people living in the state of Wisconsin. But only 52,000 of them lived in Kickapoo County. And only 10,000 of those lived in Kickapoo Falls. A lot of folks in the county came from strong German stock. They were followed closely by families with Scandinavian heritage. Followed by British stock, mostly Welsh and Scots. Politicians counted ten Catholic counties in Wisconsin. Kickapoo County was not one of them. As part of the Second Congressional District, the county was heavily Protestant, and had gone handily to Hubert Humphrey over John Kennedy in the April primary.

So yes, it was a rural county, but in the summertime when the tourists arrived, it was a real zoo. Besides the natural attraction of the Dells, we had a lot of bars in town. Plus, there were a couple of strip joints out on Highway 33—that nowhere land that conveniently fell between the small towns and their ordinances. We had drunken drivers, intoxicated boaters, traffic jams on county roads, dogfights, prostitute brawls, and the ubiquitous domestic disputes, usually involving beer. Throw in soaring heat, dive-bombing mosquitoes, black flies, and black bears, and I spent many a summer night swinging my flashlight in self-defense. And all of that was before the Sixties—when drugs, runaways, and groups of naked hippies fornicating in the woods added to our problems. Not to mention—murder.

They did the autopsies down in Madison. I swallowed hard and read the report. Michael Butler's semen was found inside Maggie's vagina. Strands of her pubic hair were found in his pubic hair. They'd had sexual intercourse minutes before they were killed. There were no signs of a struggle. There was no blood or semen but their own.

The time of death was odd. According to the autopsy reports, they were killed the evening before Karl Gutterman discovered their bodies. But the coroner put the time of death between 4 and 9 P.M. Sunset was still past 8:30. If the coroner was right, and I had no reason to doubt him, they were murdered in broad daylight. Sunset, at the latest.

Off the top of my head, I came up with five

scenarios I could present to Fats. I scribbled them in my notebook:

Scenario number 1: Murder-suicide. Maggie fucks Michael one last time. Blows his balls off. Kills herself.

Scenario number 2: Michael rapes Maggie. She blows his balls off. Kills herself. (Again, no sign of a struggle.)

Scenario number 3: Someone comes across them having sex in the field. Shoots them both.

Scenario number 4: Someone followed them into the field. Watched them having sex. Shot them when they were done.

Scenario number 5: Someone forced them into the field. Forced them into sex. Watched them. Shot them.

Maggie's fingerprints were found on the shotgun. But so what? It was Michael's shotgun. She could have handled it in their home a hundred times.

The coroner found traces of gunpowder on Maggie's right hand, implying she'd fired the gun. But that would have been easy enough to stage. Way out there, the killer could have made all the noise in the world.

They had owned their own business. Butler Travel. It was on Main Street. Directly across from Pennington Shoes. They booked vacation trips, but most of their business came from luring people to the Wisconsin Dells—families, tour groups, and such. Then Michael and Maggie saw to it they stayed at hotels and motels in Kickapoo Falls, that they spent their tourist dollars at Kickapoo Falls shops and restaurants. Was it any wonder they were so popular around town? Those postwar years are remembered today as prosperous times, and some people in the valley did have money. Lots of it. But I remember a lot of struggling farmers and hurting businesses. The bad times came and went, and then came back again. That's why the prospect of thousands and thousands of tourists every summer looked so inviting to so many. And so what if we had to sell our souls.

CHAPTER 5

THREE IN A BED

WE BURIED MAGGIE Butler alongside the husband she may or may not have shot in the balls. It was the longest funeral procession ever seen in Kickapoo Falls. They had lived their whole lives in our small town, but due to the unnatural circumstances surrounding their deaths, nobody was really sure, despite the pretty eulogies, what kind of people we were laying to rest.

That evening, I met state trooper Russ Hoffmeyer on the summit of the loftiest crag in the Dells, High Rock, overlooking the Wisconsin River. Across the water, the setting sun was slipping slowly beneath the outcroppings of natural limestone on the crests of another crag. Romance Cliff. The rocky woods around us hummed with cicadas. White birches and whispering pines swayed in warm breezes that swept down the river. It was one of those gorgeous spots on the Upper Dells accessible only by a back trail, which was known only to us locals.

The Dells is a beautiful and mysterious fifteen-mile stretch of the Wisconsin River. The enchanting cliffs and shadowed canyons were carved from sandstone by a melting glacier. In fact, geologists believe the rush of water was so great that the entire stretch was probably formed in thirty days. Legends abound among its rocky crags and swirling eddies. Fascinating stories of warring Indian factions. Hunters and trappers. Soldiers and settlers. Rivermen and lumber men. Shamans and swindlers. And crimes of an unspeakable nature.

We were both off duty. Out of uniform. I asked him for a cigarette. I took up smoking during the war. I quit when the first reports linked cigarettes to cancer. But I still bummed one every now and then. He handed me a Lucky, then flipped open his lighter. I stuck the cigarette in my mouth and bent my face toward the flame. We sat on a boulder that topped the cliff that topped the river. Hoffmeyer pried open two Leinenkugel's from a six-pack. It was the one thing we did exceptionally well in Wisconsin. We made beer. And we drank it. Schlitz, Miller, and Pabst were bottled in Milwaukee. Old Style was brewed over in La Crosse. And the Leinies in our hands came out of Chippewa Falls.

Up the bluff, the car door was left open. The radio was playing. Country-western, mostly.

The state trooper and I literally crossed paths on Kickapoo County highways. Once in a while, after a shift, I'd join him for a beer. But it had been a while, because I never particularly liked him. He'd been in the Marine Corps during the war. Saw action at places like Tarawa and Bougainville. Everybody said he was a war hero, whatever the hell that means. Anyway, he brought a lot of his Marine Corps mentality home with him. You could see it in his police work. Even a minor traffic violation was enough to get him flexing his muscles, and Russ had a lot of muscles to flex. He also kept the military crew cut, and the swagger. He was what you would call a "strapping fellow," with thick, hairy arms, and a wide, hairy chest. In the story as a whole, Russ Hoffmeyer turned out to be nothing more than a pawn. But that evening, over a can of beer, he opened my eyes and ears to a world to which I had long been blind, deaf, and dumb.

There had been rumors. Hell, even in high school there were rumors. I covered my altar boy ears to most of them. You have to understand, sex wasn't out in the open back then. It was in the bedroom where it belonged. Or so I believed. By 1960, things were changing. Everybody was promising us a new era. "A New Frontier," Kennedy called it. Senate candidate Webster Sprague hailed it, "A New Beginning for Wisconsin." A new era in politics. A new era in law enforcement. A new era where people sat around and watched other people. . . .

At the time of the wheat field murders, Hoffmeyer was going through a nasty divorce. The smallest things pissed him off. The big issues drove him crazy. I had to listen to the ex-Marine rant for a half hour about the upcoming election. I didn't even have to open my mouth, and people in town knew who I was voting for.

"What do you make of this Detective Dickerson that Fats hired?" he asked me, finally settling down and getting back to cop talk.

"I think he's dangerous."

"Dangerous? He looks kind of stupid to me."

"No, I suspect he's playing stupid . . . and that's what makes him dangerous."

"Do you still have that cabin in Door County?"

"Yes," I told him. "Someday I hope to retire there."

"How the roads up that way?"

"I'm out on the island. I sail, not drive."

"There's some great hunting up there."

"I don't hunt."

"Everybody in Wisconsin hunts."

"I don't hunt."

"War get to you?"

"What is it you wanted to talk about, Russ?"

He glanced over his shoulder, into the woods, as if we were being watched. "This is all off the record, of course."

"It is?"

"You have to understand, this doesn't look good for me . . . because I was in the wheat field that morning . . . looking at their bodies."

"So was I . . . so what?"

"Yes, but you see, I kind of had a relationship with Maggie and Michael. Something sexual . . . do you know what I mean?"

"No, I don't know what you mean. Could you be more specific?"

"You want specifics, Deputy? I'll give you specifics."

He lowered his voice a notch but upped the intensity. In fact, he spoke with an almost child-like excitement. "I'd known Maggie and Michael for years," he told me. "Christ, Maggie booked my honeymoon. I used to flirt with her. We all did . . . I mean, it was Maggie. It was innocent enough. So it starts at the Gunn Club last February . . . the Valentine's dance. I was there by myself. Everybody knew Annie and I were separated. Maggie was with Michael. I was sitting with them. Maggie and I danced once. It was no big deal . . . everybody was having fun.

Anyway, it was getting late. I was putting on my coat, getting ready to leave. Michael comes up to me, all buddylike, wants me to come over to their house for a drink. I told him it was late. It wasn't a good idea. I was being polite, but I meant it . . . it was getting late. Then he leaned into me, like he's sharing some big secret, and says, 'Maggie would really like you to come over. We've been going through a rough patch ourselves. It would mean a lot to her.' I glance over at Maggie, and sure enough, she's got that puppy-dog look on her face. So I drove over to their house for a drink. I figured, what's the harm? When I got there, Maggie was in the bathroom. Michael fixed me a drink, and he was showing me around the house. You've seen the place, it's a nondescript rambler, except that it has this huge master bedroom. And in it, they had this giant king-size bed. I mean, it was all mattress. There were no posts, or fancy foot-boards, or anything to obstruct your view . . . do you know what I mean?"

"I'm getting the picture . . . go on."

"Michael invites me into the bedroom and asks me to have a seat. There was this little couchlike thing at the foot of the bed. So I sat down there while Michael propped himself up in the bed . . . you know . . . feet crossed, hands behind his head . . . king of the castle, master of his domain, that kind of thing. It wasn't bright lights, but there was a lamp on, and we were talking small talk, about golf, about the Gunn Club . . . he wanted me to join. I think your name came up once or twice. Finally, he says, 'Maggie will be out in a minute.' I'm wondering, what the hell does that mean? We're having drinks in their bedroom at one in the morning, and Maggie will be out in a minute. I've never been in this situation before. Sure enough, ten minutes later, Maggie walks into the bedroom and crawls onto the bed. All she's wearing, that I could see, was one of those white terry-cloth robes. I mean, snow white. Brand new. But it was a short robe, up over her knees . . . and you remember what great legs she had . . . they must have been five feet long. So, she scoots over close to Michael, but they're not touching. She tucks those long legs under her, so she's kind of sitting sideways to me. Okay, two things here. Number one . . . Maggie is not talking. Not a word. She just sits there, her hair down and loose, beautiful as hell, listening to our small talk. And we're not talking to her. She's not included in the conversation. It's weird. Number two . . . the way she's sitting sideways to me, her robe is open enough so that I can see her bare tit. I mean, this big, beautiful tit is just hanging there, and she knows I can see it. So, I'm talking golf and guns to her husband while looking at her tit. Well, after a few minutes Michael and I start talking about Maggie . . . I mean, like she's still not there. You know, how pretty she is, how smart she is . . . and all this time, she's totally silent. Once in a while she gets this Mona Lisa smile on her face, but that's all. . . .

" . . . So then, Michael starts to get more specific. He starts talking about her great legs. And I tell him, yeah, I love her legs. Best legs in town. Michael goes on about her legs. Puts his hand on her legs to emphasize his point. Now this is the first time he's touched her. Then he says, 'Russ, come on over here and feel these.' Well, hell, what was I supposed to do? So, I go over and sit on the bed. Maggie stretches out on her back and extends her legs. And I mean, they were gorgeous . . . waxed and shined. So, I'm rubbing her legs, up over her knees, then up under her robe. Maggie seems to be enjoying it. And Michael . . . he's just watching, his arms folded. And then it begins . . . do you know what I mean?"

"No, I don't. Tell me."

"Michael and I begin this game of 'Captain, May I?' I asked him, 'Can I open her robe?' "

"He says, 'Sure, open her robe.' So I untie the little belt, and push apart her robe, real slow like. I mean, it's Maggie. I'm being gentle. Pennington, you wouldn't believe how beautiful that woman was. It was like staring at an angel.

She had on these white nylon panties, but other than that, it was all Maggie. You have no idea what those clothes have been hiding all these years. I asked Michael, 'Can I feel her tits?' 'Sure,' he says, 'feel her tits.' So I'm massaging her tits, and she's got these big, hard nipples. And I'm rubbing her legs, and she's moaning slightly with her eyes closed. 'Can I take off her panties?' 'Sure,' he says, 'take off her panties.' So I slide her panties off. 'Can I lick her pussy?' 'Sure,' he says, 'lick her pussy.' You know, in a way, I almost felt like some kind of circus animal performing for them, except that it was all so *fucking* erotic. I said, 'Can I show her my cock?' And Michael says, 'Maggie, the man wants to show you his cock . . . and you like cocks, don't you, baby.' Now, this is where Michael really took control. I'm on my knees with my cock out, hard as a rock, and Michael says to Maggie, 'Suck it, baby.' Then he pushes her head into my cock, and he holds it there while she's sucking. That was the only part I didn't like. Finally, I said, 'Can I fuck her?' 'Yeah,' he says, 'fuck her hard.' So I did. And it was insanely intense. And Michael just watched. After we were through, he took his drink into the living room and passed out on the couch. Maggie slipped back into the bathroom. I was left laying there. I mean . . . what's the proper etiquette in a situation like that? Was I supposed to get up and sneak out? Wait to say good night to Maggie? What?''

"And what did you do?''

"I got dressed and waited. Maggie walked me to the door. Cool and calm as could be. Kissed me good night. The thing of it is . . . I don't think I was their first guest.''

By the time Russ Hoffmeyer finished telling me about the threesome, the sun had disappeared below Romance Cliff. The exotic rock formations on the river bluffs were taking on the appearance of great shadows looming over the valley. A Patsy Cline song was playing on the car radio. "Walkin' After Midnight.''

"Have you told anybody else about this?'' I asked.

"Of course not. A gentleman has rules. But I think you should talk to Caren Sprague.''

"Webster's wife?''

"Yeah. I kind of had a relationship with her, too.''

"Was Webster there?''

"Don't get smart. I'm going through a divorce, okay. Anyway, she told me things.''

"What kind of things?''

"Some really freaky sex things. You should hear it from her. I was only half listening.''

"Did you ever go back . . . to Maggie's, I mean?''

"Couple of times Maggie and me drove out

of town. And once, I went over to the house while Michael was playing golf. Maggie and I fucked, but it wasn't the same. She fed off of him."

"Why didn't you go back while Michael was there?"

"He suggested it once, a few months back, but . . ."

"But what?"

"Well . . . when I was there alone with Maggie, there were cameras and things laying around the bedroom."

"What kind of cameras?"

"You know, movie cameras. Expensive ones. Camera lights. There was a rolled-up screen on the floor. On the dresser was a new film projector. I didn't like it. I mean, who keeps cameras in their bedroom?"

"Did you ask her about the cameras?"

"Maggie said they were filming campaign stuff for Webster Sprague."

"And you didn't believe her?"

"It was Maggie. I wanted to believe her."

"And to your knowledge . . . they never filmed you?"

Hoffmeyer's face went blank. Stone cold. "They'd better not've. I'd have killed them myself." He swallowed a mouthful of beer, hard, realizing what he had just said.

I had hardly touched my beer. My cigarette

was only a smoldering stub. I threw the butt on the ground and poured a little Leinenkugel's over it. Patsy Cline wrapped her walk. The sun was all but gone. The mosquitoes were out. I'd heard enough. I said good night. Got up to leave.

"Pennington? Do you think that's what happened? Maybe they filmed somebody. Then somebody came for their film?"

CHAPTER 6

BULL SEMEN

THE THING TO keep in mind about the wheat field murders is the year—1960. It's hard to explain how difficult it was to investigate a sex crime in those years after the war. Today police have Sex Crimes Divisions, Special Victims Units, Heinous Crimes Units, registered sex offenders, and DNA. We had none of that. If a woman was raped, she had to be found beaten and bloody in the middle of the goddamn street to warrant an investigation. And if it was her husband who raped and beat her—and it usually was—forget about it. Date rape? Spousal abuse? The terms didn't exist. Child molestation? Incest? We didn't investigate things like that. As long as nobody got killed, what went on in the home was private. I'm not trying to

make excuses for the mistakes that were made
in that wheat field, but today if two people were
found murdered in a rural county, they'd call in
the state police. Maybe even the FBI. Back then,
we were pretty much on our own.

The day that followed my talk with Russ Hoffmeyer was bright and sunny. Kickapoo Falls
woke early in those summer months. The square
in front of the courthouse was sprinkled with
people. I gave an Iowa family directions to the
Dells. Then I turned and talked with a friend.
Don't remember which friend. That was the
thing about Courthouse Square—it was nearly
impossible to get through the parklike grounds
without stopping to talk with a friendly face. An
old high school buddy. A fellow veteran. A
county employee. A farmer in town on business.
In Kickapoo Falls, people met and talked in the
square. On this day the talk was of Maggie and
Michael Butler. It was flattering that so many in
town turned to me for reassurance, but the truth
of the matter was, there was still little that I
could tell them.

I stared across the street at the Butler Travel
building. Then I loaded a shotgun into the trunk
of the squad, cleaned my sunglasses, and
cruised east on Water Street, in no particular
hurry. I swung past the new Kickapoo Junior
College on the edge of town. The kids called it

"Poo U"—it was like two more years of high school. I continued on, toward the river.

For as long as I can remember, one of the major employers in the valley was the Kickapoo Breeders Company. They sold bull semen. Kids called it the cow cum plant. I've never wanted to know the details, but apparently they extracted semen from prize bulls, bottled it, and sold it. I grew up a town boy. I had no idea how to extract semen from a bull.

Dad owned Pennington Shoes and Boots, which was built on Main Street by my grandfather in 1896. I grew up in the apartment above the store. Back then we sold more boots than shoes, but we were the only shoe store in town. Dad died while I was at school in Madison. I didn't want the store. Sold it to Bob and Grace Mackenzie. They kept the name. In fact, Pennington Shoes is still there on Main Street. Right on Courthouse Square. Been there a hundred years. One of the Mackenzie daughters runs it now.

Anyway, the reason I mention Kickapoo Breeders is because for years after our conversation, I thought of Russ "The Bull" Hoffmeyer every time I drove by their plant. I've never really understood men like him. At times, I couldn't tell if he was bragging or apologizing. I wanted to believe that everything he'd said .

the night before about Maggie and Michael was *bullshit*. But I knew in my heart it wasn't.

We searched the Butlers' house. There were no cameras found. No film. No screens or projectors. No class ring. Was there a film? Was Russ Hoffmeyer lying? Was he now a suspect? By his own admission, he had an illicit relationship with the victims. He was one of the first cops at the murder scene the next morning. Sounded like something I would do. First you kill them. Then you investigate their killing. He came to me with the story about the threesome because it made him look better than if I'd found out about it on my own. I also suspect that it was State Trooper Hoffmeyer who tipped off Webster Sprague.

CHAPTER 7

THE
KICKAPOO GUNN CLUB

RAILROAD BARON JAY Albany Gunn put up the lion's share of the investment money when the Milwaukee Road came barreling through Kickapoo Falls and guaranteed the town's survival. Gunn built a sprawling hunting lodge above the Dells. This lodge eventually became the Kickapoo Gunn Club. From its founding days, it was a club for the social elite, drawing wealthy patrons from as far away as St. Paul, Chicago, Milwaukee, and, it was rumored, Washington, D.C. On weekends, they hosted fox hunts and pheasant shoots. Several times a year they threw lavish parties. These parties were the only time nonmembers could be invited.

From the very beginning folks in the valley

called club members "clannish" and "secretive."
Over the years there were rumors about everything from political shenanigans to orgies to
conspiracies to commit murder. Since nobody
but members knew for sure what the hell went
on out there—and the members were fairly
tight-lipped—you could blame just about anything you wanted to on the Kickapoo Gunn
Club. I only blamed them for being boring.
From what I could tell, they went hunting,
played golf, and cheated on their wives. After
the war, the members carved a new golf course
out of the big woods on the river. A new Frank
Lloyd Wright–inspired clubhouse was built on
a hill above the 16th green. It replaced the old
hunting lodge as the center of activity. But golf
bores me. Talk of golf bores me. As far as
guns—I knew more about that particular subject
than any of them could ever hope to know. And
I made them painfully aware of that fact.

For years after the war, the club staged a
shooting competition: the Kickapoo Gunn Club
High-Power Rifle Invitational. They welcomed
all comers back then. We shooters had to hit a
target at one thousand yards. The bull's-eye at
which we aimed was a circle twenty inches
across. It was like putting the crosshairs on the
head of a pin. We had ten rounds and ten minutes in which to fire those rounds. With my
Springfield '03, I won that competition five years

in a row. After that, the invitational was limited to members only. Cynics called it the "Pennington Rule." It didn't bother me being excluded. I'd made my point. Besides, a sniper should never hunt the same ground twice.

The late Webster Sprague Sr., a town banker, was a founding member of the Kickapoo Gunn Club. But it was Webster Sprague III that I had come to talk with. A third-generation member of the Kickapoo Gunn Club. He built his white Colonial in a new development out on the river, right between the golf course and a wildlife preserve. I guess you could say it was where the rich lived. He was a congressman for now, running for Wisconsin's open senate seat, which found him locked in a tight race with the popular mayor of Milwaukee. But then Webster was always running for something. I remember him as class president of Kickapoo Falls High School. He was one smart politician. That morning he'd summoned me out to his house, knowing full well I'd be coming, anyway.

His daddy, Webster Sprague Jr., had sent Webster III to Yale. After graduation, he became a naval officer, but he never set foot on a boat. He spent the last year of the war in Washington. In the early fifties, he was a staff member for Wisconsin senator Joe McCarthy, another proud member of the Kickapoo Gunn Club. Webster was quick to remind his critics that John Kennedy's younger brother Bobby had also worked for Joe McCarthy.

Webster offered me a drink out on his deck overlooking the 16th hole, with the imperious Gunn Club up on the hill. Besides being on duty, and conducting a murder investigation, it seemed too early in the morning for alcohol. For me, anyway.

"How the roads?" he asked.

"The roads are fine."

Webster poured himself a scotch and water. Standing there in the sun, I thought he looked a lot like Richard Nixon. But back then, any politician I didn't like looked like Richard Nixon.

"We had a wake at the Gunn Club yesterday," he told me. "We were talking about you. Your name comes up quite often."

"So I've heard."

"That's to be expected of the man who made the longest run in the proud history of Wisconsin football."

"Actually," I reminded him, "it was the longest run in the history of American football."

He laughed at that. "It may well have been. And then, during the war, as I understand it, you were a sniper with the Army Rangers . . . parachuted into France. We know you're one hell of a shot . . . and we know you've been asked a hundred times before . . . but you really should consider joining the club. We could use a man like you."

"Use me how?"

"We have plans . . . big plans." He seemed content to let it go at that. "Terrible about Maggie and Michael," he said. He breathed a deep sigh. "Seems like only yesterday we were all in high school together. Maggie used to write to me at Yale . . . then she wrote me during the war. You know, I always felt that if it hadn't been for Michael . . . Maggie and I might have ended up together. Now, don't get me wrong, Michael was a great guy . . . I loved him : . . but that was a troubled marriage." He spoke with a perceptible quaver in his voice. Real enough, even for a politician. "Fats tells me it looks like a murder-suicide."

"Fats may have jumped the gun. Excuse the pun."

"And you're investigating these . . . killings?"

"I am."

"But I thought that's why Fats hired this Texas detective . . . Dickerson."

"Dickerson is a twit."

"Really? Some people at the club think Fats may have brought that 'twit' in to be our next sheriff."

"You might remind your friends at the club that the office of sheriff is an elected office. I think 'Detective' is as high as Dickerson is ever going to go."

A sour look fell over his face. A look born more of hostility than of sorrow. It was an intense, innate hostility directed at me personally. "Didn't you investigate my brother's so-called accident?"

My hostility, too, rose to the surface, but I kept it in check. "No, I investigated the accident of the young woman he ran off the road."

"Allegedly," Webster reminded me.

"You said on the phone we had some business."

"Yes, we do . . . but I want it all off the record." Webster Sprague took a swig of his drink, slipped on a pair of expensive sunglasses, and strolled to the rail. Looked out over his golf course. He wore a white polo shit. Tan slacks and a pair of deck shoes. Very casual. Very rich. "My wife is missing," he told me.

"How long?" I asked him, not feigning surprise.

"Couple of weeks."

"And you're just now getting around to filing a missing-persons report?"

"That's just it, Deputy, I don't want to file a missing-persons report. That's why I wanted to talk to you. I'm running for a seat in the United States Senate, for christsake. It can't get out that my wife ran off."

"First you said Caren was missing. Now

you're saying she ran off. There's a big difference."

"First of all, her name is not pronounced *Karen*, like a normal woman, it's pronounced *Car-en* . . . as in *car*. She grew up in Lake Forest, one of those hoity-toity suburbs on Lake Michigan."

"I know where it is." While he rambled on, I tried to piece together a marriage that didn't make a whole lot of sense. Finally, I interrupted him. "So you brought a Chicago girl to a small town in Wisconsin and expected her to be happy?"

He rolled his eyes and chuckled. "What was I supposed to do . . . move to Chicago? I'm a Republican." He spoke almost mockingly. "A summer place down on Lake Geneva wasn't good enough for Caren Sprague. No, she wanted to be on Cape Cod, like a goddamn Kennedy. So I bought her a summer house on Cape Cod." He was getting hot under the collar, and it didn't have anything to do with the weather. I had to listen to him rant about how John Kennedy wasn't a real war hero, and how his daddy got him the Navy Cross, and don't pay any attention to those stories about the PT boat. He downed the scotch. "Fucking women," he said, "they don't even wear dresses anymore. Things are going to change under Dick Nixon . . . you just wait."

"When did you last see her?"

"At the Republican convention in Chicago. It was the night of the acceptance speech . . . must have been Thursday, July twenty-eighth."

"Where were you staying?"

"We had a second-floor suite with the Nixon camp at the Blackstone Hotel. I went down to the Amphitheater to hear the acceptance speech. When I got back, she was gone."

"She didn't care for the speech?"

"Don't get smart."

"Nobody has heard from her since?"

"My in-laws in Chicago haven't heard from her yet. And she's not at our Cape home. Police there are keeping their eyes out for her."

"What exactly do you want me to do?"

"I would like for you to do me a simple favor. Watch police reports, et cetera . . . unidentified bodies and such. This Michael and Maggie thing has me unnerved. Caren is still my wife . . . I want to know she's all right."

"Why don't you hire a private detective, maybe out of Chicago? That might be more productive."

"Yes, I've thought of that. I just might do that."

He seemed to lighten up, as if he believed I'd fallen for his little ruse. He summoned me to his house. He felt me out on the investigation. Then he asked me for a simple favor—off the record, of course. Like I said, he was one smart politician.

Webster removed his sunglasses, twirled them in his hand. I kept mine intact. Didn't want to give anything away. "This is Fats's last election," he said to me. "Come '64, you'd look mighty good in that sheriff's uniform. We were discussing that possibility at the club. Everybody agreed, you'd be a great candidate . . . having been wounded in the war, and all. You're very popular, even though most people think you're a little off center. It wouldn't hurt to have a United States senator backing you."

"I'm a Democrat."

"That's even better. I was for Nixon. You were for Kennedy. But we agree on one thing . . . Deputy Pennington would make a damn good sheriff. The papers would lap it up."

The morning sun was getting high in the sky. The heat was on. Golf balls began to sail our way. For now, I'd heard quite enough from Webster Sprague. I conspicuously checked my watch, though the time was irrelevant. "Well, Webster, I had better go check those police reports, et cetera, for any unidentified bodies and such."

"One other thing, Deputy. There's some money missing."

"How much money?"

He paused and swallowed. "Two hundred thousand dollars."

In those days, two hundred thousand dollars was a fortune. For the first time that morning he appeared lost for words. Slightly off balance.

"Do you want to report this robbery?"

"No," he said, "that won't be necessary. The money wasn't really here in Wisconsin. I just wanted you to have the background information."

Now I took off my sunglasses. Wiped the lenses on my shirt. Made sure they were good and clean. "Did Michael or Maggie ever do any campaign work for you?"

"Maggie stuffed some envelopes," he told me, "but I couldn't get Michael interested. I think his politics were closer to yours."

"So they didn't do any film work for you . . . snap pictures . . . that sort of thing?"

"Not that I know of." He seemed surprised by the question. "Why did you ask about film?"

"No reason. I'll show myself out."

I slid my glasses back in place. Adjusted my Stetson. Walked down the steps of the deck and started around the house for the squad.

Webster Sprague followed me along the railing, looking down at me as I passed. Finally, I heard him shout behind me, "You were always an uptight little fucker, Pennington. Even for a Catholic."

CHAPTER 8

INTO THE HILLS

MY GRANDFATHER WAS born and raised on the island of Nantucket, once the whaling capital of the world. Unfortunately, by the time Grandpa came into that world, the whalers were gone. I grew up hearing stories about how Grandpa's father, after the collapse of whaling, tried to sustain a living for his family by farming the sandy soil of Nantucket, one of the few Catholics on an island of Quakers—which is sometimes how I felt in Kickapoo County. Anyway, as a result of that sandy soil, my grandfather grew up in poverty. He watched his father stare out to sea for hours on end, probably dreaming of his adventures as a young man, when the harbor was filled with tall sails and even taller dreams. My grandfather buried his people in the Old North Burial Ground. The last of the Penningtons to rest there. Then he set sail for the mainland, and the rich farming soil he'd heard of in the Midwest. I've never known exactly how it was Grandpa came to live in Kickapoo Falls, but he had saved enough money to buy some land and plant some crops. Still, when all of your farming experience is culled from a sandy island in the Atlantic Ocean, not even the rich black dirt of Wisconsin is going to save you. Grandpa failed the land, but he was smart enough to sell that land at a good price. Then he built the shoe store in town.

When I was growing up, and even as a young man, I knew that I had been born and raised in Wisconsin, as had my father. That I was a Midwesterner. Nothing else mattered. I thought I was drawn to sailing its waters because Wisconsin is a playground of water. It was only as I grew older that where my family came from became important to me. I have a tattered album with black-and-white photographs of a depressed fishing village on a distant island, the ocean ever present behind the unsmiling faces of my ancestors. My grandfather owned nineteenth-century prints of the majestic whale ships, and of whalers harpooning the great sperm whales in faraway seas. For years those prints hung rather incongruously on the walls of our shoe store in Kickapoo Falls. Today they hang in my cabin here on Lake Michigan. There's a tarnished harpoon and a rusty cutting spade out in the shed. They may be two hundred years old. In fact, the cutting spade has Pennington blood on it. Mine.

After listening to State Trooper Hoffmeyer and senate candidate Webster Sprague, I felt like I needed a bath. A cleansing of sorts. So I drove south. Away from the Dells. Away from the town and the tourists. I felt a sudden need to be part of the Wisconsin that outsiders never see. The Wisconsin my father knew, and my grandfather before him. I wanted to drive the unspoiled hills and the hollows in the morning, before it got too hot. I did my best thinking out on the road. Was the disappearance of Webster's wife related to the murders? I got suspicious of people who disappeared right after a homicide. Webster said she'd been gone a couple of weeks, but he didn't report her missing until after the murders. Even then he wanted it off the record.

Possibility number 1: Caren Sprague was in the wheat field. Witnessed the murders. Got scared. Took the money and ran.

Possibility number 2: Caren Sprague was in the wheat field. Committed the murders. Stole the money and ran.

Possibility number 3: Caren wasn't in the wheat field. But she knows who was. And the money?

The Wisconsin countryside was magnificent in those years, when most of the roads were still dirt and the best way to see the valley was on the backside of a horse. But there was a baby boom and things were changing. Millions of dollars were being pumped into road construction. The first stretch of interstate highway in Wisconsin had just been completed. New feeder routes were being opened. Old routes closed. Dirt roads got paved over. Ancient Indian trails were being drowned in asphalt. We built the new highways to accommodate the growing families in the valley. Ironically, it was those same highways our young people followed out.

I swung down Route 23 and climbed into the hills and groves that always reminded me of the wine country in France—the splendor, the beauty, the incredible peace and serenity—just before I shot out a front tire of the lead vehicle, brought the German patrol to a halt, and then gave the signal to blow the French countryside to smithereens.

Was Caren Sprague the monster from Chicago? Didn't make sense to me, that Caren forced them into that field. Even if she had, she couldn't have done it alone. No, in order to stage a double murder, and a cover-up, there had to be at least two people who walked out of that wheat field alive. Any way I cut it, I had a congressman and senate candidate in the middle of a murder investigation, right in the middle of an election.

"You were always an uptight little fucker, Pennington. Even for a Catholic."

Seemed like every time I mentioned the word *film*, people flinched.

I drove past white clapboard houses and rusty red barns. Pastoral scenes right out of New England. The sky was baby blue and cloudless. Seemed to have no limits. No beginning. No end. A lazy warmth filled the air. Summer drifting to an end. The sumac always turned first. Precursor to autumn. There were branches of brilliant red jutting out of a forest of green. I smelled the cow manure in the pastures. Then over another hill came the redolence of wild flowers and prairie grasses growing across open land. I sailed past streams of trout, and rolled over narrow bridges that crossed winding rivers with names like Kickapoo, Little Blue, and Baraboo—waters that flowed into the big Wisconsin River, and then joined with the mighty Mississippi down at Prairie du Chien.

Yes, it seemed like only yesterday we were all in high school together. Those sunny days before the war. Webster Sprague was a senior. Big man on campus. Michael Butler was a junior, but already a school leader. I was just a squirrelly little sophomore. And my classmate Maggie? Even then she was the prettiest girl in town.

Webster had always known of my feelings for
Maggie. That's why he got in that jab about
Maggie writing *him* letters during the war. Not
to mention his little reminder of *my* wounds.
Though in my heart I knew better, at times I felt
I was the laughingstock of the town.

*"There goes poor Deputy Pennington, still pining
for pretty Maggie Butler."*

But suppose Webster's feelings for Maggie
had been as strong as mine. His missing wife
was only a younger, more sophisticated version
of Maggie.

I knew Caren Sprague only enough to smile
and say hello. We didn't exactly run in the same
circles. For years, all agreed that Maggie Butler
was the most beautiful woman in the valley.
Certainly in Kickapoo Falls. Then Webster
Sprague brought Caren to town. And the debate
began. Most men believed the younger, more
fashion-conscious Caren came out on top. But I
believed Maggie possessed a natural beauty
with which few women could compete. Dark
eyes. High cheekbones. Might have had some
Indian in her. She didn't need big-city airs, or a
fancy wardrobe. Maggie could breeze down
Main Street in khaki slacks, a gray sweatshirt,
and a rubber band holding back her long black
hair, and still men stopped and stared.

I remember thinking, now that she's gone,
how easy it should be to get on with my life.

But the bewitching Maggie Butler wouldn't let go. When I was a boy, I'd ride my bicycle out of town to the nearest cornfield. It was usually in August when the stalks were taller than I was. Then I'd disappear into the middle of the field. It was a great place to play. Just me and the crows. My own little fort. My own little world. Do you remember the first time you masturbated? I do. It was in the middle of a cornfield. Can't say how old I was, but even then I was probably dreaming of her.

We were town kids, me and Maggie. It was the Depression. Times were rough. There was no money for niceties. But when I ran and played with Maggie, I felt like the richest kid in Kickapoo Falls. In the summertime, we'd wade down the creek in search of arrowheads. In the winter, we'd flop onto our backs in the middle of a snowbank and try to catch falling snowflakes with our tongues. It was in our high school years that she drifted away from me. She was growing up. And she was leaving me behind.

I followed a gravel switchback up an incredibly steep hill the locals called Sugar Bluff. About as high as you could get. At the peak, where the limestone touched the sky, I stepped from the squad and searched the countryside, basking in the sunshine. Fifteen miles in any direction, a glorious view of earth and sky. The Kickapoo

Indians had once farmed this land. But they were also hunters and fierce warriors, and they had migrated south years before Wisconsin was thrown open to settlement, leaving behind only their name.

The last time Maggie and I were together as childhood friends was atop Sugar Bluff. Webster Sprague had just gotten his driver's license. He got his daddy's car. We younger boys all piled into the backseat. Maggie sat up front, between Webster and Michael. Then we cruised the magical hills, all the way to Sugar Bluff. Standing atop the crest, staring out at the deep blue future, I boldly reached out to hold Maggie's hand. But ever so gently, she pulled away from me.

Forty years have come and gone since that day I stood alone atop Sugar Bluff, the wheat field mystery fresh in the air. Now, long twisting highways snake through the sleepy hills and the pristine valleys. Every now and then I return to Kickapoo County. Drive those highways. Still do my best thinking out there. The sparsely populated land hasn't changed much. Still the Wisconsin of my fathers. Still the enchanting land where roams the crazed spirit of Maggie Butler.

CHAPTER 9

AFTON ROAD:
PART ONE

I WAS WORKING my way out to the wheat field for another look at the crime scene. Fats was supposed to meet me there. Then the radio call came in, a call we heard about every three weeks. Usually in the warm weather months.

"Car two . . . at the end of Afton Road . . . neighbors report kids sneaking around the house. Are you in the area?"

"This is car two . . . I'll handle."

Afton Road began and ended about a mile out of town. Most deputies just drove down the dirt road with their lights on, toward the house and the barn, making themselves visible. Then the kids would split. The squad would park at the gate long enough for the neighbors and the owners to see that they had responded, that all was well, then they'd pull slowly away, never leaving their vehicle.

But I was different. The kids and their games bothered me more, even though I knew in my heart they meant no harm to the couple inside.

I coasted to a stop, just short of Afton Road. Left the squad on foot and followed a path through the woods. Using my Ranger training, I sneaked up behind the kid keeping a lookout, his eyes peering down the road for a sheriff's car. He didn't see one. I clamped my hand over his mouth, as if I was going to slit his little throat. Then I whispered into his ear. Identified myself. Told him if he didn't do exactly as I said, I'd deliver him home to his mommy and daddy in the trunk of my squad with every bone in his body broken. The urchin went limp with fear. Tears rolled out of his eyes and down across my fingers.

"I want you to yell 'Cops!' at the top of your lungs," I told him. "Then I want you to turn and run down that road . . . and don't you stop running until you get home." I let go of his mouth. The kid let loose with the scream of a banshee that frightened even me.

"Cops!"

Then the poor kid tore off for home in a sprint that probably broke every track and field record in Kickapoo County.

Three of them were inside the gate, with a

gutsy fat one crouching below a dark-curtained window. He was the one I wanted. I let the first two boys pass. They didn't even see me. Then, when the chubby mischief-maker came running through the woods to the path, I stepped from behind a tree. Grabbed him by his shirt. Lifted his pudgy body to my face. "What do you think you're doing?"

He was scared. The wet-your-pants kind of scared that comes with an unwelcome surprise. "I wanted to see the witch."

"What witch?"

"The witch married to the man inside."

"What do you know about the man inside?"

"That he's a hideous monster."

Now I was mad. "The man inside was a World War Two Marine Corps fighter pilot who fought at Midway and Guadalcanal," I yelled at the kid. "He flew planes with names like Thunderbolt and Warhawk. He played football at the University of Wisconsin, and before that he played football for Kickapoo Falls High School. And your so-called witch was a cheerleader and a homecoming queen. Now get the hell out of here . . . and don't you ever come back."

I threw the kid aside. Kicked at his ass as he rolled in the dirt. He stumbled to his feet, then ran off down the path, his tail between his legs. Yes, I was probably too hard on him. But as I said, their games bothered me more.

I stood at the front gate where Afton Road came to an end, staring up the hill at the white clapboard house with the bolted doors and the heavily curtained windows. It was a house that longed for fresh paint. The barn was barren and surrounded by weeds. A garage that had once housed a new car was now nothing but an abandoned shack. Grass had grown over the driveway. A low picket fence circling the property was gray with decay. A rusty chain and padlock secured the front gate where I stood. When I thought I saw a curtain move in an upstairs window, I knew my job there was done. That it was best that I leave.

CHAPTER 10

BACK TO THE WHEAT

WE WERE STANDING in the circle of death. Just me and Sheriff Fats. All that remained beneath the blistering grin of the sun was dried blood and withered body bits over crushed wheat. Corn-fed crows landed occasionally. Sniffed the gore of Michael and Maggie Butler, then flew off in a huff.

"Did you come in on Old County C?" the sheriff asked, breaking the silence.

"No," I told him, "I came through the hills."

"How the roads up that way?"

"The roads are fine."

He nodded toward the north hills, which hid from our view the big white farmhouse. "Karl Gutterman's going to have to harvest this wheat before long. Did your check on him turn up anything?"

"He just found the bodies. He had no idea there were people out here."

"How did they make this circle?"

"Haven't figured that one out yet, but I think this had happened here before . . . a long time ago. I was just a kid."

"You mean a circle like this?"

"I'm pretty sure. I remember a photograph. I'll check with the newspaper. I also thought I might drive down to Madison. People at the university might have some answers."

Sheriff Fats took off his hat and wiped the sweat from his big red face. In the sunlight I could see he was aging fast. Melting in his uniform. His hair had gone from red to gray. Now it was going to white. He carried a gleam of trouble in eyes old as the hills. "I picked up a rumor . . . ," he said, staring at the bloody wheat, " . . . that Michael Butler was involved with Webster Sprague's wife. This, of course, is off the record."

"God forbid somebody in this town should tell me something for the record."

"It all makes sense, when you think about it. That Caren Sprague . . . she wasn't very happy here. Webster was away in Washington a lot. Michael was a good-looking man. Pretty as Maggie was . . . his eyes were known to wander.

Might be time to write this one up for what it most probably was . . . a murder-suicide. Maggie shot Michael for his philandering ways . . . and then she shot herself."

"And what do you suppose became of their clothes? And their shoes? They didn't walk barefoot into this field."

Fats gave the questions a moment's thought. "Could have been animals carried them away. Maybe crows."

I had to pause for a second, as if I hadn't heard him correctly. "I've lived here all my life, Sheriff. Used to work for my dad in the store. I've yet to see a crow flying around Kickapoo County in a pair of Pennington shoes."

"Don't get smart. Did it ever cross your mind, Deputy, that someone may have been witness to this murder-suicide . . . and maybe they took the clothes?"

"Why?"

"Fear, would be my guess. Let's say they were all doing something sexual out here, and things got carried away. In the end, it's still murder-suicide."

"I don't know of many people who bring a shotgun to a sexual encounter. And even if that was the case . . . don't you think we ought to find this alleged witness, and bring him or her in for questioning?"

"Well, there's something I've got to tell you.

Been putting it off. People think that when it comes to Maggie Butler, you don't always operate with your eyes wide open. Fact is, more than a few people think you shouldn't be on this case. Maybe I should turn the whole works over to Detective Dickerson."

Dickerson was fast becoming a pie in my face. The more I learned of him, the more I disliked him. For example, Deputy Hess had told me that Dickerson knew guns.

"What kind of guns?" I had asked him.

"Rifles . . . you know, like you. Makes, models, stocks, calibers, scopes, marksmanship, shooting competitions. I mean, Fats found him through the Gunn Club, so I wasn't totally surprised . . . but he sounded to me like some kind of expert, you know, more military than sport. Plus, he's always asking about you."

"Asking what?"

"About your marksmanship . . . your reputation. He wanted to know if you ever shot anybody on the job. One day I caught him browsing through some of your old case files. I figure it's like one of those old Westerns. You're the fastest gun in the West, and he rode up from Texas to take you on. You know what I mean . . . this town ain't big enough for the both of you."

Now I removed my hat. Wiped my brow before the searing sun. "If you want to remove me from this case, Sheriff . . . turn it all over to your boy Dickerson . . . that's your prerogative. But stop asking questions . . . write Maggie's death up as a suicide . . . that's something I won't do."

"*Prerogative* . . . yes, that's a good word. I like it. You know, I was talking with Webster Sprague, about the election and all . . . and we both agreed that come '64, when I retire, my office would fit you well. People like you, despite your quirks. Hell, I might even retire early. That's my prerogative. Governor would have to appoint an interim sheriff till the election. Like to see that appointment go to one of my deputies. I've always admired your superior intellect, Deputy Pennington. What I haven't always admired is your superior attitude."

With that said, Sheriff Fats put his hat back on, turned, and wandered into the wheat. Faded away in a field of gold.

Fats was a hunter. The U.S. Army and the Marine Corps have three ratings for rifle proficiency. From bottom to top they are: *marksman*, *sharpshooter*, and at the top, *expert*. Like me, Fats was an expert. He'd been hunting in the deep woods of Wisconsin since he was a boy. He fought in the trenches during World War I. He was a full-fledged member of the Kickapoo Gunn Club. In short, Fats was sharp. Which is why I was so bewildered that he would consider the deaths of Maggie and Michael anything but a double homicide. Maybe it was his age.

*"I picked up a rumor . . . that Michael Butler was
involved with Webster Sprague's wife . . ."*

Fats didn't spread rumors. It was the facts he
spread around. Now more than ever, I needed
to talk with Caren Sprague. You see, Michael
was a small-town boy. A lot like me. We're born
in Wisconsin, and we die in Wisconsin. But
Maggie was different. Maggie wanted Caren's
world. She wanted a summer home on the
water, and the freedom to travel wherever she
pleased. Whenever she pleased. In our high
school yearbook, beneath Maggie's senior picture, it says: *"I want to sail to islands far away."*
Instead, she became a travel agent. Booked people on islands far away. Maggie never realized
her dreams. Perhaps she died trying. Now I was
going to avenge her death. Bring her killers to
justice. The thought made me feel a lot more
noble than I really was.

CHAPTER 11

A VOICE IN THE WOODS: FIRST CALL

I WAS AT my desk at the County Courthouse—a hot and muggy place I tried like hell to avoid. I always thought of the roads as my office. The squad room was noisy. Summertime noisy. The dispatcher was fielding radio calls. A couple from Chicago was crying about their car being stolen while up at the Dells. Probably stolen by some kid from Chicago, who was driving it back to Chicago. The woman said she didn't appreciate coming all the way to Wisconsin to be robbed. We didn't appreciate Chicago using our state as their summer playground. Of course, we believed all tourists hailed from Chicago, and back then we considered Chicago the root of all evil. Didn't matter. It was the end of August. In another week, they'd all be gone.

Across the way, Dickerson was busy at his own desk. Doing what, I couldn't imagine. I was the one investigating the murders of Michael and Maggie Butler. From what I could tell, the only thing Detective Dickerson was investigating was me.

My phone rang. I picked it up. "Pennington."

"Deputy Pennington, I hear you've been looking for me."

I put a hand over my other ear to block out the noise. "Who is this?" I asked.

"They tell me you're persistent. Even obsessive. I thought I'd save you some work."

The voice sounded ghostly familiar, even with the pretentious sexuality that was being attached to it. "Where are you, Caren?"

"You've even learned how to pronounce my name. I'm flattered."

She was right. I'd always called her *Karen*, until Webster corrected me. "Your husband is worried about you."

"The only thing my husband is worried about is getting elected to the United States Senate."

It was a long-distance call. Back then you could tell. The sound quality was bad.

"Did you hear about the Butlers?" I asked.

"Oh, yes."

"What did you hear?"

"That they died with their clothes off."

She sounded cynical, even bitter. I tried to listen for background noise. She was outside. Like a voice in the woods. Probably a phone booth. Don't ask me why, but I sensed an ocean noise. Maybe that place on Cape Cod. "Where are you?"

"I'm on an island . . . far, far away."

"Is that a slap at Maggie? Did you hate her that much?"

"I didn't hate her."

"You slept with her husband." There was no response. "When did you leave Wisconsin?"

"End of July," she told me.

"And you haven't been back?"

"Why would I come back?"

"How long were you involved with Michael?"

"If you're looking for suspects, Deputy Pennington, you might want to question my worried husband a bit more carefully. He was having a rather torrid affair with Maggie Butler. Michael liked to watch."

"And you?"

"Do you know what it's like to watch your husband make love to another woman?"

"No, I don't. Tell me."

"Perhaps you should have joined the club."

"And what club would that be?"

"Wasn't that what you always wanted . . . Maggie? Yes, I heard about you and her."

"There was no me and her."

"That's what I heard."

"Were you in the wheat field that night?"

"You mean the sex ring? I saw things."

"What things? Tell me what you saw . . ."

"Not today, lover. Some night . . . when you're home alone . . . we'll have a long, sexy talk."

CHAPTER 12

BACK TO SCHOOL: PHYSICS

IN 1960, PHONE calls were nearly impossible to trace. We had moved beyond small-town operators but had yet to advance to high-tech tracing. Caren Sprague remained a cipher. A voice in the woods. A voice that haunted me. She seemed to know a lot more about me than I knew about her. That had to change.

Labor Day came and went. The kids went back to school. The tourists went back home. The valley returned to what passed as normal. The September days stayed sunny and warm. But the nights cooled. And so did my investigation.

I was trying to keep it all straight. I started a chart:

WHO WAS SLEEPING WITH WHO IN KICKAPOO FALLS?

A. *Michael Butler was having an affair with Caren Sprague. Source: Fats*

B. *Webster Sprague was having a torrid affair with Maggie Butler. Source: Caren Sprague*

C. *State Trooper Hoffmeyer had sex with Maggie Butler while Michael watched. Source: Hoffmeyer*

D. *Hoffmeyer also had an affair with Caren Sprague. Source: Hoffmeyer (again)*

It didn't take long to eliminate Russ Hoffmeyer from my list of suspects. The state trooper was in divorce court on the day of the murders. He was on patrol that night. All of his logs were in order. Still, he claimed Caren told him things. Some really freaky sex things, but he was only half listening. Might have had something to do with cameras.

What if you were a rich man running for the United States Senate and there was film of you having sex with another man's wife? Would that lead to blackmail? And would that lead you to murder?

What happens when four people want to have sex? The answer is simple. But what happens when only three out of the four people want to have sex?

What if your husband constantly forced you into sex with other men so that he could watch? Would that lead you to murder? And then to suicide?

What if your wife, without your knowing she was there, watched you make love to another woman, while that woman's husband watched? Would that lead your wife to murder them both? Steal their clothes? Steal money? Run?

I ran over each of these scenarios while on the road. It was my day off. I'm pretty sure it was a weekday. The sun was shining. Some of the leaves had begun to turn color. All in all, a gorgeous day for a drive. I steered Highway 12 through the hills and down into Madison. Down to the university.

Built on the banks of Lake Mendota, the campus of the University of Wisconsin is one of the prettiest in America. A joy to visit. I wore my brown tweed sport coat with the leather patches on the elbow, and a pair of tan slacks, trying to look as collegiate as possible. Trying to forget that I'd flunked out of the place. I thought about puffing on a pipe. Maybe pass myself off as a college professor. But I decided I'd more likely look like a small-town deputy sheriff sucking on a pipe while dressed in ill-fitting clothes.

It was the beginning of the fall semester. On campus, the most exciting time of the year. Camp Randall Stadium was being prepared for

the first football game. The fraternity and soror-
ity houses along Langdon Street were buzzing
with new activity. There were students literally
on their hands and knees writing KENNEDY FOR
PRESIDENT on the sidewalks with colored chalk.
Other sidewalks had Nixon's name scribbled on
them, not always fondly. I pinned my KENNEDY
button onto my lapel and strolled down Langdon Street to Memorial Union, where I instinctively stopped and faced the words carved in
stone: ERECTED AND DEDICATED TO THE MEMORY OF
THE MEN AND WOMEN OF THE UNIVERSITY OF WISCON-
SIN WHO SERVED IN OUR COUNTRY'S WARS. I was
sucker for tributes like that. Always put a lump
in my throat.

The files at the *Kickapoo Falls Republic* had
turned up no photographs of a circle in a wheat
field. I was disappointed. My memory is usually
pretty good that way. So I had turned to the
university. I couldn't decide if I wanted the College of Agriculture, or the Physics Department,
or maybe even Psychology. Since Langdon
Street came to a dramatic end at Science Hall, I
decided to start with Physics.

Science Hall was right out of a horror movie—
five stories of Gothic architecture in bloodred
brick. Everything but gargoyles. In the old days
there was a morgue in the basement for medical
research and education. Bodies were brought to
the back of the building by hearse, and then

winched to the attic, where the classes were taught. Numerous ghosts were rumored to roam Science Hall.

I, on the other hand, didn't have to roam far. Up the steep stairs. Past the wrought iron gates guarding the elevator. Then down a short flight of stairs into a lecture hall. The professor was preparing for a class. He was everything I was pretending to be. Tall, slender, silver-haired, and probably Jewish. Very distinguished in appearance. He looked smart. I didn't see a pipe in his mouth, but I'm sure he smoked one. After I introduced myself, he said his name was Levine. I remember him as a very gracious man. Turned out he was a visiting professor from the University of Chicago. It was rumored he'd worked on the Manhattan Project during the war. He wouldn't confirm or deny it. He told me that he had a few minutes before the "troops" arrived, as he called his students.

I stared up at the perfectly descending rows of empty desks. Took in the smell of chalk and old wood. "How do you create a perfect circle in a field of wheat?"

The question seemed to baffle him. So I explained how I was conducting a murder investigation. I told him of the strange location where the two bodies were found, and of the condition the bodies were in when we found them.

He perked up at the word *murder*. Turned his

full intellect in my direction. "And the wheat, you say, was pressed all the way to the ground?"

"Yes," I answered. "Inside the circle, the wheat was flattened, with the stalks all lying in a clockwise direction."

"And you say it was a perfect circle?"

"Flawless."

"Without breaking the stalks?"

"Or disturbing the wheat around it."

The professor thought about it for a minute. "Well, they would have to walk in, and then walk out . . ."

"There were no footprints leading to or from the circle."

"Really? That raises two questions. How did they get into the field? And exactly what tools did they carry in?"

"If I knew how they did it, it might lead me to who did it."

"Yes, I can see how that would be helpful. I've got some bright students here. Many of them farm kids. It might be an interesting exercise . . . trampling through the wheat. Can we get back to you?"

"Sure . . . I'm a very patient man."

"Good. In the meantime, Deputy, you might want to check with the College of Agriculture while you're here. It's one of the best in the country. Agriculture Hall. Up the hill and across the Mall. Ask for John Whitman."

CHAPTER 13

BACK TO SCHOOL: AGRICULTURE

NATURALLY DRAWN TO water, I'd been sailing the isles of Lake Michigan since I was a boy. After the war I got my hands on a low-profile keelboat out of Sturgeon Bay and named her *Ranger*. She was an easy sail, even single-handedly. She had a large, deep cockpit that made her ideal for day sailing and cruising. Plus, the cuddy cabin had two bunks for an overnight. *Ranger* was very tender to about fifteen degrees of heel, and then she stiffened up significantly. Still, her sturdy design made her virtually indestructible during tough going on the Great Lakes. So you see, when I approached the College of Agriculture through the flower gardens that bright autumn day, I was more than just a Wisconsin town boy from a line of failed farmers. In my blood, I was a man of the sea.

He was dressed in bib overalls and was sweeping the floor when I walked into the laboratory, so I assumed he was the janitor. I swear, it didn't have anything to do with the fact that he was black. He laughed at me in a good-natured way. Emptied a dustpan of fresh dirt into a wood barrel and stored his broom. Then he brushed the soil from his hands and introduced himself as Professor John Escott Whitman. We walked and talked among long tables laid out with various seeds and small plants. Sunshine was strategically filtered in through the south windows.

"And you drove down here today from Kickapoo Falls?"

"Yes," I told him.

"How the roads up that way?"

"The roads are just fine."

"I'll bet that you keep them just fine."

"I do my best. What exactly do you teach, Professor?"

"Grain crops, mostly. Horticulture, and some entomology. We maintain soil experimental fields at nine different points in the state of Wisconsin. That's over five thousand acres of land. What is it that interests you, son?"

"Wheat fields."

"Wheat fields, you say. Of course, wheat is

not a major crop here in Wisconsin. Not like Kansas or Nebraska. Back before the war, farmers grew a little bit of everything, and some still do. Most farms had grinders and they would grind their own wheat. Bake their own bread. But with all the automation since the war, it's a lot easier even for farmers to just buy their bread in town. We don't see the wheat fields here like we once did."

"How about wheat fields with beautiful geometric shapes carved into them?"

"Oh, you mean crop circles?"

"You know of these?"

"Oh, heavens yes. Crop circles have been turning up for years . . . and not just in wheat . . . sometimes oat fields, alfalfa, and other grain crops."

"Who's making them?"

"Aye, there's the rub. Until recently, they were pretty much a European phenomenon. But more and more they've been showing up here in the Midwest. A lot of people believe these circles to be from out of this world . . . flying saucers and such. Another explanation, more plausible, is unusual wind patterns. A plasma vortex, an electrically charged whirlwind, like the dust devils one sees on a hot day. They collapse with a powerful downward gust of wind . . . which would explain a simple circle."

"But . . . ?"

"But that can't explain the more complex patterns. It's like saying the wind carved Mount Rushmore. No, I choose to believe the makers of crop circles are the same as the makers of Mount Rushmore . . . all too human."

"Meaning what?"

"I think farmers are behind them. Probably those Scandinavians . . . they have a very sly sense of humor."

"You mean they walk out into their fields and carve these circles?"

"No, they walk into somebody else's field in the middle of the night and carve the circles. That's the beauty of it. Remember, these circles may go undiscovered, for days. Weeks. Any footprints leading in and out would vanish."

"And you would be guaranteed a fair amount of privacy in one of these circles?"

"Oh yes, especially in the sparsely populated parts of our state, where the farmhouse might be miles from the field. Most of the circles are first spotted from the air. Pilots report them. I've never figured out exactly how they do it . . . make the geometric shapes, I mean."

"Well, Professor, when you've figured out how they do it . . . then maybe you can explain to me why they would do it."

"I'm afraid for that, you'll have to see the Psychology Department."

CHAPTER 14

BACK TO SCHOOL: PSYCHOLOGY

I TRUDGED BACK to the top of Bascom Hill to Bascom Hall. It was as high as you could get in Madison. In fact, it was said that if a student walked up Bascom Hill every day for four years, it would be equivalent to the height of Mount Everest. Whether that was true or not, the view was incredible. Exactly one mile away was the dome of the State Capitol Building. Out front of Bascom Hall was a statue of Abraham Lincoln, seated in a chair staring down at the small city. On the green that rolled down the hill between the oaks and the elms, students were lying in the grass. Reading books. Sharing a laugh. Enjoying the sunshine.

After admiring the bronze likeness of the sixteenth president, we took a seat on the steps beneath the statue. She was older than me, but I couldn't say how much older. Maybe a year or two. It's just one of those guy things, knowing instinctively when you're talking to an older woman. It probably dates back to high school when we boys were almost forbidden to talk to girls in the upper classes. Or maybe we were just too scared to talk to them. Anyway, it was Professor of Psychology Marilou Stephens who I was referring to. She had beautiful brown hair and big brown eyes. Sharp features, with really smooth skin. Right off, I noticed there was no wedding ring on her hand. No jewelry at all. And she had a great smile, one of those toothy, disarming smiles. I had walked up to Bascom Hall to talk of voyeurism. What Michael Butler had been doing, sharing his wife, went far beyond Peeping Toms. I had to know what it was I was dealing with. But now, finding myself face-to-face with a beautiful woman, an older woman, I confess, I was somewhat lost for words. I also confess that before my trip to Madison, I had to look up the definition.

Voyeur—a person who derives sexual satisfaction from observing the sex organs or sexual acts of others, usually from a secret vantage point.

"The ideal candidate for voyeurism would be

a strong narcissist," she told me. "It's the mean-spiritedness he enjoys . . . the humiliation."

As she talked, I kept glancing over my shoulder at Abraham Lincoln. I couldn't shake the feeling there was a very judgmental man sitting in a chair watching me. Finally, I dug up the nerve to start asking her more specific questions. "If you stumble across two people having sex, at a park, in a field, and you stop to watch . . . are you a voyeur?"

"Technically, it's an act of voyeurism, but I'd consider that more an act of human nature. Reality is the greatest entertainment of all. You're going to watch . . . it's just natural. Voyeurism, I believe, is when witnessing the sex act becomes more important than participating in the act."

I was impressed by how cool and calm she was, not the least bit flustered discussing a subject that she could see I was clearly uncomfortable with. I asked her, "Can you watch people act badly and yet remain good yourself?"

"I believe so. Sex doesn't cause violence, Mr. Pennington. Violence causes violence. If sex caused violence, we'd be a nation of savages. Let's face it, we're a voyeuristic society. That said, there is still a sharp divide in America between those who will accept any act between consenting adults, and those who will not."

I swear, the smarter she talked, the prettier

she got. She kept glancing down at the KENNEDY button pinned to my coat. A good sign. Like I was on the right side. I was falling in love. "Let me ask you this, Professor . . ."

"Please, call me Marilou."

"All right, Marilou . . ."

In more detail I explained what I had found in the wheat field that morning—the bodies, the shotgun, the cigarette butt, the little round holes in the wheat. It was funny, but as soon as the subject matter focused on my murder investigation, I felt more comfortable with my new friend Marilou. A lot more confident.

"And you say there were three holes in the wheat?"

"More like indents," I explained.

"Like a tripod?"

The word hit me like a plow—*tripod*. I felt stupid. Furious. How could I have not have known there was a camera out there? It wasn't a crop circle. It was a goddamn movie studio. They were using the daylight to film. A brilliant orange sunset on golden wheat in the middle of the heartland. An athletic young couple naked before a camera that was mounted on a tripod. Somebody says, "Action." Then what?

"Are you all right, Mr. Pennington?"

"Excuse me?"

"You seem to have gone pale."

"I'm sorry . . . I just had a vision, of sorts.

Tell me . . . would our voyeuristic, narcissistic friend be likely to pick up a movie camera and begin filming some of the sexual encounters he staged?"

"Almost as soon as the movie camera was invented, people started filming sex. Of course, our friend, as you called him, would feel compelled to get more extreme. More authentic. More real. The forbidden is essential to sexual excitement. 'Let's make a striptease film. Let's make a sex film. Let's make a sadomasochistic film. Let's make a snuff film.' "

"What's a snuff film?" I asked her.

"That's a film of an actual murder. Extremely rare."

CHAPTER 15

THE
LONG RIDE HOME

NARCISSISM. EXCESSIVE ADMIRATION of oneself. From Narcissus. Greek mythology. A youth who pined away in love for his own image in a pool of water. That didn't sound like Michael Butler. Not the Michael I knew. That sounded more like Webster Sprague. Yet it was Michael who had been sharing his wife the way one would share beer nuts.

I sat in my car staring up the tree-lined hill at Bascom Hall. Students were marching to class. The sun and the sky above their young heads were bright, like their futures. But my world was dark. I removed my KENNEDY button and dropped it into my coat pocket. My stomach was churning. My mind was reeling with images, none of which I could comprehend. Out there somewhere in the rolling hills of America's heartland was a film of Maggie and Michael Butler being murdered—or at the very least, of Maggie and Michael engaged in sexual intercourse before they were murdered.

I could try for a search warrant of Webster's house, but that would be risky. Besides tipping my hand, it would be politically difficult. A large number of Wisconsin judges were members of the Kickapoo Gunn Club. But what if I could find a time when Webster was campaigning down in Madison? With Caren Sprague still missing, there would be nobody home.

And what exactly would I find inside the big white house that literally sat in the shadows of the Gunn Club? Would I really be able to sit and watch a film of Maggie having sex? Or worse yet, of Maggie being murdered?

And lastly, that September day, there was the lovely Marilou Stephens. I wanted to march back up that hill. Ask the brainy beauty to dinner. I knew in my heart that she would say yes. That she was probably expecting me. But in the end, I couldn't do it. What would be the point? She was a professor of psychology. She would diagnose my wounded psyche before the salad was served.

These are the thoughts I would carry home to Kickapoo Falls. I slipped the car into drive and pulled away.

CHAPTER 16

SEX ALONG THE ROAD: PART TWO

I TELL THIS aspect of the story in three parts because that's the way it played out. Again, it doesn't have a whole lot to do with the wheat field murders, having taken place years before, but it does attest to the flaws in my character, and to my skills with a rifle. Not to mention my first run-in with the powerful Sprague family of Kickapoo Falls.

Her name was Robin Christensen. She was sixteen years old that first night I stumbled across her having sex in the back of a Ford pickup. Her partner in crime was Buster Sprague, youngest brother of Webster Sprague. I took their license plate number that night, and I made a note of their favorite spot on the Upper

Dells, about halfway between Witches Gulch and Cold Water Canyon. It was one of the perks of being a sheriff's deputy on patrol. Over the years, you learn of all the roadside hideaways where young people go to make love.

The black truck they used as a love nest belonged to Robin, or rather it belonged to Robin's father, who owned a dairy farm out Reedsburg way. Buster Sprague, on the other hand, owned a red Chevy DeLuxe convertible with a souped-up, 90-horsepower so-called Victory Six engine. Times were still hard coming out of the war. It rankled the nerves of more than a few people, including us cops, to see this rich kid tearing through the valley in a shiny new car.

Anyway, one moonlit night I pulled a sniper's rifle from the trunk of my squad. A .30 caliber Springfield M1903-A4. The same deadly rifle I'd used in the war. I removed the white cotton cloth I kept wrapped around the ten-power scope. It was called a Unertl scope, developed by a World War I German sniper named John Unertl. I climbed into the cliffs above their truck. I adjusted the leather sling and wrapped it tight around my forearm. I balanced the rifle in the Y of a tree. It was the perfect vantage point. Ever since I'd hunted deer as a child, I had a way of finding these kind of spots—where I could see, but not be seen. He had just removed her bra when I put my shooting eye up to the scope and brought them into focus. Buster was on his knees over her. I sighted the crosshairs between his shoulder blades. Robin owned perfect breasts, not really big, just beautifully rounded, and he liked to play with them. That night he sucked on them like a baby. In fact, he was sucking so hard he may have been biting her. I moved the scope up to Robin's face and watched her wince, almost in pain.

I didn't catch them in the act often, maybe two or three times a year, but over those years I did notice a dramatic change in Robin's facial expressions. She went from enjoying it to tolerating it. Like the night I aimed the rifle at them. The night I'm sure he was biting her breasts. I wanted to slip a cartridge into the breach and pull the trigger, just so that she could be done with the bastard. When he had finished with her breasts, he was back on his knees. He didn't remove her panties anymore. He stripped them from her. And I don't mean *strip* in a sexual way. It was more like he was *stripping* her of her dignity. I also noticed that he was no longer doing it to her face-to-face. He'd roll her over. Order her to her knees. Then he'd slip it into her from behind, and while doing so, he'd push her head into the bed of the truck. He was certainly having his way with her, getting more and more aggressive each time I watched. At the time I didn't trust what I was seeing. I

chalked off my police instincts to the frustration
and hostility I was feeling—that only two out of
the three people involved were actually having
sex.

The thing to remember is this—until the day
each of them died, I never had any contact with
Robin Christensen or Buster Sprague. Once in a
while I would see Robin in Kickapoo Falls, or
in the summertime I would spot her with her
friends up at the Dells. But I never approached
her. Never introduced myself. Never said hello.
She was my secret lover. And I chose to keep
our affair a secret.

As for Buster Sprague, he made a reputation
for himself drag racing through town in his fire-
red convertible. The kids in their hot rods would
come from all over the valley to challenge him,
usually on a particularly dangerous stretch of
highway where Military Road angles into River
Road just above the Dells. But their old beaters
were no match for his souped-up Chevy. I left it
to other deputies to chase down Buster Sprague.
Lecture him. Ticket him. Take his beer. As for
me, I always let Buster pass. Usually with a
slight grin on my face. Only Robin knew more
about him than I did.

In the four years that I watched them, Robin
Christensen grew into a beautiful young
woman. And Buster? He just turned into an
overaged, oversexed adolescent. I spotted him

with a couple other girls, but he always ran back to Robin.

One day she came into the County Courthouse with her father. They wanted to swear out a complaint against Buster Sprague. I didn't take the report, but I was sitting only a few feet away. In fact, I was shaking, she was so close to me. It was the strangest feeling in the world. After four years of watching Robin having sex with another man, suddenly she was sitting near me. I could smell her perfume. I could hear her speaking voice. Everything about her in the light of day was special. In the beginning, I had thought of her as a teenage whore, fucking some rich kid in the back of a pickup truck. But that morning, in the light of the squad room, I thought of her as a sweet but frightened young woman. I sat, eyes cast downward, trying not to reveal my guilt.

It turned out she had broken up with Buster Sprague, but he hadn't broken up with her. Today they call it *stalking*. There are laws against it. Back then the best we could do was a harassment complaint. Promise to have a talk with the young offender. I remember standing before the tall windows on the second-floor landing and watching Robin walk away, through Courthouse Square with her father. Daddy's little girl. I wanted to chase after her. Promise her all the protection in the world. Her personal body-

guard. But like the times before, all that I could
really do was stand about and watch.

Two weeks later, Robin Christensen was dead.
Last time anybody saw her alive was around
midnight. She had just gotten off work. Was on
her way home from a summer waitress job in
Kickapoo Falls. An hour later her daddy's Ford
pickup was found upside down in a ditch off
Highway 33. The black truck had left the road
at a high speed, struck a tree, and rolled several
times. Robin's shapely torso was pinned to the
steering wheel. Her head was in the bed of the
truck.

Bright red paint was discovered on the rear
bumper of the truck. And we were able to match
tire tracks near the accident scene to the tires on
Buster Sprague's Chevy DeLuxe. But speaking
through an attorney, Buster claimed Robin had
had trouble with the old pickup that week.
Wouldn't start. So he gave her a push with his
car, while she popped the clutch and jump-
started it. As for his tire tracks being found on
Highway 33—so what? He drag raced kids from
Reedsburg out there all the time. In the end,
there was not enough evidence to bring young
Buster Sprague to trial for the murder of Robin
Christensen. He had escaped justice from the
state of Wisconsin. He wouldn't escape mine.

CHAPTER 17

SUSPECT IN A
FIELD OF DEATH

I DON'T REMEMBER exactly when it was I realized that I had become a suspect in a double homicide. Certainly by the time I returned from Madison. A hush fell over the squad room whenever I walked through the door. Detective Dickerson was strutting about the courthouse like a rooster. Cocksure of himself. The people who liked me, began avoiding me. Even the women dispatchers, whom I'd often flirted with, were keeping their radio calls to me cold and impersonal. It was only when my favorite waitress at Lorraine's Café expressed her concerns that it finally hit home. The whole town had to be wondering about me. At any rate, by September there were parallel investigations under

way. I was investigating the wheat field murders for Sheriff Fats. And Detective Dickerson
was investigating me for the wheat field
murders.

Dickerson told Fats that while at the university I had interviewed a woman, a nigger, and
a Jew. Hard to say which species the detective
from Texas found the most worthless.

I would go out and question somebody, and
next day Dickerson would go out and talk to the
same person about my questions. For example, I
learned from the people at Butler Travel that
Maggie and Michael had driven to Chicago for
the Republican convention. Only a week before
their murder. Next day, Dickerson was on his
way to the Blackstone Hotel in Chicago.

Or Sheriff Fats would sidle up next to me.
Soft-spoken as ever. Almost bored. Say something like, "Funny about Michael being shot in
the groin like that. I guess it's something a jealous woman would do . . . or a jealous man."

Next day, it would be Dickerson's turn. "Pennington, do you own a shotgun?"

"Yes, as a matter of fact, I do."

"Where do you keep it?"

"At my cabin in Door County."

And that would be it. No follow-up. No suggestion that I actually produce the shotgun. A
day would go by, maybe two. Then, just as I'm

readying to pull away from the courthouse, Fats would stick his big, round head in the passenger-side window. "You and Maggie went to school together, didn't you?"

"Yes, we did."

"Did you date her?"

"No."

"Did you want to?"

"Of course. We all did."

"Did she have anything to do with the long and rather peculiar run you made at that football game?"

No reply required. End of conversation. They were the kind of tactics Wisconsin senator Joe McCarthy had made famous. If these thousand cuts were meant to penetrate my thick skin—they certainly did. Dickerson's suspicions made sense. He was an outsider. But why would Fats turn against me? We'd been working together for years.

One sunny day, outside the courthouse, I confronted Dickerson. "I hear you've been asking a lot of questions about me."

"Yes. You fascinate me, Deputy."

"How so, Detective?"

"You seem to leave a trail of dead bodies wherever you go."

"That's because I investigate homicides."

"Yes, but it's your so-called *cold* cases that fascinate me. It's amazing how many of your suspects were suddenly killed, before the case went cold."

"Justice in Kickapoo County can be swift and harsh, Detective. Been that way a hundred years . . . long before I came on the job."

If you're going to murder somebody in the state of Wisconsin, do it during the deer hunting season. Give your victim a rifle and invite 'em into the woods for a little sport. Put a little distance between the two of you, then shoot 'em in the back of the head. *"Whoops, sorry, it was an accident."*

That's about the end of it. The hard questions never get asked.

Was it possible they truly believed I had murdered Maggie and Michael Butler, and that I did it with a shotgun? That I did it out of obsessive love? That I marched them into the wheat field that evening at gunpoint? Ordered them to strip? Ordered them to fuck like they had never fucked before, while I smoked a cigarette and watched? And then as Michael got off Maggie and flopped to his back in a bed of wheat, his dick limp with a satisfaction I could never know, I blew his balls off at point-blank range? That would have left me and Maggie alone. Together at last in a ring of gold. Our lives had come full circle. Did I make her beg? Beg, while her husband was bleeding to death beside her.

Did she tell me she was sorry? Sorry, for all the hurt she had caused me. Did I then put the shotgun to her face, that beautiful, exotic face that haunted me since I was a boy—haunted me through four years of war, and four months in a hospital? "Good-bye, Maggie."

CHAPTER 18

A VOICE IN THE WOODS:
SECOND CALL

I HAD A bungalow at the end of Ash Street, at the bottom of the hill where the tracks followed the river out of town. Remember, I grew up in an apartment above a shoe store on Main Street. I spent the war years in a tent. To me, that bungalow felt like a mansion. At night, I would lay in my bed and listen for train whistles—the old Milwaukee Road on the run from La Crosse to Madison. For some reason I loved the sound of people going places. Ironically, I seldom traveled. Other than sailing the Great Lakes, I seldom left Wisconsin. Fats would often tell me, "You're young, Deputy, go out and see the world." I saw the world. It was at war. I liked Kickapoo Falls.

Anyway, one warm September night I was lying in bed listening for those train whistles when the phone rang. Again the connection was bad. Long distance. She had on her disconcertingly sexy voice. It would have been comical except that she was a suspect in a double homicide. I began to wonder if that was the same voice she used in the wheat field that night, perhaps taunting Maggie and Michael before she killed them. Or had she just been there to watch?

I flicked on a lamp. Grabbed a pen. After listening to a few solicitous remarks, I began with some soft questions. I wanted to keep her on the line. Milk as much information from her as I could. "Webster Sprague, your loving husband, where did you two meet?"

"I was dating a friend of his," she told me. "We were at Lake Geneva for a summer weekend. Webster showed up. He wanted me. I wanted them both. So one night we all shared."

"How romantic. After you were married . . . how did it begin, Caren? The cheating, I mean."

"Webster never really gave up his girlfriends. Rich men seldom do. So I kept in touch with old boyfriends. After we knew we were cheating on one another . . . things just escalated."

"How so?"

"We kept trying to top each other . . . excuse the pun."

"Give me an example."

"That's right . . . you're a details man, aren't you, Deputy? Here's a good one. You'll like this. Webster was in Washington for a week. I knew he had a girlfriend there, too. I was going crazy in that big ugly house on the golf course, so I called your buddy Russ Hoffmeyer. Russ and I drove down to Chicago and checked into the Drake Hotel . . . the Presidential Suite. I billed the whole thing to Webster. Must have cost him a fortune. Then when me and the big ex-Marine were naked and cozy on the largest bed I had ever seen . . . I picked up the phone and called Webster in Washington."

"Why?"

"Just to talk."

"About what?"

"About nothing . . . that was the point. You see, while I was talking to Webster on the phone . . . one of Wisconsin's finest was having me for dinner. Russ calls it his two-pillow move. One pillow for my head, and one pillow for his knees. Have you ever licked a woman that way, Deputy? You don't know how much we love that. But the most beautiful thing about it . . . Webster didn't know. He was blabbing away about Republican politics while his wife was having her privates eaten by a state trooper. That's an example of the kind of things we do to hurt each other."

"So it was only natural that you would drag others into your sick little circle."

"We never had to drag anybody. They came like children to a candy store."

"How did Maggie and Michael get involved?"

"I hated Kickapoo Falls," she said matter-of-factly. "I was going home to Lake Forest almost every weekend. One night I got back to town early and I caught the three of them in bed together."

"Maggie, Michael, and Webster?" She didn't answer. "Did you join them?"

"No. I just watched."

"Did they know you were watching?"

"That time? I suspect they did."

"The Republican convention in Chicago . . . were Maggie and Michael with you?"

"Just the last night. They had driven down from Wisconsin."

"Were they with you at the hotel?"

"We had dinner and talked. Your name came up a few times."

"In what context?"

"General gossip."

"Webster walked down to the Amphitheater to hear the acceptance speech. You stayed behind. Where were Maggie and Michael?"

"Honestly, Deputy, there was a lot of alcohol flowing that night . . ."

"What happened at the convention?"

"Is the wounded little deputy from Kickapoo Falls going to solve the big murder case?"

"What do you know of my wounds?" Again she didn't answer. "Considering the fact we were never friends . . . you seem to know an awful lot about me."

"I know that you were invited to the wheat field."

"Where is the film?"

There was a long pause on the other end of the line. A lot of static. I thought she was going to hang up. "What film?" she finally asked, not so convincingly.

"The film I need to make my case." Again there was nothing but static. I was losing her. A train was coming. I could hear the whistle. "They're trying to pin it all on you, Caren."

"Really? I heard they're planning to pin it all on you."

I could barely hear her. "Where is the film?"

"Check the house."

The train went roaring by. "Where in the house?"

"Be careful, Deputy. The boys at the Gunn Club take their politics seriously."

I confess, that last line she spoke wasn't really clear. But I'm pretty sure she said something about politics and the Gunn Club.

CHAPTER 19

THE DEPUTY AND
THE SENATOR

THE VALLEY WAS still sleeping in snow. In fact, it was snowing that morning. Early March of 1960. Almost six months before the wheat field murders. The Wisconsin primary was coming up, but nobody was talking about it. Other than the usual small-town gossip, nobody was talking about much of anything. Football season was well over. Deer-hunting season had come and gone. Baseball season was two months away. These were the dying days of winter. The sky seemed forever overcast. The air maintained its winter chill. A gray mood had settled over Kickapoo Falls.

I was just coming on duty, about to step into the squad when I saw him standing in the middle of Courthouse Square. He was watching me, as if he might want to talk. It was 7:30 in the morning. We were the only two people in the square. Saying he looked out of place would be an understatement. He looked like a cross between an athlete and a movie star. He also looked lonely, forlorn, and a little bit lost. I started across the square, as if just to say hello. "Good morning," I said to him, "can I help you with anything?"

His head was bare in the falling snow, giving him something of an angelic appearance. He wore a black wool coat over a Brooks Brothers suit. Black leather gloves and a burgundy scarf. "My name is John Kennedy," he said, extending his hand, "I'm running for president in the primary." I shook his hand. Then he reached into his coat pocket and pulled out a campaign button. Gave it to me. I liked it. It was red, white, and blue. It said, KENNEDY FOR PRESIDENT, and it was shaped like a badge.

The young senator from Massachusetts told me he'd driven up from Madison. Said he was going to speak to a civics class at the high school.

"Those kids don't vote," I told him.

"No, but their parents do."

Nobody seemed to care that he was in town. Not even the *Republic*. Personally, I'd been leaning toward Hubert Humphrey in the primary, but only because Humphrey was from neighboring Minnesota.

"Where is the infamous Gunn Club?" Senator Kennedy wanted to know.

"It's on a golf course . . . out on the river."

"I heard Mr. Nixon has been there."

"Yeah, he spoke at some shindig they had last summer."

"I suspect my invitation got lost in the mail."

I thought that was funny. In the summertime, I was used to dealing with tourists standing in the square with that lost look on their faces. So I never forgot his calm and his composure, and his sense of humor, in what must have seemed to the future president a mournful little town. Empty streets. Falling snow. Cold and desolate Kickapoo Falls.

I told him he might find some early risers at Lorraine's Café, across from the square. Other than that, I don't remember what else was said that morning. We didn't talk about being veterans, or being Catholic, or anything like that. I do remember watching him walk away, toward the café in search of a hand to shake. Maybe it's because I'm so damn old now, but he looked awful young to be running for president of the United States.

CHAPTER 20

FILM
IN A WHEAT FIELD

THE FIRST FILM is scratchy. Black and white. Only one camera. Sixteen millimeter. Every frame is a medium two-shot. The story is a male fantasy set in postwar suburbia. The acting is atrocious. The directing, almost nonexistent.

A vacuum cleaner salesman comes to the door. He's wearing a coat and tie. Thick glasses. A real nerd. He rings the doorbell. A woman answers. She's gorgeous. Wrapped only in a towel. She explains she's just stepped out of the shower, but if he insists on coming in, she's willing to watch his demonstration. The salesman steps into the living room and fires up his vacuum cleaner. You guessed it, the vacuum cleaner accidentally sucks in the woman's towel.

Now she's standing before him naked. Dark hair. Big tits. A great ass. The young American housewife. For some inexplicable reason, she's suddenly horny as hell. She wrestles the door-to-door salesman to the couch, where they appear to be having sexual intercourse. But because of the poor quality of the film, all that I can really see are the woman's legs in the air and a lot of arms wrapped around a lot of skin. The rest of the film is moaning and groaning. The reel plays out in twenty minutes.

It's what passed for a pornographic movie in 1960. No wonder my friends decided to make their own.

I learned Webster Sprague had booked a room for two nights at the Edgewater Hotel in Madison. So I took advantage of his absence from Kickapoo Falls to break into his house. My guess was that he would have a finished basement, and that's where a film projector would be found. I guessed right. The carpeting was an inch thick. The walls were dark wood paneling. A built-in bar was six feet long. A silver movie screen was built into the opposite wall. Overstuffed chairs and a leather couch ringed the room. Webster Sprague's private little theater. Six canisters of film were stacked on a bookshelf.

I rewound the film about the vacuum cleaner salesman and threaded the projector with a second film. It, too, was a bad porn movie. Not what I was looking for. I rewound that film and threaded film number three.

I throw the toggle switch and listen to the sprocket holes clicking through the projector. The screen before me flicks bright white light for two minutes. I begin to think the film is blank. Then the figure of a man and a woman can be seen on a bed. The film is black and white. They are blurry. Ghostly. I adjust the focus knob, but it isn't the projector's fault. It is the camera operator. After another minute and some muffled voices they manage to get their act together. The two people come into focus. It is Webster Sprague and his beautiful wife, Caren. They are sitting on a large bed. I recognize it as the bed of Michael and Maggie Butler. The bed Russ Hoffmeyer had told me about. The bed we found when we searched their home after their murders.

Again there are muffled voices as Webster talks to the camera operator. Then the show begins. Innocently enough to start. They are kissing. Hugging. Rolling around on the bed stroking each other's hair. Caren is dressed in a black sweater and a pair of tight-fitting slacks. Webster places his hand over her breasts. Caren begins rubbing the crotch of his pants. Soon he is stripping her, a bit too conscious of the camera. He is trying not to block the view. I'm won-

dering just how explicit these two are going to
get. I soon find out. Very explicit. They are both
naked before the camera. As the minutes roll by,
it's as if they forget all about being filmed. There
is no attempt at acting. Just a man and his wife
enjoying sex. She actually seems more comfortable than he does. On the phone, she portrayed
herself as a victim of her husband's aggression.
But in the film, she almost looks like the
aggressor.

I was watching two people, one of whom I
knew well, having sexual intercourse on film.
Again, this was new to me. But I was beginning
to think I was the last person in Kickapoo Falls
to be let in on the dirty little secret.

That film ran about twenty-five minutes. It
was an amateur production. Way too many
shots of Webster's ass, and not enough of Car-
en's. Still, it was good pornography. There
seemed to be nothing they weren't willing to
record on film. But who was behind the camera?

The next film is almost a repeat. A boring se-
quel. Again it is Webster and his wife, Caren.
Same place. Same bed. But they are dressed in
different clothes. It feels like a different day.
Caren has on a silky black dress, the kind of
dress a woman would wear to a cocktail party
in Washington. They begin by kissing. He strips
her. She helps strip him. They move slowly
along to intercourse, more comfortable before

the camera. Then right in the middle of the act,
Webster stops. He pulls out. Michael Butler
walks into the frame. He's standing beside the
bed, fully clothed. Caren reaches up for him.
Pulls down his zipper. Takes off his pants. Now
she's on her knees sucking Michael. Webster
gets on his knees behind her. Enters her from
the rear. She's got one man in her mouth, and
her husband coming at her from behind. The
film abruptly plays out, as if the camera had
been left unattended.

I was beginning to feel like a kid turned loose
in a candy store. Don't think for a minute that
I didn't want be in that bedroom in person
watching Caren Sprague getting her lights
fucked out. But even in my fantasies, I see myself watching. Never participating.

I rewound the reel and then threaded film
number five. To my surprise, this film is in living color. It takes a while for all of the colors to
come into focus, but when they do, I recognize
the scene right away. It is the wheat field. It
looks like late afternoon. Long shadows seem to
be creating problems with the lighting. Webster
and Caren are sitting on a blanket. From there
it's not much different than the black-and-white
bedroom scenes. They kiss. They strip. He
spreads her legs and enters her one way, then
he rolls her over and enters her another way.
Only this time the quality is better times ten,

except that there is still a jerking motion from the camera operator that marks it as an amateur production. There are a lot of unnecessary camera angles. A lot of playing with the sunlight. There are close-ups of their genitals, mostly Caren's. Even the sound is a big improvement, though it's mostly moaning and groaning. I don't know what it is about the film, but I have the feeling from the start that this is not shot on the day of the murders. No third person ever enters the film. It ends with Caren lying on the blanket in the middle of the wheat. She rolls to her stomach and rests her head on her arms in a classic nude pose. It almost has an artlike quality to it. Almost.

I eagerly threaded the last film, but it was a bust. Another scratchy black-and-white porn film with bad actors and vague sex.

I searched the house for an hour, looking for another reel of film, but I found nothing. I plopped into the big easy chair beside the projector. Through a basement window I could see the golf course and the floodlights of the Kickapoo Gunn Club. I turned and stared at the blank screen before me.

They would need a photo lab, wouldn't they? Some kind of film-processing center. I hardly think they would use the Rexall Drug Store in Kickapoo Falls. Could a color film like that be processed in the home? There was nothing in

Webster's house to indicate that was the case. No, more likely it was developed in Europe, and then shipped back to him.

So what exactly did I have beside a man and his wife enjoying sex? I could place Webster Sprague in the wheat field. That alone was enough to blackmail the man. Ruin his career. But was it enough to arrest him for murder? Hardly. I could also place Caren in the wheat field. Still, I needed more. I needed one more film. Now I was sure of its existence. But it was missing.

The more I thought about it, the more I realized there was something else missing from those films. Maggie.

CHAPTER 21

THE STURGEON

I WATCHED THE first of the Kennedy-Nixon debates. According to my notes it, too, took place in Chicago. September 26, 1960. It was the first presidential debate ever televised. I remember feeling good when it was over. They had both sounded smart, but Nixon looked like shit. I think it was the first time I truly believed Kennedy could win. It couldn't have been a happy night for Webster Sprague and the boys at the club.

Of course, other than the debate, I didn't have a whole lot to cheer about. Too much of the wheat field investigation was being carried out behind my back. Out of sight. Out of earshot. In the squad room there were a lot of meetings behind closed doors. Phone conversations were

held in whispers, hands cupped over mouth-
pieces. There were suspicious glances and accusatory smirks. This was odd and discomforting.
The squad room in the courthouse had always
been loud and friendly. Wide open. Now the
entire sheriff's department was tense and fur-
tive. Still, Fats couldn't have been more civil
toward me.

I only knew what I knew and I was playing
it close to the vest. I left the sex films in Webster's house, stacked on the bookshelf, exactly as
I had found them. I sneaked out of the place as
if I'd never been there. Kept what I saw to
myself.

It was hard to tell what Fats was learning
about me, what combination of facts and fiction
the weasel Dickerson was feeding him. It was
clear the diminutive detective had me in his
sights. Only a lack of evidence kept him from
pulling the trigger.

It wasn't unusual for Fats to take off in the
middle of the day and go fishing. He was the
sheriff. He could do as he pleased, and he often
did. I remember when we were kids. Fats would
take some of us older boys deer hunting. It was
quite an experience. Before we set out, the sheriff would inspect our rifles. Lecture us on safety.
Then he would deputize us. We would raise our
little hands and he would swear us in. Hand
out plastic badges. Call us all "Deputy." The

whole bit. It was about that time in a boy's life when we became just as interested in girls as we were in guns. One night around the campfire, Fats got a few beers in him, and he told us a story he must have thought we were ready to hear. It was about the war. The First World War.

"It was summertime," Fats said as he pried open another can of Schlitz, "and it was hot. Stinking hot. We were fighting in the countryside, through the wheat. After a few days of heavy fighting, there were no lines, no trenches. Everybody was lost. I got separated from the men. So I was crawling through this wheat field, trying to find my way home. You couldn't stand. If you stuck your head up . . . you might lose it. By then I was down to one bullet. One swig of water. No food. Then I heard this woman screaming . . . a terrible sound. So I began crawling toward the screams. There, in an opening in the wheat, I spotted five Huns attacking this pretty little French thing. She couldn't have been but fifteen years old. Not much older than you boys. They were stripping off her dress, and one of the Germans was dropping his drawers. No doubt, they were going to rape her. Probably take turns. What to do? I could turn and crawl away, pretend I hadn't seen what I saw . . . a young woman crying for help. Or I could fire the one shot I had left, and then get the hell out of there."

He paused for another swig of beer. We boys were on the edge of our seats, which were nothing but logs. The fire before us was throwing red-hot cinders into the air. The sheriff was telling us a true story about war. About rape and guns. We were holding our collective breath. Finally, he looked over at me, because I was his favorite.

"You've only got one bullet, Deputy. Who would you shoot?"

"I'd take out the group leader . . . maybe an officer."

"That's not a bad choice . . . but I believe I made the more humane choice. I shot the girl. I put the only bullet I had right through her temple."

I used to think about that story during my own war. Whenever I was peering through my scope with multiple choices, I would hear the voice of my county sheriff.

"You've only got one bullet, Deputy. Who would you shoot?"

I found the sheriff on the Lower Dells of the Wisconsin River. Every now and then came a break in the cliffs, where a fisherman could find a sandy beach. Fats was casting his heart out on one such stretch beneath a summer resort. Closed for the season.

"After one of those sturgeons today?" I asked him.

"Always after sturgeon, Deputy."

"It's an ugly fish."

"No, it's a beautiful fish." He glanced overhead. I could see him wincing behind his sunglasses. There was barely a cloud in the sky, only an occasional wisp of white sailing on an upper wind. September, the perfect month. "I like coming down here after the tourists have gone," he said to me. "Reminds me of the old days."

We were both in uniform. On Labor Day we had switched to our winter grays. Long-sleeved, tapered shirts. Black slacks. Silver Stetsons. Our badges were pinned proudly to our chests. The emblem of the Kickapoo County Sheriff's Department was embroidered on our arms. Fats kept us looking sharp. He hated the slovenly appearance of rural cops. He got the Gunn Club to contribute our weapons. In our holsters were .38/.44 Heavy Duty revolvers. That's a .38-caliber revolver on a .44 frame. It was designed to shoot a .38 special cartridge. The .44 frame was needed to handle the heavy recoil. Cops loved that revolver. The penetration was tremendous. Capable of stopping a car. It did, however, have one flaw. As trustworthy as it was, if that revolver was going to misfire, it would misfire in foul weather.

But that day was sunny and warm. In the middle of the river was a rocky island. One of several on the Lower Dells. Small caves were carved into its cliffs. Fats pointed that way. "Now at nighttime, the Indians would row their canoes into those caves out there with torches. The light of the fire would attract the bugs, and the bugs would attract the sturgeon. Then they'd spear 'em. Must have been some huge fish."

Fats was always telling Indian legends. In the heart of Wisconsin, there are a million of them. Especially in the Dells, where, as the Indians said, "Wave and rock and tall pine meet." It didn't matter if you'd heard the story a thousand times, Fats would tell it again.

"Dickerson said you wanted to see me. Said you'd be down here."

"Yes, Deputy. I thought it was time we compared notes . . . and the squad room being somewhat tense these days . . . I thought it might be better if we talked down here on the river."

"That's nice, Sheriff, but with all respect, I don't get to see Detective Dickerson's notes."

"Well, I'll try to fill in the blanks for you. What have you found out?"

I hesitated before I answered. But he was still the sheriff. Still my mentor. One of the heroes of my youth. "There was a camera in the wheat field on the day of the murders," I told him. "The indents we found in the wheat were made by a tripod. I believe there was a movie camera on that tripod."

"Yes, Detective Dickerson came to the same conclusion, except he thinks there was a rifle on that tripod. A sniper's rifle."

"What sense does that make? They were killed with the shotgun. Besides, a sniper wouldn't use a tripod . . . he'd use a bipod."

"And you think there is a film of this killing?"

"Yes, I do."

"Well, that would be nice. That would tell us who shot who, wouldn't it?"

"It would tell us everything except who was behind the camera."

Sheriff Fats reeled in his bait and then tossed it out again. His casting was fluid. Flawless. Like a lot of heavyset men, he was light on his feet. Almost graceful. He pointed downriver to a high cliff jutting out over the water. At the peak of the cliff, the rocks formed what appeared to be the bill of a hawk, its mouth wide open, as if screaming defiance.

"That's Hawk's Bill," Fats said. "Now, the Hawk Clan would haul their captives up to that point and perform a ceremonial dance. If a hawk was observed during this ritual, it meant the Hawk god demanded a sacrifice. Then the captives were weighted with rocks and cast into the churning water below. They did the same with their own people if they were accused of a crime. Hauled them up to Hawk's Bill. If a hawk flew over, it meant they were guilty. Then the guilty were weighted with rocks and thrown from the cliff. The river is more than sixty feet deep at that point. About as deep as the Wisconsin gets. Fast water, too. Bet there be a lot of bones down there."

"Yes, I'll bet there be, Sheriff."

"So you think they were filming these sexual games in that wheat field?"

"I think that's the way it started. Then like you said . . . maybe things got carried away. Or maybe somebody betrayed somebody."

"And where is this so-called murder film now?"

"I figure somebody involved in the killings has it."

"And that would be who?"

"My best guess . . . either Caren Sprague, Webster's missing wife, or the person behind the camera."

"War is hell, isn't it?"

"Excuse me?" I said.

"War . . . it changes a man. I had my war, you know. You boys call it World War One. We called it the Great War. There was nothing great about it—it was pure hell. Now my grandfather, he was in the Civil War. He was with the famous Iron Brigade. Seventh Regiment. Good Wisconsin men. Antietam, Gettysburg, Spotsylvania . . . they were at all of them."

"What's your point, Sheriff?"

"Do you remember that case in La Crosse, must have been seven or eight years ago? Man from Kickapoo County went up there and murdered his ex-wife and her parents in their trailer home. It was a custody dispute over their two children. The man hired a big-shot lawyer from St. Paul, and the jury let him off. They said the prosecutor hadn't proved his case. About a year later, during deer-hunting season, the man was found dead, with a bullet through his head. Sheriff up in La Crosse said that bullet may have been fired from eight hundred yards away . . . a difficult shot even under the best of conditions. So the sheriff wrote it off as a stray bullet, probably from a hunter. Thing of it was . . . the very next year, the big-shot lawyer from St. Paul was found dead with a bullet through his head."

"Some would say justice was served."

"Oh, I agree. There are people in this world who need to be shot. The future of this great nation depends on it. So why is it we could never get you to join the club, Deputy?"

"I don't play golf, I don't hunt, and I don't have a wife to cheat on."

"Yes, so you say." Fats laughed, but only briefly. He let more line out of his reel. Watched as the river carried it downstream. "Truth is, the war changed you, Deputy. Everybody accepts that. The town has tried to be understanding. People like you . . . but certain rumors about you just won't lay to rest. Now, if you hope to be sheriff one day, and we were all hoping for that, you've got to join the club and put these rumors to bed."

"Could you be more specific about these rumors?"

He removed his hat and wiped the sweat from his brow, as if he hadn't heard the question. His age was showing. He placed the Stetson back on his head. Stared out at the river. "I spent a good portion of my life building up the Sheriff's Department. I wanted to make our valley a good place to live. A safe place to live. A place where you can have a little fun, and still raise a family. Wherever I go in this state, policemen come up and shake my hand. Because I'm the sheriff of Kickapoo County. That means something in Wisconsin. Hell, it means something in Minnesota, and Chicago, and up there in Canada. We're known here for our police work."

"Yes, sir, we are."

Fats swallowed hard, as if he was trying to clear his throat of something that went down the wrong way. "Now, rumor has it, there's a murderer on my staff. A deputy who was like

a son to me. Rumor has it he killed Maggie Butler in a fit of jealous rage. Killed her husband.
Then he tried to make it look like our poor Maggie had done the killing . . . the very woman
he had murdered. The thought of it sickens me.
Angers me to no end."

"I wasn't in the wheat field that night, Sheriff.
I got there first thing in the morning, and I
found what I found."

"You know, I was in love like that once . . .
that murdering, jealous kind of love. But I was
a married man. I had children. I was too damn
old, and she was too damn young. I had to wake
up to that fact. Because I had responsibilities."

"Like I said, Sheriff, I wasn't in the wheat
field that night."

"Detective Dickerson is convinced you were."

"We've been together a long time, Sheriff.
Don't take his word over mine."

"Well then, Deputy, I suggest you put this
case to sleep."

There was a violent jerking motion on the end
of the fishing line. He'd hooked one. Fats swung
into action. Sturgeon in the Wisconsin River can
get six feet long, weigh over one hundred
pounds. Fats had a monster. Still, he wrestled it
like a pro, like a man who'd spent his life on
the river. When the great fish was finally near
shore, it leaped from the water. Fats was right.
The sturgeon was magnificent in the sparkling

sunlight. It dove, and then leaped again. I grabbed the net from the shore and stepped in water up to my shoe tops. I netted the beautiful monster and hoisted him into the air. I was so excited about the catch, I almost forgot about our conversation. Fats soon reminded me.

With his fishing reel in his left hand, he drew his service revolver with his right hand. Before my unbelieving eyes, he blasted the sturgeon to smithereens. The .38 special tore the fish to pieces. The gunfire echoed through the Dells like cannons. Fish guts and blood exploded over my uniform. The sheriff holstered his gun and reeled in what was left of the head. He drew a carving knife and sliced the line. The fish head dropped into the sand, its mouth still working, but the rest of it gone. Then Fats calmly packed up his gear and walked away.

CHAPTER 22

HAWK'S BILL

I WASHED MY face and hands in the river. Drank of its waters. Steadied my nerves. Then I walked along an old stagecoach trail, with fish guts and blood staining the uniform of which I was so proud. White-tail deer and flocks of wild turkeys scattered before me, perhaps instinctively knowing that I was once the boy who shot them dead from incredible distances. I didn't want to go back on the road. I certainly didn't want to go back to the courthouse. However, officially I was still on duty. I had some heavy reasoning to do.

The old trail took me along the top of the cliff from which Hawk's Bill juts out. I strolled to the very point of the bill, leaving only a sliver of sandstone between me and the waves below.

From that peak I could see nearly a mile of riverfront. A riot of color. An enchanting valley of painted rocks with lacy evergreens hanging spooklike over the mighty Wisconsin. The pagan Dells. I was surrounded by eerie cliffs of fantastic shapes, and tall, rocky islands in the middle of the dark, rushing water. Below me stirred the swirling eddies off Hawk's Bill, where it was said Indians were thrown to the deep if the messenger of death sailed overhead. The river itself had a brown tint to it, but not from pollution. The Wisconsin was actually a very clean river. The color came from tamarack trees along its banks. The trees secreted a natural chemical called tannic acid—the same acid that gave Coca-Cola its color. With the bright afternoon sun hitting the river, the effect was that of a million fireflies dancing above amber waves. Even with sunglasses, the sight stung my eyes, but I couldn't look away.

I was now convinced that Webster Sprague, a congressman and a candidate for the United States Senate, was involved in a double homicide. And he was probably involved in some kind of pornography ring. But where the hell was I supposed to go for help? Webster Sprague was probably the most powerful man in the county. Somehow, he had convinced the second most powerful man in the county, Sheriff Fats, that I was responsible for the murders—that my name would sully the Sheriff's Department for years to come. So far, the only ally I could garner was a scratchy voice on the other end of a phone line. And she, too, was probably involved in the murder. She was certainly involved in the sex.

Debauchery was nothing new to this part of Wisconsin. After the Civil War, legendary rivermen piloted their lumber rafts through the Dells. Then they'd saunter down to Kickapoo Falls to relax and refresh themselves. Their first order of business was usually tying up the town marshal so he wouldn't get hurt. Gambling, drinking, and whoring were a way of life in these parts. On hot summer nights the streets were often brilliantly decorated with spilled blood. In 1890, the last lumber raft floated through the Dells, and the first souvenir shop opened—a harbinger of things to come. By 1960, a quarter-million tourists a year were passing through the sandstone bluffs, mostly in the summer months. Over time, that number would more than double. And that, too, was obscene.

If Dickerson believed I had my sniper's rifle in the wheat field that day, and Maggie and Michael were killed by a shotgun, it meant he was still grasping at straws. He hadn't quite figured out how to hang the murders on me. There was something else that bothered me. Besides the suggestion that I had killed Maggie, Fats had

mentioned certain rumors, as if there had been
malicious rumors about me since the end of the
war. Small towns are funny that way.

I could see a doe and her fawn drinking from
the river beneath the sandstone bluffs on the far
shore. On the cliff above them, I glimpsed a coy-
ote as he stuck his long snout out of the pines.
One of the three would be dead before nightfall.

The people most native to this pagan land
were the Ho-Chunk people, once called Winne-
bago. Their great leader was Yellow Thunder.
Four times between 1844 and 1873, Yellow
Thunder and his people were rounded up,
loaded onto steamboats and boxcars, and removed to reservations in Nebraska. Each time
Yellow Thunder was taken, he simply walked
back to the Dells. His people followed. Finally,
in 1875, the government relented, and the
Homestead Act was extended to include the Ho-
Chunk. Yellow Thunder lived to be a hundred
years old. It was said he died in full regalia on
the shoreline at sunset, the flowing river waving
a sad farewell.

I took a long last look around at the haunting
beauty of it all. Drop me in the middle of Nebraska and I, too, would walk back to the Dells.
I searched the cloudless sky for a soaring hawk
to see if perhaps I truly was guilty. But the sky
was clear. I was feeling better about myself. Still,
I had to get cleaned up. I needed a bath.

I had just turned. Was about to head down to my squad when the first shot almost took my ear off. The second shot took off my hat. It was a military rifle. The firing was rapid bolt-action. I dove behind a pine growing out of the sandstone. Blood was spilling from my hairline. The third shot tore an entire section out of the pine. Whoever it was, and I prayed to God it was not Fats, he had me in his sights. He'd followed me through his scope until I was far enough out on Hawk's Bill that I could not retreat. This sniper wasn't trying to scare me. He was trying to kill me.

You have to remember that in Wisconsin everybody hunts. Gunshots echoing through the woods in the autumn months are not considered suspicious. I wasn't expecting help.

He was firing at me from at least two hundred yards away. Even if I could see him through the woods, and I couldn't, the best distance at which my revolver could accurately return fire was fifty yards—and to be frank, my proficiency with a rifle did not carry over to revolvers. Dear God, what I would have given to have my Springfield in my hands.

The fourth shot splintered the rest of the pine. From the exploding tree, I guessed the bullets were 6.5-millimeter shells, which are 40 percent heavier than the average bullet of that diameter. In fact, big game hunters use 6.5-millimeter

shells to bring down animals as large as ele-
phants. If he was using even a 4-power scope,
and I suspected he was, I was a dead man. With
a scope like that, and bullets like those, even a
moron could shoot like a marksman. I rolled
from pine to pine. My only defense was to
keep moving.

His fifth shot made up my mind for me. He
had me cut off from the trail, and it was just
too beautiful a day to die. I wiped the blood
from my eye. I unfastened my holster and
dropped it to the stone. I kicked off my shoes.
Then with every inch of sprint in my legs, with
every ounce of thrust I could muster, I ran and
leaped from Hawk's Bill. My reasoning was simple. The sniper was upriver. If I went into the
water, I'd come up downriver, behind the cliff.
If I came up at all.

So I was falling fast from Hawk's Bill. My
arms flailing. The swirling, Coca-Cola-colored
water was rushing up to swallow me.

I hit the river hard, and my world went cold
and dark. I was spinning in downward circles.
My arms felt as if they were being torn from
their sockets. The dark water rushed up my nose
and enveloped my brain. It was like I was dying
from the inside out. Everything seemed magnified. Internalized. Worst of all, I was sinking. As
mightily as I struggled, I could not reverse the

sickening sweep of my descent. My powers of body and mind were fast leaving me.

Indians believe there is no death, only a change of worlds. The overwhelming feeling came over me that I was changing worlds, that soon I would be dancing cheek to cheek with a thousand years' worth of human skeletons.

"Bet there be a lot of bones down there."

"Yes, I'll bet there be, Sheriff."

I know now it was a rapid current that grabbed hold of me. The Wisconsin River is famous for them. But this current, God forgive me, had a spiritual element to it. It was guiding me more than pulling me. Best of all, it was guiding me rapidly upward, toward the heavenly blue sky, and at the same time away from Hawk's Bill and the sniper's bullets. At that moment, my love for the Dells was sealed for the ages. It must have been the same warm feeling old Yellow Thunder knew as he trekked across the prairies toward his sacred rocks and water. My only challenge now was to hold my breath. Not easy to do with a head full of river water. Suddenly, through the amber waves I could see the sun, like the proverbial light at the end of the tunnel. And even before I breached the surface, I knew I was going to make it.

CHAPTER 23

AFTON ROAD:
PART TWO

IN OUR VALLEY a more bittersweet love story has never been told than the story I tell of Afton Road. Brock Carlson was older than me by a good five years. I watched him play high school football as a boy. He went on to the University of Wisconsin in Madison, where he earned the nickname "Badger" for his fierce defensive play. And while it is true that in the autumn of 1941, I made what was possibly the longest run in the history of Wisconsin football, my exploits on the high school gridiron paled in comparison to my hero. I was but a mere shadow of the football player that was Brock Carlson.

As much as we boys loved watching Brock run crazy over any football field he sunk his cleats into, we loved even more watching his girlfriend, Lila, leading the cheers for him. Lila was the classic Scandinavian beauty. A petite figure, but wonderfully curved. Her hair was a shiny blond that almost went white in the sunlight. Her face was as pure as a summer day in Wisconsin, with soft blue eyes the color of our deep-wooded lakes. For little boys short on vocabulary, there were not enough adjectives to describe Lila the cheerleader, girlfriend of the great Brock Carlson.

These high school sweethearts were married in one of the most talked-about weddings in Kickapoo Falls. Though they married just before the war, Pearl Harbor was attacked before the golden couple had any children. Brock left his young bride behind and enlisted in the United States Marine Corps, where he put all of his athletic skills and his fighting spirit into the cockpit of an airplane.

Lila waited for him. For four years she waited. Everybody in Kickapoo Falls followed his exploits. Lieutenant Brock Carlson lead his squadron in "kills" as they island-hopped across the Pacific Ocean toward Japan. He spent his last months of the war stationed in the Philippines.

I was still in a hospital tent in Europe, hoping to be sent home. Brock Carlson was an officer, and he got to come home early. Dad wrote me about it, how Lila went down to Union Station in Chicago and waited for him. What a reunion that must have been. I can see her with tears in her eyes as he steps off the train with a thousand other soldiers. He is resplendent in his dress blues. She runs to him. Throws herself in his arms. After a night at the Drake Hotel in Chicago, they rode the train back to Kickapoo Falls, where the whole town was waiting for them. On the Fourth of July, 1945, Kickapoo Falls had its biggest parade ever, with Marine Corps Lieutenant Brock Carlson as the honorary Grand Master. He and Lila rode down Main Street and past Courthouse Square in a big red convertible. Dad said there wasn't a dry eye on the street.

That fall, they moved into the farmhouse at the end of Afton Road. They had bought the property for a song, and now they set to work fixing up the old place. I went to a party there not long after I got home. In fact, I was still in uniform. Still on crutches. I remember the house as sunny and warm. All gaiety. Flowers and fresh paint. I also remember there were a lot of good-natured jokes about when Brock and Lila were going to start that family.

Within a year of our return from the war, the rumors began. Rumors about why Lila was not having children. About why Brock and Lila were both avoiding people. There were stories of bizarre behavior, terrible fights, and screaming coming from the woods behind their house. There were phone calls to Doc Hope in the middle of the night, and not-so-secret trips to the Mayo Clinic. Then one day in 1947, the doors were bolted shut at the white house at the end of Afton Road. The curtains were drawn tight. And hometown hero Brock Carlson and his lovely wife, Lila, were never seen again.

CHAPTER 24

DOOR COUNTY

IT IS SAID that only in our old age can we look back and say who we loved, and who we didn't. I loved my mother. Sounds trite, but I was just a little boy when she died. I have memories of this angelic woman holding me tight, and of an old priest leading me into her bedroom to say good-bye. I was crying. I didn't want to say good-bye. After that, the only love I knew was for a dark-haired devil of a girl from Kickapoo Falls. Her name was Maggie. Then I went off to war. Then Maggie got married. Then I was wounded. Finally, I came home.

Like a lot of returning veterans, I wanted to forget about the war. Get on with my life. But

the longer I live, the more I think about the
lives of those who were killed. Lives never
lived. What kind of careers would they have
had? Who would they have married? Where
are their children? Most of all, did I do right
by them? Did I lead a good life?

Even as a young man, I too often felt like a
writer. Only observing life. Never really participating. I had loved the beauty of patrolling
Kickapoo County. But it was a solitary patrol—
driving by myself day after day, night after
night, year after year, over the long, silent
roads. Eventually, the white lines got to me.
You can only spend so much time alone, then
you spend your life alone. Not because you
have to, but because you want to.

There were times I couldn't wait to get away,
out of the courthouse, out of town, away from
the locals and the tourists—as far away as I
could get from human contact. North I would
sail, to my cabin here on an island off the rocky
shores of Lake Michigan in Door County. In
Wisconsin, it is literally as far away as you can
get. The solitude is halfway to heaven. I am at
peace here. Always have been.

Door County is often called the Cape Cod
of the Midwest. A magical peninsula that juts
up Green Bay like a little finger. All charming
villages and enchanting islands. A lot of Chicago people summer here, but you can still es-

cape the crowds. Drive to the very tip of the peninsula. Get in a boat and sail north by northeast. Take harbor on the bay side of the island and then trek through the woods to the lake side, where, at times, the Lake Michigan waters can pound the rocks with the force of a North Atlantic wave. In fact, that's how the county got its name—from all of the ships that struck disaster trying to round its point. Death's door, sailors called it. But it's heaven's gate to me.

As I write these words on the solitary shores of this solitary island, the miles and the years on the road all melt into one another. It is only the investigative work that sticks out in my mind. Like the day I was shot at up on Hawk's Bill. The day I took the big swim. Once I pulled myself from the Wisconsin River, what could I do? I still didn't know who had been shooting at me. Why not go to the State Police, or even the FBI? Because I wasn't all that innocent.

So I just went back to work. I recovered my gun and holster. Bought a new hat. Had my uniform cleaned and pressed. Then I went back to the courthouse where, ironically, the only person who asked after me was Detective Dickerson. As much as I wanted to believe it was some kind of slight, there was no sarcasm in his voice. No bitterness. No jealousy. Sounding honestly sincere, he stopped by my desk and asked, "Are you all right?"

"Yes," I told him, "I'll be fine."

Other than that, I was treated as if nothing had happened. As if I were chasing ghosts.

CHAPTER 25

THE VOYEUR

IT OCCURS TO me I haven't written much about one of those ghosts I was chasing. Michael Butler. It's hard to write about a man I should have hated but that I couldn't help but like. He married the woman I loved. Pretty big deal in a small town. As I remember it, Michael had some kind of heart murmur. They wouldn't let him play football. It kept him out of the war. I never resented him for it. This slight medical condition gave him a vulnerable quality that girls loved and other guys couldn't understand. The thing of it is, Michael really was a good guy. He was tall and slender, and handsome, and fun to be around. By the time he died, his dark hair was thinning a bit, but other than that, he hadn't changed much since high school.

I wrote earlier that there were rumors, that even in high school there were rumors. Most of those rumors involved Michael Butler and the caves. These caves were carved out along the river at the end of the Ice Age. The most popular cave had a capacious dome shape. A hollow ledge at the back of the cave was filled with soft sand. The kids threw a blanket over it. Kind of like a rock bed. In Kickapoo Falls, a slut was a girl who went down to the caves. Though nobody ever accused her of being a slut, it was rumored that Maggie went down to the caves. Most everything I heard about the caves was secondhand. But it was said Michael Butler was the king of the cavern.

My friend Danny Irving took his girl Cindy down to the caves after he scored a touchdown against Reedsburg, as if he was entitled to it now. Must have been our senior year. He later told me he was just after some tit, but that it ended up being the first time he and Cindy went all the way. He had built a small fire in the pit. They began necking. Then they moved back to the ledge, to the rock bed. As Danny told it, he was on top of Cindy, inside of her for the first time, not believing his luck, when he turned his head and glanced into the flickering light. There stood Michael Butler on the other side of the fire, staring at them through the flames. He was not laughing at them, or even smirking. He was watching, almost mesmerized. Danny said it was spooky. He buried his face in Cindy's neck and finished what he was doing. When they got up to put on their clothes, Michael was gone.

Hard to say if a flaw in the human heart could turn a man into a voyeur, but the more I thought about it during the wheat field case, the more I thought voyeurism was the essence of Michael Butler. Watching, as his buddies played football. Watching, as his classmates went off to war. Watching, as a friend had sex for the first time. Watching, as another man made love to his wife. In fact, it struck me that perhaps Michael was not murdered first, as we had assumed. That maybe he had watched as his wife was murdered. His last act of voyeurism. The shock came when the gun was turned on him.

Michael's lover, Caren Sprague, remained the key to the puzzle. Did she have reason to shoot Michael in the balls? I saw her in a film performing oral sex on him. Yet it was she who led me to that film. Jerking men around seemed to be what she did best. I had to find her. I couldn't sit by the telephone and wait for her obscene phone calls.

She had told me she'd once run away with Russ "The Bull" Hoffmeyer. I corralled the big state trooper one morning outside the courthouse. The square was crowded with people, but the looks I was getting from those people were no longer friendly. The autumn leaves were nearing peak colors. Every now and then a leaf broke from its branch and zigzagged to the ground. The sun in the October sky shone down on me and the ex-Marine like a spotlight between the multicolored tree branches. It made Hoffmeyer uncomfortable. He didn't want to share a spotlight with me.

"Look, Pennington, I shouldn't be talking to you."

"Why not?"

"They're saying things."

"Who's saying?"

"The gang at the Gunn Club . . . Fats, Webster Sprague . . . it's all over town. C'mon, you don't want to mess with those people."

"Did you ever drive down to Chicago with Caren Sprague? Check into the Drake Hotel . . . the Presidential Suite?"

"How the hell did you know about that?"

"I figured you hadn't told me everything."

"I told you everything. . . . I just left out some of the details."

"Yeah, well, fill in the blanks."

"You got the right hotel, Pennington, but the wrong girl. I made that trip with Maggie." He glanced over his shoulder at the courthouse. Shook his head in disgust. Then he stormed off through the square.

I, too, turned to the courthouse. Standing before the tall windows on the second-floor landing was Detective Dickerson. Watching.

So why was Caren telling me stories that were obviously meant for Maggie? If Caren had the life Maggie wished for . . . was it possible Maggie had the sex life Caren wanted? More specifically, the man Caren wanted? Michael Butler?

Caren's not-so-loving husband was back in town. The election of 1960 had entered the final stretch. It occurred to me that I could use the closeness to election day to extort more information from the local congressman running for the Senate. I decided to pay a visit to the infamous Kickapoo Gunn Club. Confront Webster Sprague about his wife's indiscretions, and his own. Perhaps glean some insights into his relationship with Maggie.

Driving out to the Gunn Club that gorgeous autumn day, I really believed that the wheat field murders was a case about powerful young couples falling in love, and falling in bed, with all of the wrong people. But there was a lot more to this story than unrequited love. More than dirty little movies. As election day approached, other forces were at work. And on a scale I couldn't imagine.

CHAPTER 26

THE CANDIDATE

I COULD HEAR gunfire in the upper hills. A shooting range. At the foot of the hill, a great blue heron scoured a pond in search of a meal. Canadian geese frolicked on the banks, flamboyant in the sunshine. I passed through wrought-iron gates hanging wide open and followed the circular drive through the golf course to the Prairie-style architecture that rambled up over the hillside. The Kickapoo Gunn Club. The driveway sailed through a porte cochere, where I parked the squad and waved off a parking attendant. A practice green lay off to the left. Men draped in colorful sweaters were crouched in fierce determination, practicing their putting. In a driveway off to the right, motorized carts were lined up in rows, as if poised to mount some kind of assault. Wisconsin golfers take to the links right up to the first snow. I never understood the game. Never understood men obsessed with the game.

I marched up the stone stairs and through the pine doors. The entryway was all blond wood around jutting stones. Cherokee-red trim. The windows above flooded the oriental carpets with sunlight. The exclusive club was out of place in Kickapoo Falls, as was Wright's home, Taliesin, down in Spring Green. From a distance they seemed a magnificent piece of the natural landscape, but once inside you realized you had entered another world.

Webster Sprague was speaking at a luncheon. I strained to listen outside the double doors of a small dining room. "And finally," he told the gathering, "the election of 1960 is about morality. Who has the moral authority to lead this nation . . . and in what direction?" Then I heard him mumble some platitudes about Richard Nixon and the Republican Party.

After a friendly round of applause, the doors swung open and I got my first peek at the assembled crowd. All men. Powerful, Midwestern white men. You have to understand the times. Things were different back then. It was a man's world. Political wives were seldom seen, never heard. A man could serve in Congress for twenty years and voters didn't have the faintest notion as to what his wife looked like. I doubt many club members noticed, or even cared, that Webster's wife was on the lam. I recognized few faces. It was not unusual for Gunn Club members to take the train from Chicago or Milwaukee. Many of them resided in the affluent suburban enclaves strung like precious pearls up the shores of Lake Michigan. Places like Lake Bluff, Lake Forest, and Winnetka. Fox Point and Whitefish Bay. In Minnesota, they came down from the private clubs on White Bear Lake, Lake Minnetonka, and in Edina.

I stood close to attention as these well-dressed men filed by, holding my hat behind my back. I wanted Webster to see the uniform. See the badge. I wanted him to see for himself I was still on the job. "Mr. Sprague, can I have a word with you?" I said it loud, with a sense of urgency and authority.

"Deputy Pennington, I'd heard you were back on traffic patrol."

He was wearing a new suit, or at least it looked new to me. "You heard wrong. Dead wrong. I'm investigating the murders of Maggie and Michael Butler."

The tone of my voice and the names of the victims threw a scare into him. He excused himself from his cronies. We moved into a small sitting room. The blood-red carpeting was thick and soft. Felt like I wasn't supposed to be treading on it. The walls were decorated with fine art. Oil paintings. Undoubtedly original. Most of the works were bucolic scenes, but not of the Midwest. More like northern Europe. I couldn't help but admire the talent that went into each stroke. Yes, even a county deputy who grew up above a shoe store in a small American town could appreciate great art.

"They're priceless," Webster told me.

"How does priceless art find its way to the middle of Wisconsin?"

"You sell yourself short, Pennington. Always have. You've got that typical Midwestern inferiority complex. Too bad. You could have had some fun. I mean, real fun. Maybe you could have had Maggie."

"Did you have Maggie?" I asked.

He laughed. A laugh I didn't appreciate. "You always kept Maggie on a pedestal. Now that she's dead, she must be canonized in your mind. You're pathetic that way. Never let a woman do that to you," he lectured.

"Were you and Maggie having an affair?"

"Let me tell you something about your Saint Maggie. She was one cold, manipulative, and very shrewd bitch. And I say that in admiration. That travel business was hers. She built that business. She ran it. Michael watched. If anything, Michael was a drag on the business. A drag on her life. I wasn't surprised she killed him."

"Was Maggie with you at the Republican convention in Chicago?"

"You've been talking to my wife. Where is she?"

"Caren told me that every now and then you two used to enjoy a good movie."

Webster's face went red. Deep red. Furious red. He spoke barely holding his temper. "Do you think you're the first man to try and get into my wife's pants? You're skating on thin ice, Deputy. Where is she?"

"Are you really looking for your wife . . . or are you just looking for the money?"

"What about the money?"

"Money like that can buy a lot of votes, especially this close to election day." I was actually enjoying his anger. His predicament. On the spur of the moment, I decided to have some fun. "Let's see, according to you, Caren helped herself to two hundred thousand dollars on her way out the door. Now let's say, hypothetically, you were willing to give her another two hundred thousand dollars to ensure any movies she may have taken with her don't show up before the election. Oh hell, let's say three hundred thousand . . . just to make it a cool half million."

"Are you trying to blackmail me?"

"Who said anything about blackmail? How would I even know if such movies exist? I mean, what kind of politician would be so stupid as to film himself having sex?"

"You wouldn't understand because your wounds aren't just physical." He stepped into my face, tapped his temple with his finger. "Your real wounds are up here."

Cops never back down. I stepped an inch closer to him. "You're right, Webster, I don't understand. What is marriage? Where are your commitments to one another? What are your commitments to one another? You pass your wife around like a pretzel. She shares her husband the way she shares beer nuts. I mean, what the hell is wrong with you people?"

"I don't think you know what you're in the middle of here. You tell Caren . . . there's to be no blackmail."

"Blackmail, hell, all I have to do is whisper a few carefully chosen words into the ear of the right reporter . . . about your lovely, missing wife being a suspect in a double homicide . . . and you can pretty much kiss your political career good-bye."

"You wouldn't do that."

"Why not?"

"Because you still hope to be sheriff someday. It's the only job in this town that would validate your sorry life. Trust me, we'd take you down with us."

"Who's we?"

"I'm warning you, Pennington."

"And I'm warning you. I don't know what kind of sick games you're playing out here . . . or what kind of conspiracies you're hatching . . . but I know you were in that wheat field. I don't know exactly what your role was yet . . . but I'll find out. You might want to think about parting with that three hundred thousand dollars. With that kind of money, a man with my sorry life could move to an island far, far away."

CHAPTER 27

A VOICE IN THE WOODS:
THIRD CALL

"DEPUTY PENNINGTON, are you alone?"

"No, I'm having an orgy. Half the town is here."

"You've never been to an orgy in your life."

"How are you, Caren?"

"It's late . . . did I wake you?"

"No, I was reading a book."

"What book?"

"*Murder Me!* It's a Max Brand mystery."

"I don't know that author."

"Max Brand . . . he was killed in the war."

"Did you figure out how it ends yet?"

"All in time . . . but I think the wife did it."

"That's been known to happen. I'm lonely, Deputy."

"Yes, the ocean can be a very lonely place."

"You think you're smart, don't you?"

"Yes, I think I'm smart. You said you met Webster at Lake Geneva. You went to bed with him and a boyfriend. How did that work?"

"More details, Deputy?"

"It's late . . . humor me."

"In a situation such as that, it's up to the woman to take the initiative. We were downstairs at the bar . . . drinking, telling dirty jokes . . . it got late. My boyfriend, his name was Robb, said it's time we went to our room. I downed my drink and said, 'Why don't we all three go to our room?' Webster got the message right away, but Robb mumbled something like, 'Sure, Webster, c'mon up . . . join us for a drink.' Robb was a little slow."

"Maybe not. Come to my room . . . join me for a drink only means one thing."

"Yes, but come to *our* room . . . join *us* for a drink . . ."

"Then what happened?"

"I came out of the bathroom. Robb was sitting on one bed . . . Webster was on the other."

"And which bed did you jump into?"

"There are rules, Deputy. I was with Robb . . . I went to Robb's bed."

"And Webster stayed on his bed."

"In the beginning. Like I say, there are unwritten rules. It's important that a woman demonstrate her willingness to indulge men in all their fantasies . . . no matter how weird the script. Show some initiative . . . but do what you're told. Webster sat on his bed with a drink in his hand . . . watching."

"Watching what?"

"Watching as Robb kissed me . . . as he stripped me. Pulled my head into his lap. Then Robb liked to work from behind . . . do you know what I mean?"

"No, tell me."

"Besides doing me like a dog, he liked me on my side . . . facing Webster. Then he'd push it in me from behind while rubbing my shoulders. It was like having a back rub and a great fuck at the same time."

"And Webster watched this?"

"Oh yes, he got quite an eyefull. But you see, where some men are content to watch, Webster needed to participate."

"And he participated that night?"

"Yes, Deputy, he did."

"Explain to me . . . because I've never experienced it . . . how does a woman have sex with two men at the same time . . . if you know what I'm asking."

"Well, Deputy, I have a finely honed talent for oral sex. So the best way is to have one of them in your mouth. But if push comes to shove . . . excuse the pun . . . you can take them both in. A woman hasn't lived until she's had two men inside of her at the same time."

"The Republican convention in Chicago . . . you said Maggie and Michael drove down the last night . . . the night of the acceptance speech. At the hotel . . . who was with who?"

"It was a typical night for the four of us. I was with Michael, and Webster was with Maggie."

"But by the time the speech was over . . . you were gone, or so you say. If you were with Michael . . . what happened?"

"I don't like to talk about Michael."

"Were you in love with him?"

"From the first time I saw him."

"The first film in the wheat field . . . you were only with Webster. Why? Hello?"

"You're very resourceful, Deputy Pennington. That film was to be the first in a series."

"Escalating sex?"

"Something like that."

"So these films were not being made for your private entertainment . . . these films were made to be sold?"

"Yes, but Webster didn't know that. He's naive that way . . . he thinks with his dick. The entire series, if complete, truly complete, would be worth a lot of money."

"Why? Hello . . . still there? Who was behind the camera? Caren, do you know what a snuff film is? All right, Caren, listen up . . . this is the deal I've worked out. Webster is willing to pay for the return of the wheat field film . . . hello?"

"I'm listening . . ."

"You get the film to me . . . I get the money to you."

"How much?"

"Two hundred thousand dollars."

"And what's your take?"

"Half."

"That sounds a little greedy on your part, Deputy."

"Take it or leave it."

"When?"

"Before the election."

"You know, ever since you made that long run . . . people in that town haven't looked at you the same . . . like, maybe you're a little off center."

"What do you know about that run?"

"I'll call you."

"Don't hang up . . . hello? Caren? Damn it!"

CHAPTER 28

THE LONGEST RUN

IT'S ONE OF those local sports legends that has been repeated so often and for so many years that the truth got sidelined long ago. The story of the longest run. Some say it happened at a Packer game back in the days of Curly Lambeau. Others argue the run came during a Badger game at Camp Randall Stadium. Still others claim the record was set in the south-central town of Kickapoo Falls, but the kid was later killed in the war. I may be the only man left alive who knows the real story. In fact, now that most of the principals have died, even the folks in Kickapoo Falls have a hard time putting a name and date on the run. But I don't. It was October of 1941. My senior year in high school.

We were playing Richmond Prairie. A real

powerhouse. The game was at our field, which in those days sat off Highway 33 on the road to Portage. It was a north-south field with some of the thickest grass I've ever seen. Wood bleachers were strung along the west side. The east side was just a gently sloping hill that rolled up into the woods. People would sit over there on their blankets. Behind us were the Baraboo Hills, containing some of the oldest rock in North America. Just across the highway was a farm field. Usually cornstalks. At least it was corn that year. The entrance was framed with a wire fence beneath a big blue-and-white sign that read KICKAPOO FALLS STADIUM. A second fence kept fans out of the end zone. It was a magical place to play football. The town was proud of it. We could pack in four thousand people for a big game like Richmond Prairie.

Then there were the cheerleaders. You have to remember that before the war half of the cheerleaders in this country were boys. But it's not the boys I remember. It's the girls. God, how I loved those girls. You should have seen Maggie in a cheerleader outfit. A megaphone in her arms. Her black hair blowing free in the autumn breeze. Every kid on the team would have run through a brick wall for that girl. And nobody in town was more infatuated with her charms and her beauty than me.

In the weeks leading up to the game there

were rumors that Maggie had broken up with
Michael. That she had some secret lover. Of
course, there were always rumors about Maggie
and Michael, but there must have been some
truth to this one. Why else would I stick my
neck out before a big game and ask Maggie to
the dance? I mean, I'd always known that someday I was going to get up the nerve to ask her
out, but the opportunity just never seemed to
present itself. Suddenly, there it was.

She seemed surprised by my question. For a
second, and it was only a second, I thought she
was going to say yes. A second later, I had the
horrible feeling she was going to laugh in my
face. Finally, she put on that winsome smile that
had been melting hearts all over town. "No,"
she said, she couldn't go to the dance with me.
"It's just not possible." The thing of it was, she
didn't say why it wasn't possible. She didn't say
if she was going with Michael, or somebody
else. She just said, "No. It's just not possible."

High school is bad enough. High school in a
small town can be a living hell. I swear, within
minutes every living person in Kickapoo Falls
knew that I had been shot down by the Princess
Maggie. I had been put back into my place. I
was a reserve back. Not quite good enough to
be the star halfback. I was sixth man on the bas-
ketball team. Not quite good enough to be in
the starting five. For years it seemed, that was

me. Deputy sheriff. Not quite good enough to be sheriff.

When Maggie said, "No. It's just not possible," it was the first time I ever thought about killing her. I'd do it with a rifle. I'd do it during deer hunting season, when her death could be blamed on a stray bullet. Spot the target. Her face—that dark-eyed, dark-haired, Indian-like face. I'd rest my cheek against the stock. Eye to the scope. Check the wind. Set the sight. Relax, breath slow. Squeeze the trigger. Shoot with purpose. Shoot with moral indignation. "Goodbye, Maggie."

A little humiliation can go a long way. It took me ninety-two yards, and then some.

Night games were rare before the war. Maybe once or twice a year. The Richmond Prairie game was under the lights. Deep into the fourth quarter, we found ourselves down by four points. Our starting halfback was carried from the field with a sprained ankle. He was out. I was in. As I said, I wasn't the star of the team, or the captain of the team. I was just a small halfback. But I played my heart out. We had blue jerseys with white numerals. Leather helmets with no face masks. Not a whole lot of padding. Most of us had football cleats, but some of the farm kids played in boots or tennis shoes. But damn, it was good football. I still get excited thinking about it.

Our quarterback that game was just a junior for whom I didn't have a whole lot of respect. I just didn't think he was a very good football player. In fact, if I remember right, we called him Junior. Anyway, we were behind, 22 to 18. Richmond Prairie punted to us and the ball bounced out of bounds at our 8-yard line. There were forty-five seconds on the clock. Our undefeated season was slipping away. We went into the huddle expecting a pass play. But Junior called right-half at four. In other words, run me with the ball right up the middle. This was the stupidest call I'd ever heard. We were down four points. We had ninety-two yards to go for a touchdown with less than a minute to play, and our nitwit quarterback wanted to run the smallest halfback on the team right up the middle. I was shaking my head in disgust as we broke the huddle and moved to the line. The other thing that bothered me was that I knew there were nine other guys on my team shaking their heads in disgust. Only the quarterback, junior, seemed ignorant of the stupidity of his play calling.

Already a few people were heading for the exit gate, but most of the town folks came to their feet screaming as we lined up in a straight T formation. I could see the cheerleaders with their hands clasped beneath their chins, as if praying for a miracle.

Junior barked out the count. The center hiked the ball. I could hear our line throwing their hearts into their blocks. I always took a half step back. Planted my right foot. Waited for the blocks to develop. Then charged through the hole. This time was no different. I took the hand-off from Junior and ran right between the guard and tackle. I wasn't surprised there was a hole open; they were good blockers. It's what I saw as I ran through that hole that surprised me. I could see the cornfield across Highway 33.

Apparently, the last thing Richmond Prairie was expecting was me up the middle. They had vacated the center of the line to cover a deep pass. By the time I sprinted past their big, slow linebackers, I had only the safety to beat, and our right end was bearing down on him. I slowed up a split second for our man to pass in front of me. He flattened their safety like a pan-cake, and I was off to the races.

So what was I thinking about while I was run-ning ninety-two yards for a touchdown? Besides the fact that Junior might be smarter than I had previously believed, I was thinking about Mag-gie. About the humiliation of being told it wasn't possible to date her. About spending my school years desperately in love with a girl who probably thought I was a joke.

I sailed across the 50-yard line. The 40. Then the 30. There was no doubt now I was going to score the winning touchdown. The roar of the crowd seemed deafening. It was at that point that something inside of me snapped. In fact, if I had to trace it back, I would say it was the moment when I became a killer, of sorts. Somewhere between the 10-yard line and the end zone, I decided to keep on going. Not only to break all of the records, but to break all of the rules. I cruised right through the end zone, as four thousand screaming fans jumped up and down in ecstasy. Through the back of the end zone I ran, and with the ball still in my hand, I leaped the wire fence. Parents pulled their children out of the way as I hit the ground, still running. I broke through the standing crowd and sprinted out the entrance gate. Ran across Highway 33. I could hear thousands of gasps and screams as I dodged a semitrailer filled with wheat. I could hear the squealing brakes behind me. The blaring horn. In my mind, I could see a whole stadium of people standing aghast, their mouths hanging open in disbelief. I sprinted into the cornfield.

The corn had already been picked so that all that was left standing were the dry stalks. Now I was hurdling through golden stalks of corn in the harvest moon. Frightened deer scattered before me. I wanted to be out of sight of the crowd. I wanted to be alone. Most of all, I wanted to run.

The cornfield ended at the train tracks. Without breaking stride, I followed the tracks over the railroad bridge, across the river, and into town. I was still running, that pigskin still tucked under my arm. I cut down the hill to Ash Street, which took me around to Main Street and right through the heart of Kickapoo Falls. The streets were deserted. Everybody was at the game. I ran past Courthouse Square, the street lamps illuminating the park beneath the darkened building. I was near exhaustion by the time I reached the shoe store. I don't think I was crying, but I may have been. Even if I was crying, they were not tears of self-pity, or tears of joy. They were tears of anger.

The store was dark. I cut around to the alley and took the back stairs two at a time, up to the apartment. Once inside, I crashed on my bed. Still in full uniform. Still with the ball in my arms. Touchdown, you fucking bitch! Touchdown!

Dad got home about an hour later. I know that I was in bed. I can't remember if I was still in uniform. I do remember he flicked on the light. Saw that I was alive and well. Then he said, "Nice run." He turned off the light. Closed the door and left me alone. That was my dad.

Because I wouldn't talk about it, nobody was really sure of the exact route I took. But a couple of reporters from the *Republic* stepped it off at

2.1 miles—that's from the 8-yard line at Kickapoo Falls Stadium to the front steps of Pennington Shoes and Boots. Anyway, the story of
the halfback who kept on running hit the news
wires. And the legend was born.

1941 was also my last deer-hunting season. I
lived for it growing up. I learned how to shoot
hunting deer. I learned how to stalk. I learned
how to hide and wait. Bide my time until my
target walked into view. The Army Rangers
taught me a lot, but most of what I knew about
shooting and killing was instinctive.

On December 7, the Japanese bombed Pearl
Harbor, and the future of every boy in our class
was decided. We didn't even know where Pearl
Harbor was, but we knew what it meant. I think
it was obvious to the girls in the class that life
for them was also being determined. I remember
their faces that day. The girls seemed more
shocked than the boys. The principal urged us
to finish school and then enlist in the spring,
and most of us did ship out in the summer of
'42, but with war fever running high, there were
some boys who dropped out and enlisted right
away.

After Pearl Harbor, Michael Butler tried to enlist, but he had that heart murmur. He stayed
home. Got back together with Maggie. Led the
war effort from Wisconsin. Apparently, he vol-
unteered for every war drive imaginable. By the

time the Japanese surrendered, Michael may have been more respected around town than those of us who had served. Again, I never resented him for it. Not even when my father wrote me that Michael and Maggie had gotten married.

CHAPTER 29

THE ROAD TO MADISON: TRIP ONE

THE PROFESSOR DROVE east out of Madison, toward Milwaukee. Past one farm after another. I had left Kickapoo Falls in the early-morning dark. Now the sun was up, promising yet another rich autumn day.

"Will you be one of the policemen coming down for the rally tomorrow?"

"It looks that way," I said, feeling my usual discomfort while riding on the passenger side of a car. "My sheriff is more or less insisting. Smart politics, he calls it."

"Well, even if you're not going to vote for the man, it promises to be a good show."

Thirty minutes into the country, Professor Levine of the University of Wisconsin parked the white station wagon on a dirt road adjacent to a rolling field of wheat. A second university car was parked nearby. The farmland was owned by the College of Agriculture. I zipped up my jacket and stuffed my hands into the pockets. Again, I found myself wandering through sunlit fields of wheat, this time following the erudite physics professor. We stayed on a tractor path for a quarter of a mile. Then, suddenly, we came to a circle. A perfect circle. The stalks were lying on the ground, bent but not broken, as if they'd been blown down by a tiny tornado. The familiarity of the early-morning scene sent a chill up my spine. But this time, instead of two dead bodies, I faced two of the professor's star students, who were standing above a stake at the center of the circle. Both of the men had broad smiles across their earnest young faces.

"How did you do it?" I asked.

Professor Levine pointed to the objects on the ground. "One stake in the ground. One board. And a couple of ropes," he told me. "As I suspected, the beauty of it was in the simplicity."

"That's all they used," I wanted to know, "a board and some rope?"

The physics professor walked to the stake embedded in the ground at the center of the circle. Clothesline was wound around the stake and attached to a plank, about four feet long. Two more ropes, used for pulling, were also attached to the plank. "It's a two-person job. Whoever made your circle used a simple plank with a rope tied to each end."

The two students demonstrated as Professor Levine continued his lecture.

"This enabled them to walk upright, swishing down a four-foot swath of grain with each step. They walked backward, clockwise, pulling the plank while methodically unwinding the rope from the stake. They could work fast and barely break a sweat, because the plank is comparatively light. As you can see, using the same techniques, we made this thirty-foot-diameter circle. Neat flat swirls. A precise perimeter, and our footprints were concealed beneath the laid stalks."

"How long did it take?"

"Less than thirty minutes."

"Did anybody see you guys out here . . . wonder what you were doing?"

The two students exchanged a glance. "Not that we know of," the taller one said, "and we waited until the sun came up."

The other young man proudly chimed in. "What you do is simply walk out to the virgin wheat by following a tractor rut. Then enlarge your circle out past the tractor ruts, thus concealing your footprints beneath the laid stalks."

The professor further explained. "The first

thing we did was research the history of these
circles in our area. There wasn't much . . ." He
reached into his coat pocket and pulled out a
crumpled paper. "Just these photographs
printed in an old Madison newspaper. As you
can see from the caption . . . it says who did it,
but it doesn't say how they did it."

He handed me the fruits of his research.

The morning sun felt good, but still there was
an autumn chill in the air. I unfolded the slice of
brittle and yellowing newspaper. Stared at the
photographs. Stared at them until I felt sick. The
stake at the center of the circle seemed symbolic
of the stake that had just been driven through
my heart. It must be the feeling a husband has
when confronted with photographic evidence of
his cheating wife. Looking back, knowing what
I know now, I shouldn't have been surprised.
But I was, and it hurt like hell. The newspaper
was from 1938—the year Orson Welles scared
the hell out of the nation with his radio production of H. G. Wells's *War of the Worlds*. Two photographs appeared side by side, the photographs
I had tried to remember from my boyhood.
Seems I had gone fishing at the wrong newspaper. On the right was an aerial shot of a swirling
circle in a field of wheat. On the left was a picture of a county sheriff with his big, fat arms
draped affectionately over the shoulders of two

teenage boys. They all had big smiles on their faces. The caption read:

TRICKSTERS, NOT MARTIANS

Sheriff Fritz Galatowich of Kickapoo County stands with the two boys responsible for the mysterious Halloween circle that appeared near Kickapoo Falls. Webster Sprague, 16, and Michael Butler, 15, confess they made the circle in the wheat as a Halloween prank. The sheriff said it was all in good fun. No charges were brought against the two boys.

CHAPTER 30

THE ROAD TO MADISON: TRIP TWO

I WAS RIDING in the backseat of the sheriff's car on my second trip to Madison in as many days. We were cruising down Highway 12. My head was tilted back. My Stetson was cocked over one eye. The sun on my face felt good. Must have been mid-October, because the scenery was spectacular. The fall leaves I loved so much were at their peak. I had the window half down to take in the warm breeze. I don't think I'd ever before been in the backseat of one of our squad cars. I felt like a convict on his way to prison. Seeing the magnificent countryside one last time before being locked away.

"Now, Deputy, if you hope to be sheriff someday, this is the kind of thing you have to do. A lot of this job is politics. You may not like those politics . . . but we don't always get to choose who it is we sleep with."

"We don't?"

"No, we don't. Now, they want a show of force down there in Madison . . . five thousand cops . . . and damn it, Kickapoo County is going to show."

Fats was driving and talking, his round, fleshy wrist draped over the top of the steering wheel. He was still lecturing me like a father. Still grooming me for sheriff. Pretending nothing had happened. That I wasn't a murder suspect. That he hadn't blasted me with fish guts. Maybe even tried to kill me. In fact, until I saw the old newspaper photos, I was beginning to think that death really hadn't been all that close up on Hawk's Bill—that if it was Fats shooting at me, maybe the sheriff was just trying to scare me.

He had looked so much younger in that newspaper photograph. And handsome, too. Fats had been a good-looking guy. To us kids back then, he was a giant among men. We'd believe anything he told us. We'd do anything he asked.

We sailed silently past Old County Road C, the road that led to the wheat field. Now, in my mind, Sheriff Fats was a viable suspect in the murders. Perhaps I should have suspected him earlier. Like when I finally realized there had been a camera in the wheat field. Or when I saw that the wheat field film in Webster Sprague's house was 16 millimeter. Or when I became suspicious of the sheriff's attempts to quickly close the case as a murder-suicide. Anyway, by the middle of October, he was investigating me, so I turned around and began investigating him. Two expert riflemen taking shots at each other from the safety of distance.

I had asked Fats for the film he shot of the crime scene. Remember, he was the one who insisted on filming the aftermath of the murders. I wanted to see if it resembled the wheat field film I had seen at the congressman's house. Was it shot from the same angles? Same lighting problems? Same jerky motions from the camera operator? But Fats put me off. Said he couldn't find it. Then he told me it didn't come out. Bad film, or something.

I learned Fats had been at the Republican convention in Chicago, too. In fact, he'd stayed at the Blackstone Hotel. Same as Webster Sprague. Same as Richard Nixon. A year earlier, it was Fats who introduced the vice president at the Kickapoo Gunn Club. The topic was law and order. I remembered Caren's warning:

"Be careful, Deputy. The boys at the Gunn Club take their politics seriously."

Dickerson was riding shotgun. He was dressed in his usual cheap suit. Looked like shit. He always snapped a snub-nosed pistol to the front of his pants. Maybe that's the way they wore their guns down in Texas, but somehow I doubted it. Little bastard probably got his skinny ass run out of the Lone Star state. I wasn't yet ready to take on Fats, so I started in on Dickerson. "Tell me, Detective Dickerson, how did a sharp cop like you end up in a small town in Wisconsin?"

"Your sarcasm aside, Deputy Pennington, I was a very sharp cop in a very small town in Texas. Much smaller than Kickapoo Falls. In my book, being a detective for a county sheriff's department is quite a leap up."

"True," I told him, "but we're not exactly the Texas Rangers."

"No, you're not, but you are a fine department with a fine reputation."

"So, are you an LBJ man?" I wanted to know.

He glanced at me over his shoulder. "I could live with Lyndon Johnson in the White House, but I don't particularly like the man."

"Why not?"

"Just aren't my politics. I was, however, a great admirer of your Senator McCarthy."

I rolled my eyes. "Why doesn't that surprise me?"

"His premature death," said Dickerson, "very much saddened me. It made me want to get more involved in the political aspects of law enforcement."

"Well, you've come to the right place," I told him. "Senator Joe, as he was known around here, started out a circuit court judge here in Kickapoo County. Held court right there at our county courthouse. Some of the damnedest criminal trials you'd ever want to see. Not only that . . . Joe McCarthy was a proud member of the Kickapoo Gunn Club. Ain't that right, Sheriff?"

"Yes, that's right, Deputy."

"Never mind," I said, "that he was censured by his fellow senators and died in a nuthouse . . . he was one of our own. Ain't that right, Sheriff?"

I could see in the rearview mirror that Fats was troubled by my sardonic talk of the late Wisconsin senator. Almost hurt. "Joe was a good man," said Sheriff Fats, "but like all good men . . . he had his faults. Joe never learned that some words are better left unspoken . . . no matter how true those words may be. That even in a democracy, certain deeds need to be carried out in absolute secrecy . . . no matter how noble those deeds may seem."

There was something else I noticed in the rearview mirror. I believed we were being followed. It was more of an instinct than anything I could discern through police training, though I thought Dickerson had checked the rearview mirror one too many times. It was a big Ford sedan. New, but indiscreet. The kind of car that would be used by the Secret Service, or maybe the FBI. There were two men in the front seat. Dark suits. Sunglasses.

I also noticed Fats was doing the speed limit. Fats never did the speed limit. Fats always drove ten miles over the limit. You could set your watch by it.

Still, there's a fine line between suspicion and paranoia. I held my breath.

We drove another two miles in icy silence. I kept my eyes on the mirrors. Then Fats made his move. "I'm getting old," he said. "I gotta piss . . . can't wait."

He slowed the car and swung down a dirt road that led to a deep lake in some deep woods. I glanced out the rear window. Not far behind, the Ford sedan made the same turn.

I pulled my revolver, crossing that fine line. I cocked the hammer so that Fats could hear the deadly click. Then I stuck the .38/.44 right behind Dickerson's ear. "Don't stop the car, Sheriff."

"Deputy, what the hell are you doing?"

"I'm squeezing the trigger, that's what I'm doing. If this car stops, your little McCarthyite here is dead."

"Okay, we won't stop. You just relax now . . . I'll have to turn the car around."

"No, you won't. This road makes a big

U-turn. Puts us right back on twelve, heading south. I've pissed back here, too."

Fats kept driving, kicking up a cloud of dust. I couldn't see the other car, but I was sure that it was back there. We skirted the lake deep in the woods and then veered back to the highway. "When you hit the blacktop," I told him, "throw on the lights and lose the car behind us."

"Deputy, have you gone completely daffy? Do you know what I'm gonna do . . . I'm gonna get you a shrink and some time off."

Dickerson shook his head in agreement. "He's a nutcase from the war. He ought to be in an institution, for God's sake."

"Maybe if I wet my pants, Detective, the young deputy back there will realize what a fool he's being."

Dickerson started laughing, as if there wasn't a gun to his head. It was an arrogant, evil laugh, and for the first time since I'd met him I thought there might be a real pair of balls attached to the little bastard.

Then Fats began laughing. So I began laughing, too. Not because I'd made a fool out of myself, but because I was so damned scared I didn't know what else to do. I released the hammer and holstered my revolver. Still, as we swung back onto the highway to Madison, I kept one eye on the front seat and one eye out the rear window. And one hand on my gun.

CHAPTER 31

THE RALLY

WE FOUND a parking lot filled with police cars down at James Madison Park on Lake Mendota. Every vehicle there appeared washed and waxed—county sheriff's cars, state patrol cars, and squad cars from police departments as far away as Milwaukee, Green Bay, and Superior. Having parked our polished squad at the edge of the water, the three of us marched up Wisconsin Avenue to the State Capitol. I walked two steps behind, like a Japanese housewife. During that short walk up the hill, my mind was racing in an attempt to keep it all straight. I suspected my own sheriff was a pornographer and was trying to kill me. I had just put a gun to the head of our chief detective and threatened to blow his brains out because we were being followed by men in dark suits. I was blackmailing a Senate candidate for two hundred thousand dollars. I was holding obscene phone calls with that candidate's wife, while at the same time trying to extort from her a hundred thousand dollars of the blackmail money. And I was still investigating the murder of the only woman I had ever loved—a case in which I was apparently the chief suspect—and who it now seemed had been sleeping with everybody in Kickapoo Falls except me. The only thing I was grateful for on that walk up to the capitol, to attend a rally for a guy I wasn't going to vote for, was that my parents were dead—that they hadn't lived to see what a troubled young man their good little Catholic boy had turned out to be.

The leafy grounds of the capitol resembled a giant police picnic. Never before had I seen so many uniformed police officers gathered in one place. A stage had been assembled on the south steps, far below the white marble dome. Television crews with big bulky cameras were lining up their shots. That's where Fats gravitated to, to the cameras and the cameramen. Along the way, the hand of every cop in uniform reached out to him, as if Fats were the guest of honor that day.

"Almost as soon as the movie camera was invented, people started filming sex . . ."

I could just see the big, fat man showing his

collection of pornographic films every Friday
night. Still, for all of the crazy accusations
hurled at the Kickapoo Gunn Club, dirty movies
seemed to be one of their lesser evils. Hardly
worth killing for. If Sheriff Fats was involved in
the murders, in what capacity was he involved?
Did he shoot Michael Butler with a shotgun, or
did he just shoot him with a camera? If he was
in the wheat field that day, was it possible he
was in possession of the missing film? And what
of the morning the bodies were discovered?
Poor Maggie. There we were—me, Fats, and
Russ Hoffmeyer—standing there staring down
at her bloody face and her naked body. We three
police were supposed to investigate her murder.
Yet one of us had fucked her lights out while
her husband watched. Another had probably
filmed her getting her lights fucked out while
her husband watched. And the third, yours
truly, was being accused of taking a shotgun
and castrating her husband, and then using that
same shotgun to blow her brains out.

Besides Fats and Dickerson, I didn't see anybody that I knew, so I spent my time comparing
uniforms. I was proud to note that Kickapoo
County uniforms were among the best of them.
I had always admired Fats for that. He demanded we look sharp, a tradition I would certainly continue if I ever found myself in the
increasingly unlikely position of sheriff of Kicka-

poo County. But it was this same standard of excellence that left me wondering why Fats would hire and tolerate a sloppy little bastard like Dickerson.

About a hundred of these smartly uniformed policemen were assembling on the stage, maneuvering between the American and the Wisconsin state flags. When it was all put together, there would be a lot of cops and a lot of flags lined up behind the vice president. In fact, on television it would appear every cop in the state of Wisconsin was standing squarely behind Richard M. Nixon. I'm sure many of them were.

A roar of approval went up from the crowd when the vice president and his entourage emerged from the capitol. Beside him was Mrs. Nixon in a white hat with white gloves. I confess, I found myself applauding out of respect. Since the governor of Wisconsin was a Kennedy Democrat, Republican congressman and Senate candidate Webster Sprague was given the honor of introducing Mr. Nixon.

The capitol of Wisconsin was built on the hill of an isthmus between Lake Mendota and Lake Monona. I only mention this because the rally was held on the Lake Monona side, which put the stage facing the glistening water and the low October sun. There were a lot of sunglasses among the cops on that stage, and there was a lot of squinting from the speakers.

Webster Sprague soaked up the applause along with the sunshine, then began his introduction. "I haven't seen this many men in uniform since I served in the navy during the war. It's been a long time since I've been anywhere this safe." There was a round of laughter and more applause. "I think it speaks to the strength and the integrity of our presidential candidate that this many peace officers in one state would show up here today to show their support for a man who lives and breathes law and order. With your help, on Tuesday, November eighth, we're going to deliver Wisconsin's twelve electoral votes to Richard Nixon's column." That led to a wild round of applause before Webster wrapped up his introduction. "But you people didn't come to beautiful Madison on this beautiful day to hear me. I wish you had." More laughter. "You came to Madison to hear from the man who is going to lead this great nation into a new era. Ladies and gentleman, the next president of the United States, Vice President Richard M. Nixon."

The huge crowd went crazy. NIXON-LODGE signs appeared everywhere. A lot of people were waving small American flags as the vice president moved to the podium with the certainty of a winner. It took a good five minutes for the crowd to settle down. Then the vice president spoke. He spoke with a clear, mellow voice. He spoke slowly and confidently, with a healthy cadence.

"The pioneers who built Wisconsin were men and women with individual spirit, with faith in themselves, not thinking that they were second-rate, second-class people, but thinking that they were the best in the world. I'm tired of the Eastern establishment looking down their rich noses at your Midwestern values. Hang on to your values."

Richard Nixon was interrupted by applause at the end of almost every sentence. He was impressive in tone, performance, and style. Almost elegant.

"Don't let the Democratic candidate take Wisconsin for granted. Don't make your choice for president on the basis of the age of the candidates, on the basis of their religion, or on the basis of their personality. Don't make your choice on the basis of the party label they wear, but make it on where they stand on the great issues. If they stand closer to you, regardless of the party label, vote the man who agrees with you more than the other man. This is the way to make your choice."

In person, Richard Nixon appeared younger than his forty-seven years, and a lot less menacing. He was slim and trim, an evidently healthy man. His face was a smiling face, open and friendly. In fact, his appearance on the stage that sunny day in Madison was in stark contrast to the dark and brooding man I had watched in the television debate. I couldn't help but be impressed.

"May I turn now to what I believe is one of the great issues confronting us in the election campaign," the vice president said, in more solemn tones. "Peace in our homes. Peace in our neighborhoods, and in our towns and in our cities. Look at all of you men standing proudly in your uniforms. We can have the best Social Security program and the best health program and the best jobs that anybody can possibly imagine, and it isn't going to make any difference if we're not safe in our own homes. You men make us safe, and I salute you."

Again the crowd went wild. The vice president went on with his talk in the bright glare of the Wisconsin sun. In the tree-lined park of the State Capitol he spoke slowly and warmly, almost conversationally, with friendship and frequent applause. Although I'd burn in hell before I'd vote for the man, I was amazed. I stood there with the feeling Richard Nixon was going to win the election, feeling he was certainly going to carry my Wisconsin. It was not a good feeling.

Trapped in my suspicions, or my paranoia, I spent the rally a few feet behind Fats and Dickerson, where I could keep my eye on them both. They seemed to be totally ignoring me, the way a coach ignores a scrub. As if to say, *We're going to cut him next week, anyway.*

"Deputy Pennington, how nice to see you again. Last time I saw you . . . you were sporting a KENNEDY button, and quite proudly, if I remember."

She had caught me off guard. She was leaning into my ear and talking during the applause as the vice president wrapped up his speech. It was psychology professor Marilou Stephens from the university.

"I'm not a Republican," I tried to explain to her over the excitement. "I'm here with the sheriff . . . just kind of tagging along."

"Relax, I'm not a Republican, either, but they do put on a good show."

She was as pretty as I had remembered, and just as intimidating in my sophomoric mind. "It's nice to see you again," I stammered.

"You look different in uniform."

"Better or worse?"

"I've always liked a man in uniform." I loved her answer, and she didn't seem the least bit shy about it. "Did my psychological profile of your killer wield any results?"

I turned back to the stage where Richard Nixon was raising the arm of Webster Sprague. "Not yet, but I found it very helpful."

"Has Professor Levine contacted you?"

It was hard to hear her above the noise of the crowd. "Who?"

"Professor Levine," she almost shouted, "of our Physics Department . . . about your wheat field circle?"

"Right, yes . . . I saw him yesterday."

"I believe he's figured out how they did it . . . made the circle in the wheat. But I still don't have a clue as to why they would do it."

"I think I've figured that out for myself." I stumbled for the right words. "Maybe we could have coffee sometime and talk some more."

"Sure. How about Marco's in one hour?"

"I don't know where that is."

She pointed across the park. "It's just down State Street."

"I'll be there."

I watched her walk away, spotting friends in the crowd as she went. Besides being attractive, she was obviously well liked. For a moment I wondered what she saw in me, if she saw anything at all. Perhaps to her I was just a small-town cop with a big mystery on his hands.

The speeches were over. The rally was breaking up. Still, things were noisy, confused, and alive with five thousand cops. "She's pretty," the man said.

He was standing behind me. Dark suit. Sunglasses. I immediately noticed the bulge of a small pistol under his coat. A more anonymous-looking man I had never seen. My first guess was that he was a Secret Service agent working the crowd. I glanced back at Marilou Stephens as she moved away in the company of friends. "Yes, she is," I said.

"A friend of yours?"

"Who's asking?"

"Someone who's not a friend of yours."

It was something I learned in the army. If he's bigger than you are and you feel you're being threatened—look him in the eye and poke him in the chest. I did just that. I stepped forward, stared through an expensive pair of sunglasses, and planted my finger squarely in his chest. "I hope there's a badge to go with that gun."

"We want the wheat field film . . . and we're willing to pay for it."

That was the very last thing I had expected. I returned my finger to its proper place and glanced over my shoulder. Up on the stage, Webster Sprague was escorting the vice president back into the capitol, working the rope lines along the way. Fats and Dickerson had disappeared. If anybody was paying us the least bit of attention, I couldn't tell. By all outward appearances we were just another two cops talking over the day.

"How much are you willing to pay?" I wanted to know.

"Two hundred thousand."

"I thought I made it clear to your friend the price was three hundred thousand."

"We're not sure you have the film, or that you can even get it. Two hundred thousand. Take it, or die."

I always liked clear choices. "When and where?"

"Exactly one week from today. Be at the Butlers' grave site at midnight. Be alone. Bring the film."

CHAPTER 32

MARCO'S COFFEE SHOP

THEY CALLED IT a coffee shop, but it looked like a small diner to me. White aluminum tables were crowded about, surrounded by uncomfortable chairs with red plastic seat covers. Somebody dropped a nickel in the jukebox, and the sugar-sweet voice of Doris Day filled the room, singing that *Que Sera* song. Marilou and I had a table near the window. An assorted combination of uniformed police officers, Republican-type businessmen, and college students paraded by us on State Street, which angled from the capitol down to the university. Maybe it was Marilou, or maybe it was the caffeine, or more likely it was the arrangement for payment of the blackmail money that had me feeling stoked. I was excited, in a very dangerous sort of way. I felt like talking. "I don't think I ever came in here . . . but then, I didn't get out much."

"You went to school here?" Marilou asked.

"Just one year. The G.I. Bill . . . '46. I'm afraid I wasn't a very good student. I just couldn't concentrate on the subjects that didn't interest me." I leaned in to her and lowered my voice. My first bold attempt at flirting. "You know, of course, out there in the real world . . . there's no such thing as algebra."

She laughed at that, and the sound of her laughter warmed me.

The professor of psychology added a spoonful of sugar to her coffee and stirred. "I hear what you're saying, how insulated we are at the university. A colleague of mine who also served in the war once said to me, 'I'm constantly amazed at how removed life in the academic world is from life in the real world.' "

"So I can see how you might find it refreshing to talk with a real live cop, investigating a real live murder case."

"I find it very refreshing, if that doesn't sound too morbid."

"No. People are curious. It's only natural."

There was an awkward silence as we sipped our coffee.

"Tell me . . . did you know the victims?"

"Yes," I told her, "I knew them both. I knew Maggie better."

"How much better?"

I thought long and hard before answering. She was a beautiful woman, but she was also a psychologist. I thought it best to be bold and up front. "I was in love with her . . . before they were married."

"Ah, the plot thickens. And after they were married?"

"What do you mean?"

"Were you still in love with her?"

"She got married. I got wounded in the war."

She seemed as surprised by my idiotic answer as I was. "That's terrible," she said. "Have you recovered . . . physically, I mean?"

"Let's just say I can't have children."

"I see. I'm sorry."

"In fact, there are certain people up in Kickapoo Falls who think I'm crazy."

"Some would say you'd have to be a little bit crazy to be a policeman."

"No, they're convinced I'm cuckoo. Off my rocker. Time off for the funny farm."

"You don't strike me as mentally unbalanced. You're different . . . but people like different."

"Be careful, Marilou, your reputation may be on the line here." I was feeling more and more comfortable with her, the most comfortable I'd felt with a woman in years. But at the same time, she fascinated me. The lady shrink who wanted to play detective. "Do you think that you could spot a killer by analyzing him on your couch . . . a mad bomber, a wife beater, a vigilante, an assassin?"

"I like to believe I could spot a man with that potential."

"You said, 'man.' What if our suspect was a woman . . . a beautiful woman?"

Marilou shook her head. "No. A double homicide with a shotgun . . . that's not a woman's work. That's something a man would do. You're looking for a man."

"Then tell me something, professionally speaking. What kind of woman would have sex with two men at the same time . . . and boast about it? What kind of a woman would have sex with another man . . . while her husband watched? In fact, her husband probably picked out the man for her. What kind of woman would allow herself to be filmed having sex . . . and I don't mean acting-in-a-movie kind of sex . . . I mean real sex?"

"Would these all be the same woman?"

"Possibly . . . yes."

"A lot of people would simply write her off as a whore, but I'd say she'd be a very aggressive woman. She uses sex to get what she wants, and who she wants. And I doubt her husband picks out her men for her. He may bring them home, but she picks them out."

I had to smile at that. "You're very good. Law enforcement could use people like you."

"It's my hope that in the future the psychological profile of criminals will be become a valuable crime-fighting tool." She suddenly checked her watch. "My God, I have to run. I have a lecture."

"Maybe I'll call you, next time I'm in town."

The smile evaporated from her face. "Maybe I'll wait by the phone . . . or maybe not."

It took a while, but I had finally managed to offend her. I had said the wrong thing, or maybe I said the right thing the wrong way. When it came to women, I was the kind of guy who always said the wrong thing.

She got up to leave. Slung her purse over her shoulder. Gathered her notebooks. Doris Day was singing, *Whatever will be, will be.* Marilou stared down at me, like a disapproving mother. "Some free advice, Deputy. Don't allow old wounds to get in the way of a new life." She started for the door.

"It was a war, Professor. I didn't choose to get hit."

She turned to me before exiting. "I'm not referring to that wound."

CHAPTER 33

SEX ALONG THE ROAD:
PART THREE

I WAS THE first deputy on the scene that night. I was the one who retrieved Robin Christensen's head from the back of her daddy's Ford pickup. I bagged it. I tagged it. By then I had been with the sheriff's department five years. I was a combat veteran of World War II. I thought I'd seen it all. But nothing had prepared me for the trauma of piecing together the body parts of my secret lover—a woman I had literally watched grow up, both emotionally and sexually.

The accident was also my first official investigation. It was just a traffic fatality, but Fats passed over more experienced men and handed the case to me. He wanted results, and I quickly zeroed in on young Buster Sprague and his fire-red convertible.

As I mentioned before, bright red paint was discovered on the rear bumper of Robin's truck and we were able to match tire tracks near the accident scene to the tires on Buster Sprague's Chevy DeLuxe. But the Sprague family attorney explained away the evidence. He claimed Robin had trouble with the truck that week, and Buster gave her a push with his car. Somehow, I couldn't picture Buster Sprague using his most prized possession, his shiny new car, to be giving his ex-girlfriend a push. If he did push her, he pushed her at eighty miles per hour—the speed at which we determined Robin was traveling when she left the road. The lawyer also claimed that the tire tracks we found on the highway may indeed have been Buster's, but he drag raced kids from the valley out there all the time. After six weeks of investigative work, the county attorney informed me that I had not gathered enough evidence to charge Buster Sprague with a crime. I believed then, and I believe now, that had it been any other family in Kickapoo Falls other than the Sprague family, the county attorney would have taken the case to trial.

I was called into the sheriff's office to be told the bad news. For the most part, I kept quiet as the county attorney explained the situation point by point. It was imperative that nobody suspect I had an intimate, but distant, relationship with Robin Christensen. So I said nothing as my case went up in flames. Fats didn't say much, either, but I know he was watching me the whole time. This was my first investigation, and it wasn't even going to result in an arrest, much less a conviction. When the county attorney got up to leave, I stayed in my seat, slightly numbed by the experience. Fats closed the office door, walked up behind me in that fatherly way he had, and put his hand on my shoulder. "More than one way to skin a cat," he said.

Military Road had once run directly to Camp Randall down in Madison. If you owned a hot rod in Kickapoo Falls and you wanted to race, you'd set out north of town where Military Road angled into River Road on the Upper Dells, just above a rise of cliffs on the Wisconsin River. The drop to the water at that point was about 150 feet. It was not unusual to catch the kids dragging out there. We lost about two teenagers a year to car crashes in that long stretch. It wasn't just the valley kids. In the summer, they came from miles around.

The thing that made that particular stretch so dangerous was a natural rise in Military Road, and then a sudden dip in the River Road. Because of this deadly configuration, you could, with enough speed, get your car airborne. The kids loved it. But there was precious little room for error. Too much speed, a few beers, the darkness of night, a car full of screaming teenagers, and the results were too often fatal. Years later I thought it could easily have passed for the ominous stretch of road in that Jan and Dean song: "Dead Man's Curve."

A sniper doesn't hunt. A sniper waits. He waits patiently for his prey to literally cross his path. Move into his crosshairs. Sometimes he waits hours. Sometimes days. For Buster Sprague, I waited weeks. I would have waited years.

It didn't take a whole lot of surveillance to know when Buster was on the prowl, especially in the summer months. From the high bluffs on the opposite side of the river, I estimated my distance from the deadly intersection to be five-hundred yards across open water. The wind would be a factor. I had no night scope back then, but the lighting was favorable. I had what the Indians called the moon of the silver canoe hanging above me in a starlit sky. I could see headlights cruising down Military Road. I only had to pray Buster had the lead over his latest opponent when he hit River Road. This would be a fast-moving vehicle. I had but one shot.

The Springfield '03 was a bolt action rifle, with a twenty-six-inch barrel and a telescopic sight—extremely accurate at eight hundred to a thousand yards. Its accuracy was owed to its rigid construction. Other than the firing pin, there were no moving parts. During the war it was issued primarily to snipers. Without making a sound, I nestled between the rock and the pines. Pulled a cartridge from my pocket. It was a needle-nosed bullet. The copper jacket had been polished by hand. I rolled it in my fingers, as I had been doing for years. Then I slipped the bullet into the breach. Slid the bolt home. Wrapped the leather sling tightly around my forearm. I nestled the nine pounds of smooth, oiled walnut into my shoulder. Rested my eye to the scope.

I slowly moved my scope along Military Road, watching and waiting. Spend enough years on night patrol and you can guess a vehicle type by its headlights. I soon put the crosshairs on the headlight of a Chevy DeLuxe and followed it as it sped down Military Road. Buster was clearly in the lead. I estimated his speed to be nearly ninety miles per hour when he got airborne over River Road. I compensated for the wind down the river. My heart was pounding with revenge. The crosshairs were rising and falling on my target. Finally, my concentration overruled my heart. I dropped the crosshairs from the right headlight to what I guessed was the right front tire. With purpose and moral indignation, I squeezed the trigger and sent a .30-caliber missile screaming across the river at two thousand feet per second.

Buster Sprague and his Chevy Deluxe hit the blacktop hard, igniting a shower of sparks. The car fishtailed out of control and then did cartwheels going over the cliff. Buster must have been cruising on a full tank of gas, because his hot rod exploded in a ball of flames when it hit the river. With the fiery illumination, the towering rocks and cliffs appeared as the Dells from hell. Dante's Inferno. Then the flames slowly died as the car headed for the deep. Only fiery gasoline trails remained, flickering along the dark, rushing water like lightning in the sky.

The second car screeched to a halt about a quarter mile down River Road. I watched as the kids ran to the edge of the cliff. Stared down at the river in disbelief. In the official report, the kids said they heard what sounded like a single boom, an exploding tire, and then the car hit the blacktop. It veered wildly out of control and sailed over the cliff. One kid said he could see Buster pinned to the steering wheel. He was on fire. That he appeared like a candle blowing crazily in the wind, as he tried unsuccessfully to escape the burning car in the seconds before it sank to the river bottom.

State divers were unable to retrieve the sunken hot rod. The water at that point in the river was just too fast. Too deep. So they never discovered the .30-caliber hole in the tire. But they did manage to fish out the charred remains of Buster Sprague, who became a dubious legend in the valley. Webster waxed eloquent at his little brother's funeral. Then they cremated the rest of him.

When the investigation into Robin's death had gone cold from what the county attorney called a lack of evidence, Fats never badgered me. Never lectured me. He merely set it aside as a cold case. "These things have a way of playing out," he told me.

A week after Buster Sprague's crispy remains were pulled from the river, Fats again called me into his office. He congratulated me on the way I had handled the accident involving Robin Christensen. Justice, he believed, had been served. Then he closed the books on the case, and once again invited me to join the Kickapoo Gunn Club. Again, I respectfully declined.

Buster Sprague wasn't the first criminal suspect to be served justice Kickapoo County style. And he wouldn't be the last.

CHAPTER 34

A VOICE IN THE WOODS:
FOURTH CALL

IT WAS JUST before midnight. I was standing in the shadows near a phone booth off Highway 33. Behind me was a truck stop that had been built after the war. There was not a lot of activity at the truck stop, but it was still open and well lit, which made me feel a wee bit safer. I was waiting for the phone to ring. I could see the lights of the stadium in the distance. The lights were out, but the stark silhouettes of the elongated poles stood in the moonlight beneath the hills like the fence posts of a concentration camp I had seen during the war. Every once in a while, an eighteen-wheeler roared down the highway and its headlights revealed the bleachers and the goalposts. Then, just for a moment,

I was again young and innocent and sprinting down the field for the winning touchdown. My father was in the stands. And Maggie, too, was filled with all of the zest that life had to offer, as she led the uniformed cheering from the sidelines.

The stadium's days were numbered. Highway expansion was threatening its existence. A bond referendum was before the voters in November—to build a new high school east of town, with new athletic fields and a new football stadium. There was a baby boom, and Kickapoo Falls was growing. Everybody had big dreams.

I pulled the note from my pocket. Read it one more time. It was typewritten and had just arrived in the mail the day before:

BE AT THE PHONE BOOTH AT THE TRUCK STOP ON 33 AT MIDNIGHT ON THURSDAY ILL CALL YOU BE CAREFUL

There was no signature, but the envelope had been postmarked in Hyannis, Massachusetts. Cape Cod. I assumed the note was from Caren Sprague. Would a killer ask me to be careful? But what if the note wasn't from Caren?

It was one of those phone booths that when you pushed the door closed, an interior light popped on. Like stepping into a spotlight. I couldn't escape the overwhelming feeling that I

was being set up, that the minute I stepped into
that booth, a bullet would crash through the
glass. Was it a federal agent who had approached me at the rally, asked me to meet him
in a cemetery with the wheat field film? Did a
congressman have that kind of pull? Or was the
anonymous-looking man in the sunglasses just
a mobster? Or worse, a gun nut from the Gunn
Club? I searched the hills overlooking the truck
stop. Even in the light of day, those hills were
a sniper's paradise. I reasoned they'd be less
likely to shoot a uniformed cop, so I waited
dressed to the nines. I kept one hand on my
holster. I kept my squad car parked in plain
sight. In the dark, I strained to see the watch on
my wrist. The second hand pushed past midnight. I looked up at the phone booth. Silence.

It then occurred to me to step into the booth
and disable the lights. I swore at myself for not
thinking of it sooner. If I was going to meet men
in dark suits in a cemetery to collect blackmail
money, I was going to have to think a whole lot
faster and a whole lot smarter. As the investigation into the wheat field murders sailed deeper
and deeper into uncharted waters, I could almost feel my smarts drifting away. My paranoia
was eating away at my brain like a cancer. I
was convinced somebody had rifled through my
desk at the courthouse. I had the spooky feeling
somebody had searched my home. It would

only take one stupid move to hang myself, and I had already survived several stupid moves.

I walked out of the shadows. Toward the phone booth. Then the phone went off, like an alarm clock. The ringing seemed abnormally loud and I almost jumped out of my skin. I froze in place and watched it ring. Two times. Then it rang a third time. And a fourth. Finally, I stepped quickly toward the booth and lifted the receiver, keeping the door propped open with my foot. "Pennington," I yelled.

"Relax, lover, we're alone."

In an open phone booth on the side of the road, she was even harder to hear. The static of a long-distance call. The put-on sexuality of her speaking voice. I was mad. She was jerking me around again. "Why am I standing out here on the highway?"

"They tapped your telephone . . . home and work. They're also monitoring your radio calls."

"Who is . . . who's they?"

"One of those secret government agencies . . . you know . . . the one that protects the president, and stuff."

"Why would they do such a thing?"

"You've been tagged a killer, lover."

"They have nothing on me. If they did, I'd be in jail by now."

"What if I told you . . . you were in the film."

"That's not possible."

"When was the last time you saw Maggie alive?"

"Courthouse Square, day before the murders."

"Were you alone?"

"Yes," I told her. "We were in the square but the conversation was private."

"What was she doing at the courthouse?"

"She said she was divorcing Michael."

"I'll bet your little heart jumped right through your chest. Is that when she invited you to the wheat field?"

"Guessing games, Caren, you're playing guessing games."

"With her husband out of the way, did you think you had a chance? Were you so in love you allowed yourself to believe Maggie was going to leave a failure like Michael to marry a failure like you?"

"Perhaps you were afraid she was leaving Michael to marry Webster."

"You think you're smart, don't you? Did it bother you that so many other men had sex with her, but never you? Would it bother you to know that I had sex with her?"

"Did Michael watch?"

"Yes, Michael watched."

"And was Fats behind the camera? Hello . . . ? Caren, I've made the arrangements. Webster's people are going to pay the money. Hello . . . ?"

"Two hundred thousand . . . like you said?"

"Yes, two hundred thousand. But I need the film . . . we don't have a lot of time."

"First get me the money . . . then I'll get you the film."

"I need the film at the payoff."

"So give them a film. What are they going to do, view it there in the graveyard?"

"How did you know that . . . about the graveyard?"

"When I get the money . . . you get the film. Then if your conscience is still bothering you . . . you can turn the film over to Webster."

"Are you trying to get me killed?"

"Good-bye, lover . . . I'll be in touch."

CHAPTER 35

OAK HILL CEMETERY

OAK HILL CEMETERY rolled up a gentle climb northeast of Courthouse Square. The burial ground was bordered with a wrought-iron fence, and that fence was adorned by a neighborhood of large Victorian homes set back from red-brick streets. Today they call it the historic district. Back then it was just the spooky end of town.

We had reached the end of October. The clear night air was tinged with a winter chill. The first snow couldn't be too far away. Fresh leaves coated the graves. A thousand different shaped headstones, headstones from as long ago as the pioneer days, were strewn about the cemetery in imperfect rows. In the light of the Halloween moon, the bare branches of the tall trees had the appearance of spindly arms and arthritic fingers. A cold wind was blowing through those trees— not a strong wind, but enough to stir up the dry leaves and mask foreign sounds.

On the slope of the hill just beneath the crest, I found the ground where I had been instructed to wait. The grass had still not grown over the graves of Michael and Maggie Butler. Their final beds were dressed with simple white markers. Their permanent headstones had yet to be set in place—which seemed appropriate, since their true ending had yet to be written.

As was my usual custom on a stakeout, I arrived early and set up watch in the darkest shadow I could find. See, but not be seen. I felt like an interloper. There was a small Catholic cemetery on the outskirts of town where they interred the bones of heathens like me. I had slipped a black leather coat over a black T-shirt. I wore black slacks and black shoes. I did everything but apply blackface. I checked and double-checked my revolver, then strapped it to the belt beneath my coat. I grabbed my heavy metal flashlight. I had to drive down to Madison to find a canister of movie film that resembled the film cans I had seen at Webster's house. But Caren had a point. How would they determine they had the correct film? More likely, they were just going to shoot me.

Still, I dreamed of the things I could do with

a hundred thousand dollars. In fact, if I didn't need the wheat field film so damn bad, I could cheat both of the Spragues. Keep for myself the whole two hundred thousand. Leave Kickapoo Falls behind. I had no family. Few friends. Maggie was dead. For all I knew, Fats was a pornographer, maybe a murderer. My chances of ever being elected sheriff seemed slim to none. Why not take the money and run—to Jamaica, to Barbados, to any one of those tropical places I read about in those glossy magazines?

Why not? Because all that was the stuff of dreams. What the two hundred thousand dollars really bought me was a one-way ticket to Caren Sprague. When I got my hands on the lousy bitch, she would do a lot more than hand over the film. I pictured her tied to a bedpost, an anonymous man in a mask stripping her. I was watching. She was begging for my help. I kept demanding of her the truth.

Between her tales of sexual encounters, Caren Sprague seemed constantly to be playing mind games. Reminding me of things she shouldn't have known. True, Webster could have told her things while they were married, but she knew my phone had been tapped. She really tripped up when she mentioned the meeting in the cemetery. Was it possible, indeed probable, that Webster's missing wife was playing both sides of the fence—that I wasn't the only party she was dialing up in the middle of the night?

Caren wouldn't have been in that wheat field without Webster, unless she showed up uninvited. She had all the reason in the world to kill Maggie. She believed Maggie was about to steal her rich husband. I saw it going down like this: The camera was rolling. Caren stepped through the wheat and gave them what they wanted. A murder on film. She blasted Maggie in the face with the shotgun. Michael's last act of voyeurism was to watch his lifetime companion murdered in cold blood. Caren read his love for Maggie in his face. She turned and shot him between the legs.

So what was Caren doing with the Butlers' shotgun? And what about the advice I got from Marilou Stephens? *"That's not a woman's work. That's something a man would do. You're looking for a man."*

I had three suspects. Fats, Webster, and his missing wife, Caren. Two out of three of them were men. What if Webster pulled the trigger, Fats filmed the murder, and Caren watched? Maybe it went down like this: Maggie was in the wheat field. Michael was in the wheat field. Both of them were naked. Fats was in the wheat field, but behind the camera. Michael and Webster argued. Webster picked up the shotgun and

shot Michael, right in the balls. Maggie
screamed. Webster wheeled and shot Maggie in
the face.

What other combinations were there? My
mind was swimming with possibilities. How
about Fats stepped out from behind the camera
and picked up the shotgun? How about some
lunatic broke into the Butlers' home, stole the
shotgun, and headed off for the wheat field? But
every time I came up with a plausible scenario,
I came up with at least three questions that
poked holes in that scenario. Hell, it didn't matter what combination of possibilities I came up
with; I still needed that film—the real film, not
the phony piece of shit I was holding in my
hands.

And there was one other piece of the puzzle
gnawing at my brain. Why would the Secret Service be interested in me? Caren said it was the
Secret Service that tapped my phone. I thought
it might be the Secret Service tailing us to the
Nixon rally.

The apparition emerged from the midnight
shadows near the entrance gate. He appeared so
fast, I never saw his approach to the cemetery.
He walked straight toward me, carrying a briefcase. If he had any trepidation about paying
blackmail money in the middle of a graveyard,
it didn't show in the ghostly way he moved. I
stepped from my own secret shadow. Stood in

the dirt of Maggie's grave. Blocked his path. He kept coming. I held up the flashlight and switched on the light. Shined it in his eyes. "That's close enough," I told him.

Still, he moved to within two feet of me. "Is that the film?" he asked. It was the same anonymous-looking man from the Nixon rally. The same dark suit. The sunglasses were gone, but his eyes were well hidden behind a thick pair of lenses.

"Yes," I told him, "this is the film."

"Here's your money."

He popped open the briefcase and showed it to me. I shined the light that way. I had raided gambling joints and strip joints. I had captured bank robbers with the stolen loot still in their hands. But never before had I seen so much cash so neatly arranged in one compartment. I didn't know the rules of etiquette when it came to blackmail. It seemed rude to count it. He slammed the briefcase closed. Then he held it out to my face with one hand. I took possession of the money and handed him the film. He stuffed the canister beneath his coat, then turned and walked away. I killed the light, and he vanished as fast as he had appeared.

It was all too easy. Too fast. I was standing in Oak Hill Cemetery with a briefcase filled with two hundred thousand dollars. That's when the questions started up in my mind. What if only the top bills were real? What if it was all counterfeit bills? What if someone was waiting to kill me in the shadow of a tree, to take back the money? It was time to run. I took a long last look at the sorry grave on which I was standing.

I ran up and over the hill. Started for the back fence. Every tree branch appeared to be pointing an accusatory finger in my direction. Every headstone seemed like a human head shouting, "Stop, thief!" The Halloween moon was now like a spotlight shining down on an escaping convict. I ran through the fallen leaves. I grabbed hold of the wrought iron and climbed the fence as best I could with a heavy flashlight and a briefcase full of cash. I flipped over the black iron tips at the top and tumbled down to the sidewalk. Dropped my flashlight. The briefcase slipped from my hand. I reached out to grab it, but a foot slammed down on my fingers. I screamed in pain. Then I went for the gun beneath my coat, only to find a snub-nosed pistol a quarter inch from my nose. I didn't even have to look up. I knew it was Dickerson.

A flashing red light popped on across the street. Then another red light was twirling behind me. Yet a third squad car rounded the corner, its siren going. Within seconds I was bathed in a circus of lights. Headlights. Squad lights. The lights of popping flashbulbs. I stayed on the sidewalk, down on my knees. Dickerson reached over and relieved me of my service revolver.

Fats stepped from his sheriff's car. His shoes moved my way as if carrying the weight of the world. He stood over me like an executioner. Other deputies crowded around. I kept my head down. I had sunk as low as a cop could go.

"I swear," said Fats, in a voice filled with sorrow, "this is the saddest damn day of my life." I couldn't look him in the eyes, but I could hear him choking back the tears. "There comes a time," he said, "when we have to separate the wheat from the chaff. Deputy Pennington, you are under arrest for the murder of Maggie Butler, and for the murder of Michael Butler . . . and just for good measure, Deputy, I think we'll throw in blackmail and extortion."

CHAPTER 36

THE ARREST

IMAGINE THIS: YOU enlisted in the army, and you believed you served with honor during World War II. You were even wounded. Came home on crutches. You weren't the biggest hero in your small town—that honor went to a former football star and Marine Corps pilot—but you were warmly welcomed home. Despite the quirks in your personality, you were given a badge and a gun and a job for life with the county sheriff's department. Then, suddenly, it all comes crashing down. You are arrested and charged with murdering one of the most prominent couples in town. Now you are the most despised, most hated man in the river valley where you were born and raised.

Well, I don't have to imagine it—I lived it.

Once upon a time, I knew what it was like to be scorned and spat on by the very people I had sworn to protect and serve.

A picture of my arrest was plastered across the front page of the *Kickapoo Falls Republic*. I still have that picture. Every few years I dig it out to remind myself of how far a man can fall. When I began putting this story to paper, I dug out that old newspaper photograph one more time and spread it across my desk. It is yellow now, and brittle. Faded and torn. Scotch tape holds it together. In the photograph, I am still a young man. I am on my knees on the sidewalk in front of the cemetery. My head is down. My hands are folded in my lap. My trusty flashlight is on the ground before me. A briefcase can be seen lying on the sidewalk beside me. It is nighttime and I am the only person in the photograph that can be clearly identified. The people hovering over me are all arms and legs. The witchlike hands of Detective Dickerson can be seen dangling at his waist, his snub-nosed pistol in one hand, my service revolver in his other hand. For drama, there is no escaping the heavy, weary legs of Sheriff Fats towering over me. Once again, on the first day of November, 1960, a Wisconsin murder was making for some great headlines.

The Madison newspaper did a full-page spread on my arrest, and made much of the fact that I had been the lead investigator on the very murders for which I was now charged. A Milwaukee paper said I had stalked Maggie Butler for years. Murdered my childhood sweetheart. The Chicago papers reported that I had been under surveillance by the Secret Service because of my Army Ranger past.

Many believed then, and still believe today, that sniper warfare is morally wrong. Repugnant. Unworthy of a role in the United States Army. Why? Because a sniper shoots first, and shooting first is somehow considered un-American. In a sense, sniping is considered premeditated murder. The enemy has no chance to return fire. No chance to surrender. It's like shooting somebody in the back.

After my arrest, rumors about me began to surface like dead fish in the river. A virtual chorus of people, once my friends, were now clucking their tongues while shaking their heads.

"I'm not surprised . . . considering his past."

"I warned Fats years ago there was something wrong with that boy."

"Remember when he scored that touchdown . . . and then just kept on running?"

Not only did I stand accused of a double homicide, blackmail, and extortion—I was being cursed at for poaching black bears and deer, window peeping with a telescopic sight, and shooting the tires out of cars up on Dead Man's Curve. I never did most of those things. Still, what I did in the war, my skill with a rifle, was coming back to haunt me. Big time. It didn't seem to matter that Maggie and Michael were killed by a shotgun at close range. Or that for months the sheriff of Kickapoo County, the man who arrested me, was insisting the wheat field killings were a murder-suicide—that Maggie shot Michael, and then turned the gun on herself. All that seemed forgotten at the first word of my arrest.

CHAPTER 37

KICKAPOO COUNTY JAIL

THE KICKAPOO COUNTY jail was housed in the basement of the county courthouse. A pretty stark lockup. There were four windowless cells—three single-person cells, and a larger cell with four bunks and a metal table. A sink and a toilet. No matter what month of the year, the cells were cold and damp. There was one low-watt lightbulb in each cell. These lights were embedded in the ceiling and turned on and off from upstairs. A steel door was at the foot of the stairs. The stairs led up to a back hall, which led to a back driveway. Prisoners were brought into the courthouse through the rear of the building, keeping them away from the press and the general public. I was thrown into the big four-bunk cell. I guess it was professional courtesy. They tossed in a blanket and a pillow. In the summertime the cells were constantly occupied. But with the onset of cold weather, I had the entire bunker to myself.

Since being locked up, I hadn't really been questioned. Remember, this was 1960. Before Miranda rights and public defenders. Hell, I didn't even get the one phone call that all the bad guys got in the movies. One court appearance, and then into the pokey I went. Sat in my cell and stewed. No fresh clothes. No shower. No shave. I was made to feel dirty, but that's the way I wanted it. Fats was still playing the role of the crushed father. Wouldn't talk to me. I was told Detective Dickerson would question me when he had completed his investigation.

With the presidential election only days away, news of my arrest faded fast. I spent my nights dreaming about what I would do to the lovely Caren Sprague if ever I got my hands on the bitch. Most people count sheep when they can't sleep. When I can't sleep, I lay awake and dream of killing. Looking back now, it should have been as plain as the nose on my face that I was being set up, but my paranoia had gotten the best of me. Caren, I suspected, had cut a deal with Webster. She would get the money. He would get the film. They would both get me off their case. Or maybe, just maybe, she had cut that deal with Fats.

Finally, on the seventh evening of my stay, the metal door at the foot of the stairs clanged open. Dickerson walked into the cell area by himself, leaving the stairway door behind him wide open, a clear violation of jailhouse rules. He unlocked my cell, pulled open the bars, and left the keys dangling in the lock. Another obvious violation of our rules regarding prisoners. It was almost as if he was daring me to make a run for it.

I stayed seated on my bunk. Refused to stand because it might be interpreted as a sign of respect.

Dickerson reached into his shirt pocket and lifted out a pack of cigarettes. They were Lucky Strikes. "Smoke?"

"I quit."

"Yes, but you still bum one every now and then."

"Where's the sheriff?"

The diminutive detective returned the pack of cigarettes to his pocket. "Home packing. Says he has business out of town tomorrow."

"On election day?"

"I thought that was odd, too." Dickerson plopped down on the bare bunk opposite me and loosened his tie. I could see his nasty little pistol protruding from its holster. He propped a foot up on the mattress and draped his arm over it. A pretty relaxed posture. Almost the way I would question a suspect. He looked different sitting across from me, but that may just have been my new perspective. I was his prisoner. He was my jailer. He appeared more confident than arrogant. More like an investigator, and less like a fool. "I don't like you," he said. "I want to make that clear."

"I don't like you, either." Boy, what an intelligent conversation for two grown men to be having.

"I think you're an arrogant, sanctimonious smart-ass," he went on. "I think you walk around with more dark secrets than anybody in town."

I was about to tell him what I thought of his 4-F ass when I wisely thought better of it. "Speaking of secrets," I said, "who was your Secret Service friend?"

Dickerson shrugged his shoulders. "The vice president of the United States was going to be in the area. We had a murder suspect among us . . . a suspect who had been a sniper in the war. We all agreed that the best way to keep an eye on you was to bring you along."

The thought that somehow I was a threat to national security amused me. "What did you think I was going to do . . . shoot Nixon? Sorry, I don't take my politics that seriously."

"We do."

Those two little words, trivial as they seemed

at the time, would haunt me for the rest of my
life. *We do*. They haunt me as I write this. But
at the time, they meant nothing. My mind was
elsewhere. I was trying to clear myself of murder charges.

I told the detective from Texas, "You don't
have one scrap of evidence that ties me to what
went on in that wheat field."

"Poor choice of words, Deputy." He reached
into his coat pocket and pulled out a scrap of
paper. "We conducted a second search of the
Butlers' home," he said. He held the paper up
for me to see. "Oldest police trick in the
book . . . we ran a pencil back and fourth over
the top page of one of Maggie's notepads," he
explained. "This is what showed up."

To: Deputy Pliny Pennington,
Would you like to watch?
Come to the wheat field around sunset.

He continued holding the note to my face, as if
it were a crucifix. "It's Maggie's handwriting . . .
but as you can see, Deputy, there are no directions
to the wheat field."

"And that tells you what?"

"That tells us you already knew where the
wheat field was."

"How do you know I ever got that note?"

"We don't. You would have destroyed it immediately. You're smart, that way. Which is why I don't understand the blackmail. That seemed stupid."

"Not so stupid. There is a film out there of the murders . . . of that, I'm sure. My plan was simple. Use the blackmail money to secure the film . . . use the film to solve the murders."

"That's not a bad plan."

"Thank you."

"You must want that film pretty bad."

"I want to know who killed the Butlers. I want some justice."

"Of course, I could argue, you want the film because you have a starring role in it. Or maybe you got greedy . . . thought you could get the film and the blackmail money."

Even while begrudgingly earning my respect, the little bastard was starting to piss me off. "I confess, the thought of keeping that money crossed my mind . . . but my main objective was the film."

"Tell me then, Deputy, in your mind, who is in this film . . . other than Maggie and Michael Butler?"

"I believe, Detective, that our esteemed congressman, Webster Sprague, and/or his wife, Caren, are in the film."

"And what are they doing?"

"One of them is murdering the Butlers . . . the other is watching."

"And who's behind the camera?"

It was a logical question, but it surprised me coming from Dickerson. His line of reasoning was now following mine. Still, I feared another trap. I didn't answer him.

He sat up on the bunk. Leaned forward. Rubbed his hands together while he glanced over his shoulder. Checked to make sure we were alone. Then he lowered his voice until it was barely above a whisper. "Look, I don't believe for one minute you killed those people. A lot of people in this town want me to believe you killed them . . . but I'm having a real hard time with it. So why don't you help me out, Deputy?"

"You might make a real detective yet, Dickerson."

"Let's pretend I'm not there yet . . . who was behind the camera?"

I thought long and hard before answering. But I was desperate for friends. So I chose my words carefully. "Halloween, 1938. That *War of the Worlds* scare. The Madison newspaper printed a photograph of two boys and a man, beside another photograph of a Martian crop circle discovered in a Kickapoo Falls wheat field. The two boys were Webster Sprague and Michael Butler. I believe the man in that photograph to be our man behind the camera."

"And did this man just happen to arrest those two boys way back then?"

"The man thought the prank was harmless. The man didn't arrest anybody."

"I see. And do you still have this newspaper photograph . . . which, you understand, would be circumstantial, at best?"

"I still have the photograph."

"And what other evidence is there?"

"In Webster's house . . . there are other films . . . dirty little movies, if you will. One of those movies was shot in the wheat field. I'd be willing to bet the mother lode of those dirty movies are in the man's house . . . maybe even the murder film."

"I can't get into those houses. No judge would issue me a warrant."

"I could get into those houses . . . at least one of them."

There was a long pause as we stared at each other. He didn't trust me. I still didn't trust him. Finally, Dickerson turned. Stared at the open bars. Looked over his shoulder at the open door leading up the stairs. "You've got until sunup," he whispered. "With or without the evidence, you surrender yourself to me in the morning."

"Where?"

"On the Upper Dells. Witches Gulch. It's closed for the season. There won't be anybody up there but me, you, and the spooks. But be warned, Deputy, until then you're a fugitive. Considered armed and dangerous."

Then the detective got up and left. He slammed closed the bars to the cell door. He slammed closed the metal door at the foot of the stairway.

I listened as he marched up the stairs. When all was deathly quiet, I got off my bunk and wandered over to the bars. There, dangling in the lock, was a full set of keys.

CHAPTER 38

A VOICE IN THE WOODS:
LAST CALL

HARD TO SAY how long I sat in that cell staring at those keys dangling in the door. Seemed like hours. My brain, already racing, went into overdrive, completing a study in contradictions. Dickerson was a rat. Dickerson was a good cop. Dickerson was going to help me arrest Sheriff Fats and Webster Sprague. Dickerson was waiting at the top of the stairs to shoot me as I tried to escape. Finally, having weighed all my options, I did what any caged bird would do with the door left open. I flew.

It was strange to be on the run. A fugitive in my own town. The first thing I did was head for home. Picked up my rifle and pocketed some

shells. I grabbed my flashlight. I threw a fatigue
jacket over the black T-shirt I had been wearing
for seven days. I didn't know how long I had
before I would be reported missing. I also had
to figure in the distinct possibility that Dickerson was setting me up. It seemed the fashion-
able thing to do. I had no idea how to get into
the home of Sheriff Fats, but I did know how to
break into Webster's house. If they were going
to ambush me, that's where it would come—at
the big white Colonial in the long shadows of
the Kickapoo Gunn Club.

It was cold and cloudy. I stayed off the roads.
Stayed away from cars. I moved stealthily
through the woods and the farm fields, just like
a deer, only now I was the hunted. I worked
my way to the golf course, then cut across the
fairways until I lay on the crest of a hill overlooking the Sprague house. The place was dark,
not a light on anywhere. Maybe Webster was
already in bed, but more likely he was out doing
last-second campaigning. In less than twelve
hours, people in Wisconsin would begin trek-
king to the polls to pick a new president.

I lay on the ground with my Springfield and
my flashlight. In combat mode. I was tired. I
was scared. My breathing was erratic. Once
more, I was the scout out ahead of the patrol,
lying alone on a field in France, waiting for a
German patrol. It was as Dickerson had noted.

I was harboring dark secrets in a town flooded with dark secrets.

The detective was a strange one. Friend or foe, I still didn't know. In the morning he wanted me to be at Witches Gulch, a long, narrow, and spooky passageway between two rocky bluffs. In the summertime, it swarmed with tourists. At nighttime and wintertime, it was a haunted cavern fit only for men who feared neither God nor Devil.

What was my plan? I really had none. Break into the house. Get the one wheat field film I'd already seen. Then find Caren. The Spragues owned a summer home on Cape Cod. I was sure that's where she was hiding. But police on the Cape had checked the home, said it was vacant. Still, some clue to her exact whereabouts had to be in the imposing house before me. I would find what I could find, then make my way up to Witches Gulch.

I was about to move down the hill to the house when the first wet flake hit my cheek. I held out the palm of my hand. In seconds it was clustered with flakes of snow. Giant flakes. Damp and heavy. I put my bare hand to the ground. It was cold enough to stick. I was screwed. In the snow, I'd be about as hard to track as an elephant through a field of mud. I got off the grass fast, down the hill and into the house.

In the basement theater, with the thick carpeting and the dark paneling, I found the canister of film I knew to have been shot in the wheat field. It was right where I had left it. Strange as it sounds, I wanted to see it again. I threaded the projector. Hit the toggle switch.

Once again, the wheat field comes into focus. Within minutes, Caren and Webster Sprague are naked on a blanket. Then he is inside of her. The film seems better the second time around. I pay more attention to detail, especially Caren's role. All woman. All erotic. He pulls out and rolls her over. She comes to her knees. Her shapely hips are high in the air. He reenters her from behind and she shrieks with joy. She rests her head on the blanket, her face to the camera.

Then the phone rang. Went off like a burglar alarm. Like a knife cutting down my spine. It shrieked at me, the way it shrieked that night on the side of the road, the night I waited for her call at the truck stop. Not all ringing telephones sound the same. The truly ominous calls always have a shrill to their ring. I knew it was her. But she couldn't possibly know I'd be at the house. Or could she?

After seven earsplitting rings, I lifted the receiver from the cradle. "Hello . . ."

There was the usual long-distance static, but no voice. Just silence. The kind of silence that follows surprise. I kept quiet. Just listened. I turned and watched her image up on the silver screen.

She is at once raw and beautiful. The camera pans down the arch of her back and then closes in on her lovely face. Her long black hair is flailing about her shoulders. At every thrust, she moans with pleasure. Her outstretched arms are off of the blanket and her fingers are grasping straws of wheat.

Finally, she spoke. "Hello, lover. You get around."

"It's all coming down, Caren."

"What do you mean?"

"They didn't buy it. They let me go. Webster is going to be arrested in the morning. We're searching the house now. We expect him to accuse you of the murders."

"Webster is the man you want. Please leave me out of it."

"Then tell me what I need to know. No more secrets."

"Sex thrives on secrets."

"No. No more games. The Republican convention in Chicago . . . you said you were with Michael. Webster was with Maggie. Webster walked down to hear the acceptance speech. When he got back, you were gone. Maggie and Michael were hightailing it back to Wisconsin. Why? What happened?"

"Maggie found out the boys at the Gunn Club

were formulating a backup plan in case Nixon lost. At least that's what she told Michael."

"What kind of plan?"

"They said they could live with Johnson, but like hell if they would live with Kennedy."

"What does that mean?"

"I think that's when your name came up."

"My name? For what reason?"

"We all got scared and left."

"What happened in the wheat field?"

"Webster wanted Maggie dead . . . because she knew about the plan. They wanted it all on film. Apparently, there are private collectors in Europe who pay big money for such films. Webster saw it as a win-win situation. He promised to pay Maggie and Michael big dollars if they'd be in one more movie."

"But you took the final reel and ran . . . why?"

"Insurance. I was next."

"They're still looking to kill you, Caren. You have to turn yourself in. I can help. Where are you?"

"Did you love her . . . I mean, was it real love?"

"Don't start—"

"I mean, think about it. How was it possible to be so in love with a woman who didn't care if you lived or died?"

"I'm coming for you, Caren. I'm bringing you in."

"I'll be waiting. You'll be surprised."

Then she hung up. I glanced up at the screen.

Webster turns her on her back for the cum-shot. He pushes her knees apart. Soon he is spent. Through with her. The dark-haired beauty rolls to her stomach. Rests her head on her arms in a classic nude pose. She stares into the camera.

CHAPTER 39

INTO THE WOODS

I FOLLOWED THE edge of the golf course as it followed the edge of the river. Below me, the white house was bathed in red snowflakes. The flashing lights of squad cars from the Kickapoo County Sheriff's Department surrounded the property. In the distance, I could see what I guessed were the twirling red lights of state patrol cars coming fast down the highway. In fact, the last thing I heard before I disappeared into the big woods was the unmistakable voice of my hero and my mentor, Sheriff Fats, as he addressed his young deputies. "Boys, this is something I have to do myself." That declaration of self-pity was followed by the unmistakable sound of a .30-caliber cartridge sliding into the breach. Followed by the sound of the bolt sliding home.

I had just enough time to grab the film and get out the back of the house. My guess was, Dickerson had indeed set me up. Or maybe he meant to help but got cold feet at the last minute. Point is, they knew exactly where to look for me, but they were too slow and I was too fast. I was running with the canister of film in my coat pocket. I carried the flashlight in my hand like a war club. My Springfield was slung over my shoulder. I hugged the tree line, knowing my tracks would be harder to find in the dark. A handful of cartridges jangled in my pockets. I hoped I had grabbed enough. If they called out the dogs, I would have to kill them.

The falling snow was coming straight down. No wind. No ice. No mix of rain. Just a gentle snowfall lulling the land into a long, deep sleep. The first thing I did was head for the nearest cornfield. Rested between the dead stalks. I would work my way up to the Dells. If I cut cross country, if I moved at a brisk pace, I could be up where wave and rock and tall pine meet by the time the sun came up. Find Dickerson. Or maybe kill Dickerson. One or the other. From there, maybe I could steal a car. But then what?

When you're running for your life, it's hard to think of anything but survival. The phone conversation with Caren Sprague kept racing through my mind, but I had a difficult time making sense of it. Was it possible Maggie was not killed over sex games—that instead, Maggie was killed in a deadly game of politics? Could I believe anything Caren Sprague told me? Even on the run, even trying to weigh the enormous implications of what she had said, I couldn't stop thinking of the sex goddess starring in the film that I was carrying in my pocket. She was naked in the wheat field. On her knees. The sun was golden across her back. Her body was literally pulsating with sex. If somehow I got out of Wisconsin alive, I knew what I would do. I would make my way to Boston. Assume a new identity. Then I would work my way down to the Cape. It might take years to find the bitch, but it would be well worth the effort. Worth the risk.

CHAPTER 40

WITCHES GULCH

ELECTION DAY. TUESDAY, November 8, 1960. That long, fateful day broke sunny and white. So white and bright it stung my eyes. I'd forgotten to grab my sunglasses. Hardly the first thing you think of while on the run at night. I had reached the Upper Dells just before dawn. Dozed off in a bed of pines, the branches serving as a teepee. Awake, I crawled from my nest and hobbled to the edge of Sunset Cliff above Witches Gulch. I put a hand to my forehead to shield my eyes and gazed out over a winter wonderland. The valley of the painted rocks had been painted white. The towering pines. The sculptured cliffs. The rambling stretches of rocky banks. Everything in sight was pristine white. Only the Wisconsin River had escaped the ghostly shroud of snow—but even the dark, rushing waters were made more picturesque by the soft white blanket that covered its shores. I was the only living creature in sight, and just for a moment on that luminous wintry morning, I was afforded a rare glimpse of an ancient time—a time so long in the past that even the Indians had yet to discover the enigmatic Dells.

With a rifle slung over my shoulder, I had marched ten miles across rugged terrain through a falling snow. And that was after wasting away in a dank jail cell for seven days. I was cold. I was hungry and wet. My back ached. My feet hurt. The fingers on my hands were freezing numb. I stood in the sunshine and soaked in the rays. But I had precious little time to enjoy the warmth. Against a background of unbroken white, my army green jacket stood out like the bull's-eye on a target.

Fats would be in his hunting mode. He, too, had a Springfield '03 with a telescopic sight. I knew he would be tracking me. Not hard to do in the snow. Only the sheriff's age and his health could keep him from catching up with me. That's if he tracked me all the way. There was the real possibility that he would simply drive up to the gulch with Dickerson. Shoot me, or cuff me. How far was I willing to go? Who was I willing to shoot?

Every summer, countless people entered the

gulch on the river between Sunset Cliff and the high bluff across the way called Signal Point. But there was also a rugged trail that led down the cliffs at the rear of the gulch—a back door, if you will. I made my way east along the southern cliff. Deer tracks marred the snow, and a rabbit had hopped by before dawn, but other than that, there were no footprints leading down into the gulch.

Most of the spooky legends in the Dells had sprung from that enchanting stretch of river where the evergreens grew right out of the rock—that sweep of dark water that raced by Witches Gulch, from Louis Bluff, through the Narrows to Black Hawk Island. Even the old rivermen from the logging days swore to their mothers they would never, in their drunkest state, traverse that haunted stretch of rushing water at night. My father had told me some of the stories. Fats told me others, like the one about the battle cries of a Sioux war party that could still be heard echoing through the canyons. On stormy nights, he went on, there could be heard, between claps of thunder, the tortuous screams of a Ho-Chunk brave as his scalp was cut from his head. In Witches Gulch, there was rumored to be the horrible laughter of a hag, followed by a bony hand extending a flickering candle through a gap in the rocks. At night, temple bells were said to be tolling in the pagan

Dells. And more than a few loggers reported seeing a ghostly white phantom emerging from the darkness of Chapel Gorge and sailing out over the water.

Cynics in the valley believed the ghost stories were cooked up for the biggest monster of all—tourism. When I was a kid, I believed every one of them, and more. As I started my descent down the snowy cliffs and into Witches Gulch, those stories came back to me in frightening detail.

A wooden walkway was built through the gulch in 1875. A trout stream ran beneath and beside it. I managed to reach the pine boards without breaking my neck. I held my rifle out before me and began a slow patrol along the narrow opening between the two rocky bluffs. Icicles hung like teeth from the narrow passageways. In some places the two cliffs came within a foot of each other. In other places the walls opened into capacious domes of yellow and pink sandstone—almost cathedral-like settings, where the musical waters swirled into whirlpools. Despite its splendor, it was not good terrain for my Springfield. No sight lines. Too much rock. Too many curves. I did have the benefit of daylight filtering in. And it was dry. Much of the snow had been unable to penetrate the gulch. I appeared to be alone. The first to arrive. I searched for a place to set up, where the deadly advantage would be mine.

There was little chance Fats or Dickerson would be arriving by the river, so I set up on an overhanging cliff facing the rear of the gulch. It was about eight feet above the boards. A depression in the soft stone granted me a measure of cover. I nestled into the dome made of rock. A geological wonder shaped by wind and water. A sliver of sunlight cut through a gap in the high cliffs. Across the expanse of sandstone was just that one narrow opening where the walkway and the stream filtered through. They would have to come down that wooden path and step into the light, and into my sights. I could use the rock before me as a bench rest for the rifle, though at that short range it would be like taking a shotgun to sleeping moose. More important, with me up on the cliff and one of them down on the floor, we could talk. Maybe negotiate. The dark, shadowy gulch had a resonate echo, which might account for some of the ghostly sounds.

The air around me was sweet with the redolence of pine and fern. Still, chill winds whistled through, and my aches and pains only multiplied while I sat. Every muscle twitched with cold and fatigue. Every sound felt booming. Eerie. My thoughts returned to how it was

I ever got myself into this predicament. Seemed I'd spent my life in a blind with a rifle. Waiting. First I'd hunted squirrels. Then I tracked deer. Then I ambushed Germans. Besides being a good marksman, the Rangers had wanted men who had both outdoor skills and strong moral character. No hotshots. No loudmouths. No braggarts. Those types tended to fold when the going got rough. The Rangers wanted us quiet types behind those rifles. Men who did more thinking than talking.

I was dreaming of those days, while at the same time watching the walkway through the gulch, when the first shot rang out. The stone a foot above my head exploded into shrapnel. Bits and pieces of the soft sandstone rained down upon me. Then I could hear the echo of metal on metal as his bolt was drawn to the rear and he chambered a second round. The son of a bitch was above me. He was shooting through the slender gap in the high cliffs. He couldn't possibly have an angle on me. I had made sure of that. But that didn't stop him from trying. A second shot again blasted the rock above my head. The echo of the rifle fire was maddening.

I put my scope to the sliver of sky above me and searched the pines for a shadow, a hat, the barrel of rifle, anything to pin down his location. When at last I thought I saw an ominous shadow jerk forward, I squeezed the trigger.

Killed a pine tree. Its chips went spitting into the snow. The report of my rifle was followed instantly by his own. Again, high and away. He was doing what I was doing. Guessing, with no clear shot.

Again I put my scope to the snowy cliffs above me and searched. I was hoping it was Dickerson up there. Just show me your skinny neck, I prayed. They flop around a lot when you shoot 'em in the neck. Kind of bleed to death and suffocate at the same time.

I waited. I waited for what seemed like an hour, though it was only a matter of minutes. I knew what had happened. He had realized he had no angle on me, and if he attempted to move to a better position, I'd take him out. In effect, we had pinned each other down. That also told me I wasn't shooting against Dickerson. I lowered my weapon. Decided to shoot off my mouth instead of my rifle.

"How the roads up that way, Sheriff?" There was no answer. "Where's Caren Sprague?" I shouted. My voice echoed off the rock as it bounced its way through the gulch and up to the cliffs.

The answer came back equally loud and impressive. "The things you don't know, Deputy."

"I'm not coming in, Sheriff. I'm going to find her. I'm going to retrieve that film you shot."

"Don't make me kill you, Deputy. You're not the man I'm after."

"Who are you after, Sheriff?"

"Sometimes a man has to grab history by the throat."

"What does that mean?"

"That means there's not a problem in this country that can't be solved with a Bible in one hand and a rifle in the other."

"So are you going to bless me or shoot me?"

He sent another .30-caliber shell into the sandstone above me. Particles of stone drifted into my eyes. Then he was yelling down at me again. "I want you to know . . . I didn't shoot at you that day up on Hawk's Bill. If I had, you'd be dead. There are other forces at work here."

"Yes . . . Caren told me about the plan," I yelled back. It was like talking to a ghost.

"Well then, Deputy, I guess now I have to kill you."

"A good sniper recognizes the shot that can't be made. You once told me that, Sheriff. So why don't you throw your rifle down here . . . because you're under arrest."

"For what reason?" His voice was booming. Like God demanding an answer.

"Conspiracy to commit murder," I told him.

"Murder who?"

"Michael Butler."

"Well now, Deputy, it seems one of us killed a Butler . . . which one did you kill?"

"I hated what you people were doing to Maggie."

"You're totally blind when it comes to that woman. Maggie Butler was a thieving, lying, whoring bitch!"

I shouldered the Springfield and sent another shell crashing through the pines above. And boy, that was stupid. I took a deep breath. Wiped the sand from my eyes. Checked my coat pockets. One canister of pornography and three shells. Now every shot would have to count.

Then Fats began laughing. It began as a soft chuckle, but soon reached a frenzied pitch. "So this is it," he crowed. It was an evil, haunting laugh, and it struck me that perhaps, all those years, Fats had been the horrible hag of Witches Gulch. When the last echo of laughter bounced off the last rock, he shouted down, "Any regrets, Deputy?"

"I wish I'd applied for an absentee ballot."

"Don't get smart."

I searched the cavern before me. Eight feet to the ground, and a mad dash across the walkway. But to where?

It was like Fats was reading my mind. "There is only one way out of here, Deputy."

He was right. Unless I went down the river, in which case I'd be a sitting duck when sighted from the cliffs, back through the gulch was the only way out. "Don't you have a plane to catch?" I asked.

"I can wait. You ain't but half a man, anyway."

There it was. Whenever Pennington got too big for his britches, remind him of his wounds. Small towns are evil that way. Everybody in town has one specific weakness, and everybody else in town knows what it is.

So I was pinned down in Witches Gulch. An accused murderer. A fugitive. Armed and dangerous. Fats might not have been up there alone, and even if he was, his deputies couldn't be too far behind. I had to make a break.

I decided to go for the river. If I could reach the mouth of the gulch without getting killed, I could force Fats out along Sunset Cliff. Then it would be a fair fight. I'd have at least one good shot at him.

With the same determination I had showed on Hawk's Bill, I sprang from the cliff with the rifle in my hand and dropped to the walkway. But my legs had little left in them. They buckled like a rag doll. The Springfield hit the boards and flew from my hand. I retrieved it on hands and knees and was scrambling to my feet when Fats's next shot nearly split the rifle in two. It was jolted from my hands and spun along the walkway, smoke oozing out the breach. A lucky shot, or an incredible shot, but he'd put a bullet

right through my Springfield. Other than as a
club, it was worthless. I waited for the next bullet to hit me in the back of the head. A sniper
has no rules regarding eye contact. But the bullet didn't come. I stood, slowly, and turned. My
hands in the air. I gazed up between the bluffs.
There in the sunshine stood Sheriff Fats on a
bank of snow, his rifle to his shoulder, his crosshairs boring a hole in my forehead. He was in
full uniform—his badge pinned to his winter
coat, the Stetson set atop his head. His chubby
face was red from exhaustion. Red from the
cold. He looked older than I'd ever seen him.
More lethal, too. It was the point in the story
where one of us was supposed to confess. But I
decided, to hell with it. There being no doubt
in my mind he was going to shoot me—I was
determined to take my secrets to my grave.

And I would have, had Fats not been shot in
the back.

The old giant fell like a redwood. Rolled like
a boulder. He toppled down the bank of snow
and dropped twenty feet into the gulch. He
crashed over the railing of the walkway, spilling
blood across the boards. Then I watched in as-
tonished disbelief as he crawled to his knees.
Attempted to stand, one hand over his bloody
uniform, one hand pointing at me. The bullet
had entered his back and exited his stomach.

"Traitor," he cried.

He stumbled my way. "A damn traitor." His eyes were on fire. "Why did I ever trust you?" I couldn't really tell if he was talking to me, or through me. "I was a fool . . . just an old fool."

For as long as anybody could remember, he was the sheriff of Kickapoo County. A living legend. And those were the last words out of his mouth.

"I was a fool . . . just an old fool."

The next shot took off the back of his head.

CHAPTER 41

DEATH OF A LEGEND

FATS LAY ON the pine boards like a beached whale rotting from the head down. By then I had seen much death in my young life. My buddies in the war. My enemies in the war. The woman I thought I loved. Now the sheriff—my idol, my mentor. Most of them had died violently, at the hands of a rifle. Died too young.

I waited for my savior to show himself on the snowy banks of the high bluff, but there was nothing up there in the sun but frosty silence. Suddenly, with the wintry wind whipping through the cavern, Witches Gulch began to live up to its spooky reputation. I was convinced I could hear the cries of that Sioux war party, followed by the tortured screams of a helpless boy. I thought I heard the horrible laughter of the hag. And finally, clear as a temple bell, I heard ghostly footsteps marching down the wooden walkway.

I reached over the fallen body of Sheriff Fats and pulled his service revolver from its holster. Aimed it toward the dark opening in the rock. I waited. My finger was ever so gently squeezing the last fraction of slack from the trigger as the eerie sound of the footsteps worked my direction.

At last, the devil with the bony hands stepped from the shadows. But it wasn't a disembodied candle he carried. It was a cheap Italian rifle with a 4-power scope. Probably mail-order. In his other hand was the black briefcase that I recognized to be from the payoff in the cemetery.

I lowered the revolver. "You're a man of many surprises, Detective Dickerson."

"As are you, Deputy."

"Why did you do it?"

"He was going to kill you . . . and I figured, I might be working for you someday."

"Is that the money?" I asked.

Dickerson laid the briefcase at the feet of the dead sheriff and popped it open. The two hundred thousand dollars in cash was still stacked neatly inside. Envelopes and papers were scattered atop the cash. "I found it on his office desk, among other evidence. Fats had the money. She has the film. He was taking her the money when you got loose."

"Where is she?"

Dickerson stood with a long envelope. Red, white, and blue. "Fats had a plane ticket," he said. "United Airlines out of Chicago. Destination . . . Boston. Check it out."

He handed it to me. On the back of the envelope that contained the airplane tickets were directions down to Hyannisport. Beneath the directions were the following handwritten notes:

- *money*
- *equipment*
- *JFK*
- *ferry to Nantucket*

It was Fats's handwriting, all right. He'd been scribbling me notes since the day I pinned on the badge. Still, it took me a minute to decipher its meaning. "Fats was a photographer," I told Dickerson. "*Equipment* probably refers to his camera gear. *JFK* means shoot pictures of the candidate."

"Yes, I'm sure that's what it means. Take the money and the squad car and go to Chicago. You catch that plane. If she's on that island, bring her back here. Make her pay for what she's done. I'll pick up Webster Sprague. Just to be on the safe side, I'll alert the Secret Service."

I reached into my coat pocket for our two suspects, who had traveled with me all night. Turned them over to the detective. "Here's an earlier film they shot in the wheat field. I'm sure Fats was behind the camera."

"I'll tag it as evidence." Dickerson closed the briefcase and handed it to me.

I took a long, last look at the sheriff of Kickapoo County. There wasn't much left of the man I knew. I looked over at Dickerson, his hand wrapped securely around the barrel of his mail-order rifle. Cheap but deadly. "Funny," I said to him, "even while he was shooting at me just now . . . Fats wanted me to know that he wasn't the one trying to kill me that day up on Hawk's Bill."

"There's only one way his job will ever be yours," the detective declared, "that's if you wrap this thing up. Bring that woman in . . . dead or alive."

Then, as I was walking away with the money and the plane tickets, I heard Dickerson add, "Radio me some help up here."

CHAPTER 42

AFTON ROAD:
PART THREE

THERE WAS ALWAYS a kind of arrogance about Lila Carlson. Not malicious, more the natural arrogance that comes with natural beauty. The golden girl who married the golden boy. When she disappeared behind the bolted doors on Afton Road, some thought it was her comeuppance. A failing marriage, perhaps. A philandering husband. Maybe an illegitimate child. But the truth proved more awful than all of that.

It was Doc Hope who finally put all rumors to rest, it being illegal to conceal a contagious disease. While serving in the Philippines, Brock Carlson had contracted leprosy.

The entire town was shocked. The initial

shock was followed by concern. Soon, as happens in small towns, that concern grew into fear. Almost panic. We learned of a leper colony in Hawaii, and everybody talked of how nice it would be for Brock and Lila to live out their lives together on a Pacific island. A collection was taken up, and not even I can remember if it was a sincere attempt to help them, or if it was just a cynical ploy to get the two lepers out of the valley. Officials from the health department approached the house with special transportation tickets, but a shotgun blast fired over their heads from a front window sent them retreating down the road. The odd thing about it was this—the health department workers swore it was Lila Carlson who had fired the shot from an upstairs window. At any rate, the decision was made to leave the young couple alone.

Over the years, not even the town doctor was allowed past the surrounding fence. Doc Hope would simply get a note from Lila describing a specific ailment, then he would leave the appropriate medicine in a bag at the front gate. The same with their groceries, and other needs. Their phone had been disconnected, probably ripped from the wall. Store owners in town would get a simple note in the mail. Deliveries were made to the front gate, along with a bill, which was paid promptly by mail every month. Neighbors in the surrounding hills said the goods would sit outside until nightfall. By morning, they had been brought in. Once in a while somebody would report seeing a figure clad in a heavy coat and cap wandering about the backyard near the woods, but even that was rare.

Among the children in town, horror stories about the house on Afton Road grew more outrageous with every passing year—stories of monsters and witches, and of people being murdered in the woods behind the house. On Halloween, a deputy had to be posted at the end of the road to keep the older kids from venturing toward the house on a dare.

Brock Carlson of Kickapoo Falls, Wisconsin, one of the true heroes of my childhood, finally succumbed to the disfiguring disease in 1966. Lila requested that a simple pine casket be delivered to the house. Next day, Doc Hope and four workers from the state health department dressed in protective garb were allowed to enter the house to remove the casket. The old doctor told me about it one day, how Lila was seated in a chair in the front parlor, dressed all in black. Her face was hidden behind a heavy black veil. Her hands were covered with black velvet gloves. Before her was the casket. It was closed.

Doc Hope turned to her for permission. "We have to be sure . . . it's the law."

But Lila said nothing. Sat in stony silence. With that lack of response, the doctor opened the casket and peered inside. The tears in his eyes reflected both sorrow and revulsion.

The closed casket was taken directly from the house to Oak Hill Cemetery, where it was interred immediately. Lila stayed behind.

She lived another twelve years. When a delivery of milk and groceries were left untouched at the front gate, neighbors called the sheriff's department. I assumed the task of breaking down the door. Doc Hope, then retired, was with me, as were a man and a woman from the state health department. We donned masks and rubber gloves.

Once through the door, we called her name, but there was no response. We threw open a curtain to shed some light on the situation.

I had expected the house to look like something out of *Great Expectations*, with Miss Havisham still in her wedding dress, a veil hiding her hideous face. But the house was pristine. Cleaned and dusted. Filled with the pride a woman takes in decorating her home. Wildflowers cut from the woods, probably in the cover of dark, graced the tables. There was candy in the dishes. With the sun shining through the window, she could have been expecting company at any minute. In fact, the house was not at all different from when I had attended a party there some thirty years before.

We found Lila in the bedroom, as if asleep in her bed. Her shiny blond hair had turned a brilliant shade of white. The natural lines of aging creased her face, but even those were soft and faint. Other than that, she was as pretty as the day they had retreated to the house and bolted the door. Though we did not know it then, or we chose not to believe it, leprosy is perhaps the least infectious of all the contagious diseases. Lila Carlson had been spared the horror that ravaged her husband. Her death was one of loneliness.

I think about them now and then, buried together on the side of a hill, there being no mention on their stones of the curse that had plagued them in life. And as much as I idealized Brock Carlson in my youth, it is Lila Carlson I find myself wondering about on lonely nights. How her love for her husband was so great, so true, that she took to *her* grave *his* pain and humiliation.

The house and barn at the end of Afton Road were burned to the ground. In their place, the forest service planted a stand of pines. A conifer forest of cleansing needles and cones. It worked. The trees are tall and thick now. There is no trace of a home. No outline of a yard. Today the area where the dirt road comes to an end is known as Leper Woods, though few people actually remember why. I would drive down that road sometimes. Stand where the gate used to be. And there, beneath the stately pines, I would marvel at the love between a man and a woman.

CHAPTER 43

TAKING FLIGHT

IT WAS THE first time I had ever been on a commercial airliner. I still have the ticket stub. United Airlines. Flight 176. Chicago to Boston. The last time I was on an airplane before that, I jumped out of the damn thing. In the dark over France. A rifle strapped across my chest. Now I was flying first class. A drink in my hand. A Chicago newspaper spread across my lap.

AMERICANS GO TO THE POLLS

Experts Say Nixon-Kennedy Race To Be Close
Record Turnouts Expected

According to the article, the young senator from Massachusetts would cast his ballot in the morning. In Boston. From there he would travel to the family's summer home on Cape Cod to await the returns. Hyannisport. The same place I was headed. But I was no longer a fugitive, or a threat to national security. On this flight, I was a deputy sheriff again, being sent out of state to apprehend a murder suspect. I folded the newspaper and set it aside. One more time I pulled the airline ticket from my coat pocket and read the handwritten notes hastily scribbled on the back of the red, white, and blue envelope.

- *money*
- *equipment*
- *JFK*
- *ferry to Nantucket*

In my mind, I kept telling myself the same thing I told Detective Dickerson—that *equipment* and the reference to *JFK* were about photography. The *money* and the *ferry to Nantucket* were about Caren Sprague. I had come to accept that Fats was a pornographer. Perhaps a conspirator. But I still couldn't bring myself to believe that our county sheriff was some kind of hired assassin. What I did believe was that somewhere on that far-away island I was going to find the woman who I suspected had walked out of that wheat field with blood on her hands and two hundred thousand dollars in her pocket.

Before hightailing it to Chicago, I had had just enough time to return to my house, jump in the shower, and put on some clean clothes. I traded my fatigue jacket for a sportcoat. Packed my duffel bag. I called it a duffel bag, but it was really my sniper bag from the war. Other than my Springfield, it was one of the few mementos I had hung on to. During the war I'd carried rifle parts in it—binoculars, telescopic scopes, and bullets that with one good shot would literally separate your head from your shoulders. Now I was tossing in socks and underwear. I packed my revolver. For some reason, perhaps my own peace of mind, I checked the batteries and then threw in my flashlight.

Out the airplane window it was cloudy and gray. We had caught up with the storm that had blanketed us with snow. Little could be seen of the Great Lakes below. The pilot announced the weather in Boston was better. Sunny and warm. I pulled the briefcase out from beneath the seat in front of me. Popped it open.

From the sheriff's file atop the money, I picked out a color photograph of Caren Sprague. Maggie's nemesis. Her evil twin. I studied it. The picture looked as if it had been snapped for some glossy magazine. She was standing beside a city highway, probably Chicago. Attired in the proverbial little black dress and wearing silver heels, she was slightly bent over, her hands on her long, slender legs, as if checking a run in her nylon stockings. Her black hair was blowing freely in the wind. Her eyes were as dark as night. Her lips were full and moist, with just the hint of a fleeting smile. Everything about her posture was provocative. Everything about the photograph screamed sex.

I finished my drink. At last, I had a date with the monster from Chicago. Again, my plan was simple. I find Caren Sprague. Hand over the money. She hands over the film. I place her under arrest. If she resists, I shoot the bitch.

Also in the file was the pencil-scribbled paper taken from Maggie's notepad. I placed it over the photograph. Over Caren's face. Read it for the hundredth time.

To: Deputy Pliny Pennington,
Would you like to watch?
Come to the wheat field around sunset.

The note repulsed me and excited me at the same time. No wonder my name kept coming up. At last, I was to be included. In a perverted way, it was like being recognized for years of service. My position within the sheriff's department could no longer be ignored. My standing in town was on the rise. The respect I had earned had made me a player in even their simplest plans. But as often is the case, it is the simple plans that go wrong. Like that night in the wheat field.

CHAPTER 44

SLOOP OUT OF HYANNISPORT

YES, I KILLED Maggie Butler. Justice demanded it. Why else would I be writing this? I remember staring into those dark, haunting eyes of hers in the very last second of her life—just before I drew blood from her very heart. In those eyes that I once believed were pure and good, I saw hatred and evil. Lust and greed. The small-town girl I had worshiped, had spent my life in love with, was nothing short of a monster. Immoral and without a conscience. Profane beyond description. She had invited me into her circle of debauchery. Invited me to bear witness to her lechery and her treachery. Pray tell, face-to-face with this monster, what would you have done? What action would you have taken had you stared into those hellish eyes of hers, only to find yourself staring back? In my heart was an uncontrollable rage. In my hand was a weapon. But before you condemn me, allow me to finish the story.

It was dark by the time I reached Hyannisport. On the East Coast, the polls had already closed. I stuffed the briefcase into my duffel bag, slung the bag over my shoulder like a sailor of old, and hiked down to Hyannis harbor. Found the Steamship Authority. A large ferry was tethered to the wharf, but it didn't have the buzz of a ship that was going anywhere. I checked my watch. It was near 8:30. I had been hoping to make it to the island by nightfall. Find an inn. Begin my search at dawn.

A batch of schedules for the ferry service were planted in a wood box outside an office door. I grabbed one, unfolded the paper, and tried to make sense of the fine-lined grid. The harbor lights were sparse and dingy yellow. I strained my eyes to find the departure times. Finally, I gave up. Looked around.

Lights were on in the harbor office, but there was nobody inside. In fact, there was nobody in sight. The wharf was deserted. The air was still. The sea was calm. It was as if you could hear for miles. The aroma of fresh fish and salt air was intoxicating. For all of the years I spent floating down the Wisconsin River, for all of the summers I spent sailing Lake Michigan, those magnificent bodies of water could not compare with the power I drew from the sea. The blood of my ancestors still coursed through my veins. For a moment I simply breathed the Atlantic air and let myself get lost in an oceanic trance.

"And where would a stranger like yourself be headed this time of night?"

He had sneaked up behind me, and I was mad at myself for being caught off guard. "Nantucket," I told the man.

"Nantucket," he said, sounding somewhat bemused. "Last ferry left at eight. Next ferry leaves at nine."

"Nine tonight?"

"Nine o'clock in the morning."

"Damn it," I mumbled.

"Wanted to be there tonight, did ya?"

"Yes," I told him. "It's very important."

"Got a sloop down the wharf. Making a run to Nantucket tonight. We could always use an extra hand."

This fisherman, as I thought of him, was New England to the core—an old salt in his late fifties. Not a big man, but rough, like the sea. His fingers bore the scars of fishhooks; his palms the calluses of rope lines. On the wharf, as on the water, his gait was one of mastery. A walk of pride.

I would learn as we boarded that his sloop

was built from spruce in Friendship, Maine, around 1900. These Friendship Sloops are fairly common on the East Coast. Nothing fancy. A workhorse on water. Sailboats built for fishing. This sloop had a big gaff-rigged mainsail and two jibs. A clipper bow was capped by an elongated bowsprit. There were thirty-one feet on deck, with an eleven-foot beam. According to the fisherman, the sloop drew five-and-a-half feet of water. Top speed—six knots.

"How long a trip then?" I asked.

"Nantucket be thirty miles out . . . with a good wind, be about a four-hour trip. Not much wind tonight. The calm before the storm. Tomorrow be rough."

His shipmate was waiting for us in the pulpit of the bow, though he appeared to be more of a passenger than a sailor. Dressed in a navy blue windbreaker and black tennis shoes, he was a big man whose muscles had gone to fat. His bullhead countenance and the razor-close haircut gave the shipmate the appearance of a military man. Awkward out of uniform. As we set sail, no introductions were offered. None were made.

After helping hoist the tall mainsail, I took a seat on the cabin roof, midship, my feet resting atop my duffel bag at the toe rail. The fisherman was at the stern, behind the wheel. The burly shipmate, as I call him, remained perched at the

bow—like a lookout. My flashlight and my revolver were inside the bag. Packed last. I was
beginning to wish I had strapped the revolver
to my belt. Beneath the hawklike stare of the
shipmate, I slowly reached between the draw
strings and drew my flashlight. My security
blanket. From my breast pocket I took out the
color photograph of Caren Sprague. Handed it
back to the fisherman. Shined the light on it.
"Have you ever seen this woman?"

"Nope . . . can't say I have. Pretty girl."

He handed back the photo. I turned into the
icy stare of the shipmate, then thought better of
asking. I placed Caren Sprague back into my
breast pocket.

Despite the lack of a good breeze, we were
soon out upon the dark, murky waters of Hyannis Harbor, sailing toward Nantucket Sound.
Every once in a while I was warned to duck as
the boom swept past my head. Suddenly, the
feeling washed over me that all of this was just
a little too timely. Too convenient. I didn't have
my sea legs yet. No sense of direction. I was
nervous. A small fish in new waters. I turned
back to the fisherman, trying to make conversation. "Exactly how do we get to Nantucket . . .
I mean, what are the directions?"

"You sail?"

"Lake Michigan . . . Superior."

"That must be fun. Nantucket's a simple trip in calm winds. The magnetic course is one-seven-five. The reciprocal course is three-five-five. Once we clear the channel, we stay west of Bishops and Clerks Tower. Sail past buoy seventeen. When we enter the channel to Nantucket Harbor, pay attention to the buoys . . . there's a nasty sandbar. You'll see the Coast Guard station to starboard."

In my mind, I was recording everything he told me.

"See that string of lights?" the fisherman said, pointing port side at Hyannisport. "That's the Kennedy place. Old Joe has been a regular on the Cape for thirty years. I'll bet that place is hopping tonight. Here, take the binoculars."

He handed me a powerful pair of binoculars. They were military. I admired them for a moment before putting them up to my eyes. Behind the lights I could make out three or four simple white clapboard cottages. Nothing before me appeared regal, or even presidential. What appeared to be the main house was ablaze in lights and activity. I could see men moving back and fourth before the large windows that faced the sea. But that's all I could see. I would need a scope to make out who was who.

The fisherman talked as I scanned the nightscape. "That's Marchant Avenue you see there. Comes to an end right at the Kennedy place. And out there on the dock, that's the family yacht, the *Marlin*."

I lowered the binoculars. "You seem to know a lot about the Kennedys."

"Like I said . . . family's been here more'n thirty years. I think it was 1927 that Joe Kennedy bought the old Malcolm cottage. They've been buying up land and houses ever since."

I returned the binoculars and dug from my coat pocket the schedule for the ferry service. Studied it under the glare of my flashlight. Then I began to think out loud. "Says here, the last ferry to Nantucket leaves at nine P.M."

"That's the summer schedule," said the fisherman. "It's fall."

"Where does it say that?" I didn't get an answer. Just one of those cold Yankee stares.

I turned back to the shipmate. Now he was perched at the bow with a rifle resting in his arms. A Springfield M1903-A4, with a Unertl scope. Same as mine. A rifle rare among civilians. He wasn't pointing it at me—yet. He was just cradling it in his arms, the way I cradled my rifle, with the ease and comfort of a trusted friend.

"What's the rifle for?" I asked him, trying to sound calm.

"Sharks," he said.

"Have to be one hell of a shark."

"You think you know it all, don't you?" The shipmate had an accent, but it was more Southern than New England.

"I know you ain't no sailor."

"And you know a sailor when you see one?"

"I know an army sniper when I see one."

The thing to remember about a combat situation is that it's usually over in seconds. But in the minds of the combatants, it seems like hours. Especially in hindsight. All three of us sensed the moment was at hand. We all made our move at the same instant. And every single move seemed incredibly slow and magnified.

The shipmate shouldered the sniper's rifle, the barrel and scope clearly aimed at the Kennedy compound.

The fisherman reached beneath his jacket for an automatic pistol.

I had just enough time to reach into my duffel bag.

"You've only got one bullet, Deputy. Who would you shoot?"

I stood at midship like a cross. With my left hand, I extended the flashlight toward the stern and shined the powerful light into the eyes of the fisherman. With my right hand, I extended the revolver and squeezed off one shot. Sent a .38 into the gut of the shipmate. He doubled over, screaming profanities. Then he struggled to aim the rifle over the port side.

Now pistol shots were coming from behind me. I swung behind the mast. The fisherman was shooting blindly. I worked my way along the starboard side, firing shots into the stern. I saw the fisherman weaving in and out of the spot of my flashlight. When I fired my last shot, I saw him flip backward, over the rail. Felt the heavy splash of the water.

Now I turned my attention back to the big shipmate, down on his knees, blood all over the bow. He was like a man possessed. Paid no attention to me. He had his orders. He wrestled the rifle to his hip. Pointed it again at the cottages in Hyannisport. I grabbed hold of the boom and gave it a shove. The mainsail swung nearly full circle, clipped the shipmate's head, and sent him somersaulting backward into the sea. The Springfield crashed to the bow. Slid along the rail.

The sloop was floundering out of control. I was knocked to the deck. Crawling on hands and knees, I secured the sail and worked my way back to the wheel. I steadied the ship. Pointed it in the right direction. Then, just when I thought I was back on course, that I had won the day, I was attacked from behind. The fisherman had crawled from the sea, like the Creature from the Black Lagoon. He was covered in seawater and blood. His eyes were on fire. In his hand was a filleting knife, its blade sharp as a razor. He lunged toward me, and I had barely enough time to turn and grab his wrist. Had to fight like hell to stop him from filleting my face. Even with a bullet in him, he had remarkable balance. On dry land, I'd have tossed him like a salad. On the ocean, I couldn't get the son of a bitch off me. I kept working my knee into his midsection, guessing that's where he'd been shot. I finally pinned him up against the wheel. Forced the knife from his hand to the deck. I could feel him weakening. Dying. One more time I brought my knee into the pit of his stomach. He doubled over. Almost a forced surrender. But I was in no mood to take prisoners. I flipped him overboard, then slipped and fell to the deck.

By the time I got back on my feet, I was seasick. Disoriented. Luckily, I hadn't been stabbed. Hadn't been shot. The lights of the Kennedy compound shone to my left. The bowsprit was still pointed toward Nantucket Sound. In the distance, I saw what must have been the lights of Bishops and Clerks Tower. Past that would be buoy seventeen. I couldn't see much in the dark, murky waters of Hyannis Harbor, so I simply prayed that this time the fisherman and his coconspirator were once again united. Somewhere in the deep.

CHAPTER 45

GHOST SHIP

ONE MORE NOTE about that night in Hyannis Harbor. I was being followed. A ghost ship was keeping pace off my starboard side. My first thought was Coast Guard. They would be reacting to the gunshots. But the lights coming from this ship were not searchlights. They were signal lights. And they were signaling me. It was just too damn dark, and the ship was too far away for me to judge what kind of force I was up against.

I retrieved the Springfield from the deck and hauled it back to the stern. Popped the bolt and checked the breach. I had three cartridges. I put the rifle to my shoulder. The scope to my eye. I spotted the signal light, probably a flashlight like mine. I was on water now and none too sure of my aim. The crosshairs wavered on the light. I squeezed the trigger. Across the darkened water, the phantom light exploded. Vanished.

I hurried along the rail to the bow. Again, I shouldered the rifle. Snuggled up to the stock. Aimed into the dark, to where I'd last seen the light. I allowed for the speed of the ship. Guessed at the wind. Then I waited for the muzzle blast I knew was to come. Sure enough, within seconds the soul of a rifleman aboard the spectral ship sent a shot across my stern. I instantly zeroed in on the flame of the blast. Returned the shot.

I'll never know if I claimed any spirits that night. But the ghost ship slipped back into the shadows of the sea and haunted me no more.

CHAPTER 46

THE HOMECOMING

I HAVEN'T BEEN back to Nantucket since that
deathly gray day. But I've read about it. Jewel
in the Atlantic. Summer resort for the rich and
the famous. A living history. Believe me, it was
none of those things in 1960. Back then, it was
nothing but a depressed fishing village. Remote
and forbidding. All past, and little future. An
island of squandered dreams.

I woke wobbly and tired, the sloop tethered
to a long, decaying wharf. The seas had turned
choppy overnight. By dawn, they were rough.
The morning sun was unable to penetrate the
thick layers of clouds. A cold, heavy mist filled
the air. Winds were on the rise. Temperatures
were in decline. The November storm that had
blanketed Wisconsin in a purifying snow had re-

loaded over the Great Lakes. Picked up moisture and speed. It bypassed Washington, but hit Philadelphia and New York hard. A classic nor'easter— powerful and dangerous, and true on course up the Atlantic seaboard. Cape Cod and Boston were next up in the counterclockwise spiral of the storm's path.

I stowed the Springfield below deck, along with my flashlight and my duffel bag. I slipped another six bullets into my revolver. Tucked the revolver beneath my belt. Covered it with my sportcoat. I was ill dressed for the weather. I turned up my collar to keep my neck dry. Then I climbed onto the deteriorating wharf and the welcome feeling of a more firm footing.

It was a bleak-looking island. Noisy gulls flew over the harbor in search of breakfast. Strange birds bobbed along on top of the water. At a row of crusty shacks on the waterfront, I spotted a trio of men standing in a doorway. Commercial fishermen, by appearance. Their ears were tuned to a radio inside. Their eyes were turned to the skies. Election news and weather reports were breaking at the same time. My approach met with three icy stares. Nothing I had to say could possibly be more important than what they were listening to on the radio. It wasn't the homecoming I was hoping for. But then, as a Pennington, I'd been away for two generations. I was cold and wet, and a bit seasick. I must have looked like hell, even to them. "Good morning, gentlemen."

"Mornin'," said two out of three of them.

I fished out the photograph of Caren Sprague. Handed it to the tall one in the middle. "Have any of you seen this woman on the island, recently?"

"Wish I had . . . hell of a woman . . . but can't say as I have."

The other two took a quick glance, then shook their heads no. "She in some kind of trouble?"

"No," I told them, "just an old friend."

They returned the photo with no further comments. I, too, could hear the radio inside. The announcers had that breathless tone to their voices. I recognized it from the war years—that everything they had to say was of earth-shattering importance.

"By the way," I asked, "who won the election?"

The tall one did all of the talking. "Still can't say for sure . . . but sounds like Kennedy."

"Really?" I was pleased. Almost giddy. "Did you happen to hear how Wisconsin voted?"

"You from Wisconsin?"

"Yes."

"Well, Wisconsin went to Nixon. Looks like Minnesota is going to Kennedy . . . and they're still fighting over Illinois. It's close."

I thanked the three reticent men and turned

away from the waterfront, toward the base of Main Street. Then I thought of something else, and they being the only three souls in sight, I decided there would be no harm in my asking. "One more thing, if you don't mind. If I wanted to look into some family history while on Nantucket . . . where would I go?"

The tall one pointed to the top of the town. "You'd do best by hiking up to Sunset Hill."

"And that would put me where, exactly?"

"That would put you in the cemetery."

CHAPTER 47

THE HEADSTONE

I FOUND A café off Main Street. Stopped for breakfast. Sat at the counter and ordered coffee and Quaker Oats. There, too, a radio was on. One minute they were talking storm warnings, the next minute they were talking politics. In record numbers, the American people had gone to the polls to pick a new president, but more than twelve hours after the polls had closed, the results were still uncertain.

I showed Caren's photograph to the waitress, a hardy woman with a friendly disposition. "You know, I think she's been in here. I really do."

"So you have seen her?"

"I wouldn't swear to it on a stack of Bibles, but, yes, I think I've seen her."

"Recently?" I asked.

"Maybe this past summer . . . because she's still fresh in my mind."

"How big is the island?"

"About fourteen miles long. Maybe three miles wide. That's more ground than you might think. If she's in town here . . . she shouldn't be too hard to find. But if she's out on one of the points—Quidnet, Sconset, Madaket—you might be here a while. Pretty desolate out there. Nantucket is a good place to hide."

With that promising lead, and some hot food in my stomach, I walked the cobblestoned streets in deteriorating weather. Ducked in and out of stores and shops without much luck. I quickly learned that island people were similar in nature to members of the Kickapoo Gunn Club. Fairly tight-lipped. Those willing to talk said they doubted she was around town—that a woman that young and pretty, and an off-islander to boot, would surely be noticed.

Around noon, I popped into a drugstore in the heart of town, where Orange Street and Centre Street came together at Main. I paid a quarter for a map of the island. Outside, under the overhang, I tried to get my bearings. The cold mist had turned to a light rain, with the promise of even worse. Across the way, I watched a man in a gray slicker chase another man down the street, both of them headed toward the wharf.

He was shouting after him. "It's over," he said. "Nixon conceded. Kennedy is president."

Strangely, because of their island reserve, I couldn't tell if the man was pleased or disappointed.

With my search for Caren Sprague as cold as the weather, I decided to attend to some family history. Just for the hell of it. I followed the narrow winding streets up to Sunset Hill. Nearly every cottage along the way was gray-shingled, with a roof-mounted walk. Perfect for viewing the sea.

Behind me stood a windmill among rolling fields of tall grass and shrubs, and wildflowers wilting in the weather. Beyond the belt of mist before me was a spectacular view of the town and Nantucket Harbor. I could see the lighthouse at Brant Point, and beyond that, the wide expanse of ocean. The white sails of a skiff were in a race with the storm for the coastline. A red-tailed hawk sailed overhead, then dived toward the beach. My eyes watered in the wind. My hands were turning red from the cold. I stuffed them into my pants pockets and wandered down the lane and into the Old North Burial Ground.

The graveyard sat on a windswept hill, surrounded by a split-rail fence. Few trees. Many of the simple white headstones were a hundred years old.

URIAH COFFIN
BORN IN NANTUCKET
MAY 14, 1777
DIED IN THE CITY OF NEW YORK
APR 12, 1861
AE 83YRS 11MOS

ELIZA
WIDOW OF
URIAH COFFIN
BORN AT NANTUCKET
JULY 4, 1787
DIED IN NEW YORK
MARCH 4, 1874

I moved from row to row, marveling at the archaic names, the family plots, and the dates from so long ago. In Wisconsin, a hundred years old was considered ancient. Before civilization. A hundred years ago on Nantucket, the island had already passed its glory.

The wind and rain were putting a damper on my search for long-lost Penningtons. I was just about to give up. Head back into town. Then I stumbled across the headstone. Though, like many of the others, it was a simple white stone, this marker was hard to miss. It had my name on it.

PLINY PENNINGTON
BORN
MARCH 30, 1802
DIED
APRIL 6, 1859

I stood before the grave with my name carved on it and thought of how many times in the past few months I had flirted with death. The leap from Hawk's Bill. The wild ride down to the Nixon rally in Madison. Witches Gulch. The sloop out of Hyannisport. I did some quick math in my head. By my reckoning, the man buried before me would have to have been my great-great-grandfather. Odd, my own father had never mentioned him. Or maybe he did, and it just didn't register. I knew only that *Pliny* was an old family name I wouldn't be passing on. Still, it was like finding my own grave. Disconcerting, to say the least. I needed a break from the day. A break from the weather.

I didn't want to go back to the sloop and the rough seas. So back in town, I found my way to the Atheneum Library, where I spent a very quiet, and a very warm, afternoon learning as much as I could about this small and rather peculiar island that I now found myself wandering.

Nantucket was an Indian word. It meant "faraway land." The warming influence of the Gulf

Stream provided the island with the longest growing season in New England. The first English settlers were farmers and sheepherders. Apparently, only the foolhardy refused to give up on the land. The rest of them took to the sea. More specifically, to the hunting of whales. Chasing their own death, the fictional Captain Ahab and his crew of the *Pequod* set sail from Nantucket, in their search for Moby-Dick.

In the early part of the nineteenth century, whaling made Nantucket one of the wealthiest communities in America. But that wealth came at a heavy price. Voyages were long and dangerous, often lasting two to three years. Women were left to run the town, unheard of in the nineteenth century. In fact, almost a quarter of the women on the island had been widowed by the sea. Surprisingly, despite deep Quaker roots, the use of opium on the island was widespread—particularly among the women.

Benjamin Franklin's mother was from Nantucket.

That lighthouse out on Brant Point was the second-oldest lighthouse in America.

In the summer of 1846, a fire wiped out one-third of the town, including the entire commercial district and most of the waterfront. The town was quickly rebuilt, largely in brick.

But as the whaling ships got bigger, and the demand for whale oil got smaller, the heart of the whaling industry sailed across the sound to New Bedford, New London, and Sag Harbor. The island went into decline. In November of 1869, the last whaling vessel left Nantucket Harbor, never to return.

Finally, feeling drowsy, I closed the book on Nantucket. Laid my head down on the library table. Closed my eyes and listened as the storm battered the windows. Without intending to, I drifted off to sleep. A long-day's nap.

CHAPTER 48

ABIGAIL

THEY WOKE ME when the library closed up at 5 P.M. It was already dark. The cold rain had turned to a pelting sleet. I felt that my search for Caren Sprague was probably over for the day. Quite frankly, I was feeling homesick. The thought of spending a stormy night aboard the sloop did not appeal to me. In fact, ancestors be damned, I was beginning to think Nantucket was a rather macabre little island. Before leaving, I asked the librarian if she could recommend a place to stay. She suggested the Coffin House at Broad Street. Having already seen my name carved into a gravestone, I was in no mood for morbid jokes. But as it turned out, the largest boardinghouse on the island was indeed called the Coffin House.

Being from Wisconsin, I found the sleet less daunting than the rain. As I ventured into the weather, I soon discovered that it was the wind whipping through the narrow streets that created most of the havoc.

I ended up before the Coffin House on a dark, deserted corner. I was, in fact, about to go inside and inquire about a room, when my eyes were drawn to an ethereal light coming from up on a hill. It was not a lighthouse. More of a faint beacon. So I turned my back on the Coffin House and made my way up to Church Street. This side street was appropriately named, because that's what was there—a big, beautiful white church, with soaring windows fronting a tower that climbed four stories high. The imposing church stood over the town like a celestial guardian. The light, probably a lantern, was coming from atop the tower. I stood at the foot of the hill on which the church was built, gazing up at the haunting light as it crept slowly down the windows in a zigzag pattern.

When the light was about halfway down the tower, I suddenly saw her. My heart pounded with recognition. My head swelled with anger and loathing. At long last, I believed, she was found.

There must have been a floor up there for her to stand upon, but from the outside looking in through the storm, she appeared as if floating in the tower window. It was the figure of a young woman. In a black dress. With dark hair. I was too far away to make out the specifics of her face, but every bone in my body told me that my search for the voice in the woods was finally at its end.

She remained in the tall cathedral window like a statue, her bewitching gaze cast down upon me. I tried to remain calm. Started up the brick walk toward the large double doors. I was straining my neck, staring straight up at her. She moved not a muscle. The sleet was peppering my eyes. Soon she was towering directly over me. I broke into a run.

I burst through the doors, into the vestibule. A wood stairway stood off to my left. I went to it. Raced up the stairs. On the second level, I found a choir loft with a huge organ. I ran up another flight, taking the steps two at a time. I was in the tower now, where I guessed she must have been. But the apparition was gone. I moved to the window where I believed she had been. Stood before the glass. Watched as the northeast wind pushed ghostly shadows up and down the winding streets.

I peered up another flight of stairs, only to see a lantern descending. My first thought was of the bony, disembodied hand with the flick-

ering candle that was said to haunt Witches
Gulch. But this light had a flesh and clammy
old hand attached to it.

The wiry man held the lantern up to my face.
"Storm coming," he said to me. "Closing her
up."

"I'm sorry . . . do you work here?"

"And pray here. Barker's my name."

"I saw a woman, upstairs, in the window."

"Young thing, pretty, dressed in black?"

"Yes. Do you know who she is?"

"That would be our Abigail." He kept right
on walking, down the stairs.

I trailed after him. "How long has she been
here?"

"More than a hundred years now."

I followed Barker and his swinging lantern
down the stairs. Obviously, it was his light that
I had seen in the tower. "A lot of strange things
going on," he said. "I hear this morning they
pulled a man's body right out of Hyannis
Harbor . . . not far from the new president. Had
a bullet hole in him."

I didn't comment on that tidbit of news. We
passed through the vestibule and into the
chapel, past row after row of box pews. All of
them numbered, the remnants of a bygone era.
The interior of the church was decorated with
large columns and recessed pilasters. A chandelier that must have been seven feet in diameter

hung from a classic tin ceiling. The ornate chandelier flickered off and on with the storm. It was all very simple, but at the same time, quite grand. A house of worship in quintessential Protestant New England. Once again, I was feeling like an interloper.

Another diminutive man stood beneath the pulpit. He was popping batteries into a flashlight. Dressed in a black turtleneck with gray slacks, he had a full head of fine silver hair, with wise gray eyes firmly set in a weather-beaten face.

Barker introduced us. "This is the Reverend Smith. And this here is Mister . . . ?"

"Pennington," I told them. I fixed another button on my sportcoat and shoved my hands into the pockets, hoping the reverend would not notice the revolver stuffed in my pants.

"Yes," Barker said. "Mr. Pennington, here, says he saw our Abigail up in the tower."

"That doesn't surprise me." He shined the flashlight in his face. "Tonight would be the night for it."

"I didn't really get a good look at her."

"Nobody ever gets a good look at Abigail."

Thinking Caren was probably using a different name, I asked, "How old is this Abigail?"

"Well, let's see," said the Reverend Smith, satisfied his flashlight was now in working order, "the church was built in 1834. Abigail was a

young bride . . . probably sixteen or seventeen . . .
that would make her about . . . one hundred and
forty years old."

"Are you telling me I saw a ghost?"

The reverend smiled at me, the way one
would wink an eye. "Her young husband was
a first mate on a whaling vessel, as the story
goes, returning home from his first voyage since
they were married. Abigail could see the ship
rounding Great Point in the teeth of a nor'easter.
So the young bride ran through the storm and
into the tower here to watch the ship enter the
harbor. But, encountering one of the severest
gales ever experienced off Nantucket, the ship
never made it. Got caught up on the Nantucket
Bar. Was torn apart in the storm, right before
Abigail's eyes. All hands lost."

"Blast that bar," said Barker. "It was the death
of this island, you know. How you gonna keep
up a harbor if you can't get ships in and out?"

"Anyway," continued the Reverend Smith,
"people have been seeing Abigail up in the
tower ever since . . . whenever there's a
nor'easter."

Barker nodded his head, as if every word of
the story was the honest-to-God truth. "Monster
nor'easter," he said, "must have been twenty
years back. Before the war, anyway. I was in
here by myself, closing up the shutters, just like
tonight, and the organ started up. Now that's a

five-ton organ up there, with nine hundred pipes."

The Reverend Smith corrected him. "Nine hundred and fourteen, to be exact."

"Yes, well, all nine hundred and fourteen of those pipes began wailing in the middle of the storm. Sounded like the Devil's brigade marching out of hell. I nearly jumped out of my skin. I ran up the stairs to the choir loft, and no sooner did I get up there, than that organ stopped dead. Saw Abigail's skirt disappearing up the tower stairs. Well, I yelled right up those stairs after her. Gave her a good tongue-lashing. Bawled her out, ghost, or no ghost. Woman darn near gave me a heart attack."

As I had been doing all day long, I pulled the photograph of Caren Sprague from my coat pocket and handed it to the Reverend Smith. "Have you ever seen this woman?"

He examined it closely, a spark of recognition in the gray of his eyes. "You know, this looks like that mainlander woman."

Barker leaned over his shoulder. "No, that ain't her." He squinted his tired eyes as he studied the picture. "Way too young to be her."

"I didn't say it was her, I said it looks like her."

"Who are we talking about?"

"An older woman than this. I've seen her in here."

"Worshiping?"

"No. Mostly climbing the stairs, and staring out the windows . . . out to sea. Not all that unusual for island women."

"I suppose not. Where would I find this mainlander woman?"

Revered Smith stole another glance at the picture in his hands. "Like I said, don't think she's the woman in your picture here, but I heard she's been renting Captain Monaghan's house . . . down on Orange Street."

CHAPTER 49

THE BEGINNING OF THE END

THE MOST SUPERSTITIOUS people in the world are people of the sea. There was a beautiful young ghost standing in the church tower window. There was a grave with my name on it. There was a boarding house called the Coffin House. In fact, most of the homes on the island were still said to belong to people dead a hundred years. Everybody I met was of a fearful and gloomy nature. The Reverend Smith watched my anxious departure from his church. He left me with the following words: "I only hesitate, Mr. Pennington, because I fear no good can come from your finding her."

It was like Barker had said. *"A lot of strange things going on."*

The wind was screaming. Howling. The rain

had turned to sleet, and then back again to rain. I ran directly into the storm. Down through the narrow, sandy streets and out onto the long, straight wharf. Then the street lamps went out. The world went dark. The town behind me was now without power, giving Nantucket the appearance of a gray and desolate rock. The Friendship Sloop was bobbing up and down in the white and ghastly crest of the surf, thumping her side hard against the rough logs. I jumped aboard, needing all of my balance to keep from tumbling to the deck. Or even worse, falling into the sea. I ducked down into the cabin, escaping for a moment the fury of the gale. Found my duffel bag.

It may seem silly to all but those of us who have patrolled our miles on rural highways, largely at night, but there was no way in hell I was venturing up to that house on Orange Street without my flashlight. It had less to do with the sudden darkness and the weather than with my own instincts and experience. My own superstitions. In nearly fifty years of police work, never at night did I step from that squad car without that flashlight grasped firmly in my hand.

I held the long metal cylinder before me. Felt the security of its heft. I flicked it on. Checked the powerful beam. I fought to keep my balance as the light danced crazily around the small cabin. I reached down and lifted the briefcase, in which lay the money and the files. Then I thought better of lugging blackmail money and evidence through the town and the weather, toward an uncertain destination. I returned the briefcase to the duffel bag. Tucked it snugly inside. It was then, over the roar of wind and water, that I became aware of a loud and gradually increasing sound. A submerged thumping sound was coming from the ocean side of the sloop. This would be but the first of the extreme horrors and dread that I would encounter on that dark and stormy night. I climbed to the deck.

It was raining sideways. A freezing, machine-gun rain. I struggled over to the starboard side and clung for my life to the rail. Each rolling wave promised to be my last. The water heaved up over my legs, and then tried with hellish might to pull my feet from beneath me and drag me into the sea. I could see that a line of rope was cast overboard, and that this rope was stretched taut. Something, I believed, that should have been tethered to the deck was under the water. Banging against the hull. I waited for a break in the surf, and then I grabbed hold of the line. It was indeed attached to a heavy object. I gave it good, strong pull and could feel its slow rise to the surface. Suddenly, and without warning, the sea rose like a wild beast and forcibly hoisted the ghastly object of

my efforts out of the water and onto the deck.
Onto me.

He seemed to be alive, though all of my
senses tried in vain to assure me he was dead.
So it was that once again I found myself wrestling with the fisherman out of Hyannis Harbor.
The fisherman, whose sloop I had comman-
deered. The fisherman who, the night before, I
had cast into the sea—not once, but twice. He
had somehow managed to grab hold of a line
beneath the water and tethered his arm to his
beloved sloop. Tangled there, I dragged him
through the dark seas, all the way to Nantucket.
Not even in death would his soul be severed
from the soul of his ship.

He was covered with seaweed and slimy sea
creatures. I struggled to get him off me. His skin
had the feel of cold wax. I clubbed his skull with
the flashlight. Even above the storm, I could
hear the bone plates cracking beneath his hairline. Finally, I kicked his rotting corpse into the
stern. Into a corner.

I fell to the deck, gasping for breath. I shined
the light on his face. It had been eaten at by
fish. An eye and an ear were missing. Something
live was dangling from his nostrils.

I struggled on hands and knees to the rail and
then climbed onto the wharf—cold, wet, and
scared. I took one last look at this dispirited

character, lying like some dead sea serpent in the stern of his own boat.

Then, with the wind roaring in my ears, I set out to find the mainlander woman.

CHAPTER 50

THE HOUSE ON ORANGE STREET

TWICE, AS I struggled up the dark street, its cobblestones slick with rain and ice, the electrical power was restored to the town. Street lamps flickered on. Windows lighted from within. Then, just as fast, the power went out again. All was dark, but for the candles and the lanterns that burned preternaturally inside the shuttered homes.

At the top of Main, I heard so strong a gale blowing landward that I turned back to the wharf. I could see that the sloop had torn loose from its mooring. It came about in the harbor, as if on command. Now, bowsprit to the open sea, it sailed along against the fierce wind. And though I would not swear to it in a court of law, in fact, I did not even mention it during the official investigation into the bloody events of that night—in a brief stab of light, I saw what appeared to be the shadow of the fisherman standing at the helm of his ship as it disappeared into the tempest—taking with it my duffel bag, the briefcase, the money, the sniper's rifle, and the entire case file on the wheat field murders.

I felt a chilling ache in the pit of my stomach. It was as if the gods of the sea were conspiring against me—family history be damned. My troubles sprang from a land in the heart of the continent. I had no business dragging my mysteries into the Atlantic. I shook my head in wonder. Sheer amazement. Then I resumed my search.

As I had learned that afternoon at the Atheneum, and as I have mentioned before, Nantucket was once one of the richest communities in America. This wealth was most reflected in the elegant brick Colonials and the giant clapboard mansions that lined many of the streets in town. Especially Orange Street. It was there, on the east side of Orange, that many of the ship captains built their fine homes. On this gentle slope above the town, the seafaring men of Nantucket could escape the stench of the wharf, but still keep an eye on their ships.

I found the house number I was searching for

about halfway up Orange, just past a stone alley. Built in the Greek Revival style, Captain Monaghan's three-story home was white clapboard with black shutters. Two dormers peaked out of the roof, and a platform, often called a widow's walk, ran along the back, offering a bird's-eye view of the sea. On the north and south of the house were two wide chimneys. These, too, were painted white. White pillars, standing like sentries, guarded the front door. It looked as if somebody had attempted to close the shutters on the first floor, but was unable to complete the job. The shutters at the far south window banged incessantly against the ledge.

The house was dark, and I had scant reason to be there. The men at the church claimed the woman staying in the house was from the mainland. Resembled the photograph of Caren Sprague. A waitress at the café swore she, too, had seen the subject of my search, though she couldn't recall when or where. Mostly, I was operating on my own gut instincts. Those instincts, ever since seeing the familiar-looking apparition in the tower window, told me that I was at the right place. I remembered the very last words Caren Sprague had said to me before she hung up the phone.

"I'll be waiting. You'll be surprised."

I don't like surprises. I walked up the stone steps and rapped on the door. The heart of the storm was now beating on the island. A mixture of rain and sleet whipped by crazy winds pelted my back, chilling my bones and killing my spirits. I knocked again. Harder. There was no answer. I grabbed the door handle, put my thumb to the latch, and pushed.

Inside, all was dark. I called, "Hello . . ." but I might as well have been speaking to the wind. Still, good cops can sense when they are not alone, and my senses that night, after wrestling with a corpse, were operating at full sail.

"Caren . . ." I shouted.

But there came no reply from within the house. I closed the door. Drew my revolver. Shined the flashlight before me and ventured inside.

The large house had a musty smell to it. Unloved, and unlived in. I was only a few steps inside the front hall when electrical power was once again restored to the town. I jumped at the sights and sounds. Only one lamp had been left burning at Captain Monaghan's house. It was a small lamp, glowing on a corner table of the living room area, just inside the doorway. A pack of Lucky Strikes and a book of matches lay beside the lamp. A grand piano sat in another corner, but it was draped with a white canvas. The ceiling was eleven feet tall. The hardwood floors at my feet must have been a century old. There were no carpets or rugs to cover the knots and the stains. The walls and woodwork were all painted white, as was the mantle above the fireplace, but it was a dirty white. Curtains hanging to the floor before the shuttered windows were lace, but a ghostly, ungainly lace. The room cried out for life.

On the floor, propped up against the cold fireplace, was an oil painting of a considerable nature. This portrait captured the striking visage of a sea captain. I shined my light on it. Guessed it to be the face of Captain Monaghan—though I couldn't help but wonder if, in life, any man could be as wise and noble as the gray-bearded man appeared to be in the painting.

And that brings me to the strangest part of this particular room in this particular house. The painting of the captain had been removed from above the fireplace so as to expose the bare white wall. Expose the wall so that it could be used as a screen. For in the very heart of this century-old room stood a 16 millimeter movie projector. Loaded with film.

CHAPTER 51

THE SNUFF FILM

I FLIP THE toggle switch. The room is bathed in flickering bright light. Scratchy white frames spin noisily through the sprockets. I pray the power holds. The film begins.

Above the fireplace, the summer sun is setting slowly over a field of wheat. Golden hues fill each frame. The sunny wheat field of my native Wisconsin stands in stark contrast to the nor'easter raging around me.

Michael Butler is sitting on crushed wheat at the center of the crop circle. He is fully clothed. A short-sleeved shirt. Khaki slacks. Penny loafers. His arms are wrapped casually around his knees. He appears to be enjoying the sunset. Perhaps it is the passing of the months, or maybe I can't shake the image of his face frozen in terror, but I have forgotten what a good-looking man Michael was.

At first, she is difficult to see. Almost ghostly, as she walks out of the sun and into the frame. A beautiful woman strolling through a field of wheat. She is coming Michael's way. She is almost angelic. A messenger from heaven. But the woman turns out to be the Devil. It is Caren Sprague.

At this point, every single frame has the innocuous appearance of an art film.

She enters the circle in red high heels. Stands above Michael. Runs her fingers through his thin brown hair. She is wearing a silky red dress. Short and sleeveless. Surrounded by the golden hues, the red dress sometimes appears fiery orange. She reaches down and removes the high heel from her right foot. Then she places the ball of her foot between Michael's legs. He doesn't move. Just watches. She repeats the gesture with her left foot.

Now, standing in her bare feet, she turns her back on him and gazes into the setting sun. She stretches. She sways. She plays with her long black hair. Then she reaches down and pulls the dress up over her head. Tosses it into the wheat. Her back is to Michael. Her back is to the camera. Her back is wonderfully curved and tanned all the way down to her fire orange panties. Her legs are long and fluid.

She turns, as if tired of the view. Michael watches, intently.

Tan lines accent her breasts. They are full and round. Her nipples stand out, brown and hard. She towers over Michael. Sticks her thumb beneath the band of her panties. She stretches her panties out just far enough for Michael to peek inside. Then she snaps them back.

Caren spins slowly in the setting sun, executing some erotic dance moves. Then she is back before Michael's face. Her legs are spread apart. After more teasing and preening, she finally peels the panties from her legs and tosses them alongside the dress.

She lifts her breasts with the palms of her hands. She tweaks her own nipples. She drops both of her hands between her thighs and pulls them apart, so that Michael can see. He seems in a trance. Then Caren drops to her knees. It is in this feline position that she is at her most sexy. Every man's fantasy, which is exactly what the film purports to be.

Now she strips Michael Butler of his clothes. He doesn't help her, but he doesn't resist. I realize I am watching role reversal. She is the aggressor. Michael is passive. She tosses his clothes onto her clothes. She lies him on his back. Still on her knees, she takes him in her hand. Handles him the way a woman would handle a delicate flower. He is hard. So she takes him into her mouth.

Only then does Michael respond. He lifts his arm and gently strokes her long black hair, while she sucks away at him. All of this is beautifully filmed. Beautifully timed. The setting sun is providing perfect rays of light. Not too bright to spoil the mood. Not too dark to prevent quality viewing.

Cigarette smoke wafts into the frame. An unwelcome intrusion. Somebody nearby is smoking. Watching.

Now has come the time for Michael to return the sexual favors. Caren goes to her back. Michael is on his knees over her. He parts her legs. Crawls between them and drops his mouth to her belly. Then he licks his way down to her thighs, where at last he presses his tongue inside of her.

She throws her legs over his shoulders, and Michael wraps his arms around them, supporting her weight as he performs oral sex. This act goes on far longer than I could have imagined.

Still on his knees, Michael moves to her side. Hovers over her. He takes her right hand and places it between his legs. She grabs hold. Then he takes her left hand and places it between her own legs. The microphone must be built into the camera. The sound quality is poor, but Michael can be heard to mutter, "I want to watch."

With that request, Caren pumps him up and down with her right hand. Then she inserts two fingers of her left hand inside of herself. Michael seems in heaven.

At last, it is time for intercourse. Caren assumes another catlike position—on her knees, her arms stretched out before her. Her hips are high in the air. Her nose is just above the wheat. Michael is now hard as a missile. He enters her from behind. Reaches around and takes hold of her breasts. The sex act is long and extremely intense. Even with the poor sound, the moaning and groaning has a desperate quality to it. Almost a final act. Spent at last, Michael pulls out. The camera pulls back. Lingers over them.

Caren Sprague, unashamedly naked before the disappearing sun, flops to her back and stares into the darkening orange sky. A few feet away, Michael Butler, totally naked, falls to his back, oblivious to the rolling camera. Both of them seem to be in a state of sexual euphoria. But I am scared. Confused. Cold with fear. These are the exact same positions in which I found the two bodies. Something is wrong here. Something is terribly wrong. I cannot watch, but I cannot turn away.

The murderous events unfold fast, but in a slow-motion kind of way. The camera pulls back even more, showing the unsuspecting couple languishing in the wheat. Then it jerks forward, toward Caren, signaling something is amiss. Caren Sprague rises to her elbows. Looks directly into the lens. A baffled smile crosses her face. She is being filmed from the waist up now. Her eyes suddenly turn away. Burst open wide. In the last split second of her life she realizes what is happening. A shotgun barrel appears in the frame.

"No, please . . . don't do this . . ."

These are her last words. A blast rocks the field. The camera jumps as her face explodes before my eyes. She is thrown onto her back, while the camera lingers over the whole bloody mess.

Now the camera swings around wildly. Blurs the action. When the operator regains control, Michael Butler comes into focus. He is still on his back, struggling to his feet, backpedaling, his hands out before him. Pleading. Begging.

"Oh, Maggie, why? Why! Why! Why!"

Again, the shotgun barrel enters the frame. Michael can't get to his feet because of the soft footing. The shotgun ends up right between his legs. The blast is instantaneous. Again, lacking even a modicum of compassion, the camera lingers.

Michael is still breathing. His eyes are filled with tears and questions. His chest is heaving. His arms and hands, hovering above his bloody thighs, are twitching violently. He is in shock, a state I witnessed often during the war. It is hard to guess how long Michael Butler lies there in indescribable agony before he mercifully drifts into the big sleep—where I find him the next morning.

CHAPTER 52

THE DEPUTY AND
THE DEVIL

SO YOU SEE, in a way, I was in the wheat field that night. The film, to me, was so visceral that even after all of these years, when I look back on it, I do not see myself standing in a Nantucket house watching a movie. I see myself standing helplessly at the edge of the wheat. Frozen in the summer heat. Unable to move. Unable to prevent the tragedy I know to be unfolding. Like the times before, all that I could really do was stand about and watch.

The film came to an ambiguous end. The camera pulled back to reveal both bloody bodies lying in the crop circle. Then it panned up and across the wheat field. Into the sunset. And then nothing. No killers. No conspirators. Just scratchy white frames spinning noisily through the sprockets.

Suddenly, as if on cue, the island again lost power. Everything went black. I was left standing in the dark with a heavy flashlight in my hand and a revolver stuffed under my belt. I was feeling shell-shocked. Benumbed by the second of the three horrors to befall me that night. There was an incessant banging against the side of the house. The nor'easter throwing shutters about, like feathers before the wind.

"You were always an obsessive little bastard."

I spun around when she said that, but in the doorway there was nothing to be seen. Just that voice in the woods. "Obsession has its rewards," I answered, into the darkness. I was just about to raise my flashlight when she struck a match. The sight of her face above the flame sent shivers up my spine. She lit the cigarette dangling from her mouth.

"I didn't know you smoked."

"The things you don't know about me, Deputy Pennington."

When the match went out, I raised the flashlight and caught her face in the beam. If ever I believed I was face-to-face with the Devil, it was then. She blew a stream of smoke from her mouth. Her head, with its shock of black hair, seemed disembodied. Her eyes displayed a tinge of red at the center of the irises. Her normally dark complexion seemed to radiate a sallow yellow. All of this was in the beam of a flashlight in a darkened room on a stormy night.

"Over here," she said, "there's a candle."

I pulled the beam in the direction she pointed, until it landed on a sconce attached to the wall. Maggie Butler struck a second match and lit the candle. The room glowed gold, almost like a wheat field at sunset.

"Where's the money?" she wanted to know.

"It went sailing."

"Don't get smart."

She moved to the other side of the doorway and illuminated another candle. She was clothed in a black dress from another time—a relic she had probably discovered in the attic. It fit her well, showing off a still shapely figure. But even bathed in candlelight, I could see that Maggie was growing old before her time. The years and the weather, and surely the events of the past three months, had taken a toll on her once soft skin. A hardness gripped her eyes.

"You've cut your hair," I said.

"Yes. Do you like it?"

"No."

"Too damn bad."

"Maggie Butler," I stated, for the record, "you're under arrest for the murders of Caren Sprague and Michael Butler."

"Why do this, Deputy?"

"Because . . . it's the way I am."

She didn't flinch when I announced her arrest. In fact, her calm was frightening. She strolled to the fireplace, where another pair of candles hung on the wall. Pointed to the portrait of Captain Monaghan. "They say his spirit still walks this house. On lonely nights, I especially feel his presence." She struck a match. Fire framed her face. "I saw myself growing old in Kickapoo Falls," she told me. "I felt suffocated and trapped. A bit of voyeurism seemed a fair price to get out of Wisconsin, don't you think?"

"No. It's my home."

"Well, this girl wanted out of Squaresville."

"Is that what we are to you, Maggie . . . squares?"

"Yes."

"I guess that would make me the biggest square of all. Why, then, was I to be invited to the wheat field?"

With no more emotion in her voice than she would lend to a cooking recipe, she struck one last match and brought a flame to the last candle in the room. "You weren't invited to the wheat field, Deputy. I wrote that note so that you would take the fall for the double murders."

"You're making my skin crawl, but I'll bite. Why me?"

"You'd become a little too successful. Too popular. The Gunn Club wanted you out of the sheriff's picture. Though he would never admit it, Webster always believed it was you who killed his brother."

"Are you suggesting even Fats wanted me framed?"

She tossed the spent matches into the fireplace. "Wake up, Deputy. Fats wasn't grooming you for sheriff. He was grooming you and your magic rifle for the Gunn Club. When you wouldn't join . . . yes, as much as it hurt him, he wanted you arrested."

"So then, after you wrote the note, my so-called invitation to the wheat field, you never sent it to me."

"Of course not. You built a career on being underestimated. There's more to you than meets the sniper's eye. The sheriff and I understood that. Webster never did. With you in the wheat field, you'd have found a way to muck things up. We couldn't risk it. Easier to frame you for the murders."

"You and Fats were that close?"

Maggie stood before the fireplace. Beneath the glowing candles. The portrait of the noble sea captain was at her feet. She took another drag on the cigarette between her long, lissome fingers, then she let the smoke slip out, slowly, between her pouted lips. I noticed the class ring, still attached to her finger. KICKAPOO FALLS HIGH 1942. I could just see her in the wheat field, removing the wedding ring from her hand and slipping the diamond onto the warm and bloody corpse of Caren Sprague, but she lacked the heart to part with her high school ring. Maggie had been happy in high school. I doubt she'd been happy since. She noticed the sentimental stone had captured my attention. "My parents couldn't afford it," she told me, holding up the ring. "So the sheriff bought it for me. And over the years I paid him back."

"You were the secret lover he told me about?"

"Since I was seventeen."

"And Webster was your lover, and Russ Hoffmeyer was your lover, and Caren Sprague was your lover, and Michael, the man you took a shotgun to, was your beloved husband."

"Just another small town in America."

"Why film it? The murders, I mean?"

She moved toward the movie projector. "We'd been filming sex for years. Things just escalated to the point where the sheriff and I had distributors in Europe." She ran her hands over the reels on the projector, as if they were rare antiques. "Overseas, this film is worth a fortune. Sheriff Fats went back the next day and filmed the aftermath right in front of your eyes. He tried like hell to get the autopsy filmed. There's never been anything like this—color film of an actual murder—and I've got the most valuable piece of the puzzle."

"And you double-crossed Fats to get it?"

"I suppose."

"You've got nothing, Maggie. Fats is dead. Webster is in jail."

For the first time that evening there seemed a tincture of sorrow in her eyes. A touch of regret in her voice. "Did you kill him?"

"Fats? No, but I gave him my best shot."

"I guess then . . . it's just me and you." She laid those dark, beautiful eyes on me, in a way I had once dreamed. "Isn't that what you've always wanted?"

"I'm bringing you in."

"Deputy, do you have any idea how much money we're talking about here? I have two hundred thousand dollars. You should have another two hundred thousand with you. And we have the film. If we play our cards right, that's over a million dollars."

"Something tells me there was a lot more to your plan than a million dollars."

She turned away from me when I said that. Tossed her lit cigarette into the fireplace. Hot red ashes danced in the hearth. Maggie strolled to one of the shuttered windows with the long lace curtains, near the covered piano. Outside, there was no cessation of the wind on this island of restless spirits. The pounding of the shutters against the house seemed relentless. "I wanted to kill my husband's lover. Webster wanted to kill his wife. When I found out the Gunn Club wanted to kill a presidential candidate . . . I got scared. I had the two hundred thousand dollars for Michael and I doing the film. I took the money and I ran. You know the rest."

"Why this godforsaken island?"

"Oh, but you should see it here in the summertime. People are drawn to water. It's gold waiting to be mined. Webster and the boys at the Gunn Club have been buying up land. We have big plans for this godforsaken island."

"You mean, you're going to do to Nantucket what you did to the Dells?"

She turned to face me. "That's right, you're one those purists, aren't you? You never cared for what we did *for* the Dells. Perhaps we should have left Kickapoo Falls to die, along with a hundred other ghost towns that litter Wisconsin's highways."

In every storm there comes out of the clouds one gust of wind so strong, so violent, that most damage is done in that one terrifying instant. Directly behind Maggie Butler, the shutters were thrown into the window with such overpowering force that the glass shattered. Exploded inward.

I jumped back before the pressure and the flying shards of glass. But Maggie just stood there, as if the wind at her back was little more than a summer breeze. Now the nor'easter was inside the house. The lace curtains were flying about the room, like crazed spirits tethered to the walls. The candle flames were going wild, stretching for the ceiling. Cigarette ashes leaped from the hearth and flew about the room.

"It's time to go, Maggie."

"Follow me. There's something I want to show you."

CHAPTER 53

THE DENOUEMENT:
WIND

I TOLD MAGGIE that night that obsession has its rewards. But that was untrue. Obsession is an illness. A crippling disease. My lifelong obsession with this woman was bitter and blinding. Corrupting. Then, on a stormy night in the Atlantic, the blinds were forcibly lifted. For the first time in a lifetime, light filtered through my thick skull, and I could see with newfound clarity that this woman of unrequited love, the woman I had all but worshiped, was inherently evil. Guilty of the most unspeakable crimes.

Before I thought to object, she almost floated out of that windblown room. Maggie moved swiftly up a flight of stairs. I followed after her. On the second-floor landing, she breezed down

the long hallway to another flight of stairs—
moving farther and farther ahead of me. On the
third floor, I clung to a railing and shined my
flashlight down the hall. But I caught only the
seam of her black dress as she disappeared
through an attic door, and up yet another flight
of stairs. I went to the opened door. Suddenly,
I was in the embrace of a freezing wind as it
raced down the stairs. I shined my light up this
narrow stairway at the top of the house. The
steps seemed to climb directly into a copper-
colored cloud. What could not be seen in that
beam of light was Maggie.

Now I could smell smoke drifting up from
below. I feared the worst. I started up the stairs.
Right into the maw of the relentless squall.

I found myself outside, on the wooden platform that jutted out from the roof of the house.
The widow's walk. I stood above the town that
stood above the harbor. I was even above the
treetops. Cloud-to-cloud lightning was added to
the storm, and every now and then—between a
mixture of freezing rain and driving snow—I
could see giant ocean waves crashing down on
clusters of jagged rocks. I grabbed hold of the
railing and hung on for dear life. I ran my flashlight in a half-circle.

"Maggie," I yelled. But my voice was barely
audible.

It was then that I was struck from behind, the

back of my head sliced open. I dropped to my knees. Grabbed at my wet, sticky hair in an attempt to stop the bleeding. I felt the swift kick of a boot. It laid me out on the platform. A long pole was dropped into the beam of my light. The pole was attached to a sharp metal blade coated with blood. My blood. This, I would later learn, was an old cutting spade, once used to slice open whales and strip them of their blubber.

Now she had her hands beneath my coat. I heard her talking over me. "You should have a revolver in your pants, which, if rumors are true, is the only thing in your pants that works."

I felt my gun slip away. Next, she picked up the flashlight. Then she kicked me again. "Get up," she ordered.

I struggled to my feet, holding the back of my head. The warm blood spilling down my back mixed with the freezing rain, leaving me faint and nauseous.

She shined the flashlight in my eyes, as I had done to so many others over the years. Still, I could make out the revolver in her hand. It was pointed at my gut.

"Look at you, Deputy Pennington. Overpowered by a woman. I mean, you even fucked up being a war hero. Now, Brock Carlson and Russ Hoffmeyer—there were a couple of real war heroes."

In a way, she was right. Snipers don't get dirty. Even after I had accepted that she was pure evil, that she had, in cold blood, murdered Caren Sprague and then turned the shotgun on her own husband—I still did not draw my weapon against her. I was never much of a warrior. I'd let her float out of that downstairs room without a whimper of protest. What she had wanted to show me was the sharp end of a cutting spade.

So there we stood in the fury of an Atlantic blizzard. A boy and a girl from Kickapoo Falls, Wisconsin. I wish I could write about what was going through her head in those final minutes. Did she despise me? Pity me? Did Maggie hate me? Because I hated her. Love and hate are the same emotion—and at that moment, I hated that woman with an intensity that words cannot describe. She had corrupted everybody she had come into contact with. Sheriff Fats. Michael Butler. Webster Sprague, and others. Most of all, I believe, she corrupted me. Not in the same way as the others. My corruption was more insidious. More hidden. Psychological damage from the safety of distance. How many times, I wondered, when I laid those crosshairs on another human being, was it really Maggie Butler that I was lining up in my sights?

Though I am unable to tell you what she was

thinking while we faced each other out on the widow's walk—I can tell you what was said.

"Did you really love me, Deputy? Because, I'm curious . . ."

"No," I told her, coming to my senses, "I loved a face . . . and I loved the idea of loving that face. But that's all you've ever been to me, Maggie . . . a hollow and empty face that I filled with all of my silly dreams."

I glanced down at the .38/.44 revolver in her hand. Called to mind our weapons training. As trustworthy as that revolver was, if it was going to misfire, it would misfire in foul weather. Maggie pulled the trigger, expecting me to die. But there was no exploding cartridge—only the sharp click that a cop recognizes instantly. Maggie, however, was baffled. She glanced down at the gun in her hand with a look of betrayal. A look that lasted just long enough for me to lunge forward with a lifetime of pent-up anger.

I grabbed her gun hand and forced it into the air. Maggie squeezed the trigger a second time. This time it fired, sending a .38 slug into the heavens. Her hand and fingers were locked securely around the revolver. Too tight for me to rip it away. So I tore the flashlight from her other hand. She squeezed the trigger again. The shot exploded in my ear. I raised the heavy flashlight high above my head and, with all of the force I could muster, I brought it crashing down upon the face of Maggie Butler.

I opened a gash beneath her eye. Blood gushed out her cheekbone. Still, she would not release the gun. In fact, she fired off another shot. Another shell exploded in my ear. I was furious. I could feel her wrist breaking in my hand. Still, she would not let go. Again, I smashed the flashlight into her face. I did it again, and again. I may have been crying while doing this, I do not recall, I only remember beating in her face with that flashlight as we both sank to the boards—blood flying in all directions, my revolver locked in her hand.

I collapsed on top of her. Almost laughed at the pathetic thought of it. All of my life I had dreamed of laying my body across the body of Maggie Butler. And now I had.

Though she still gripped my gun in her hand, she had stopped moving. Stopped breathing. I pushed off of her, repulsed by *her* blood all over *my* face. I found myself on my backside, back-pedaling, unable to get firm footing. Oddly, the same way Michael had died in the wheat field. Finally, I gave up. Lay there. Exhausted. Staring directly into the blizzard. Sweating in the freezing cold.

Now it was snowing hard. The wind was bringing it down at sharp angles. The heavy white flakes fell across my brow, melted in an instant, and bit by bit rinsed away the blood of Maggie Butler.

I could hear windows exploding beneath the roof. Not from the storm, but from the fire. I lifted the flashlight and shined it across Maggie's prostrate body. She was on her back, all blood from her shoulders to her hair. I prayed the loathsome bitch was dead. But as so often happened in my life, my prayer went unanswered.

Her chest heaved, and I could see her sitting up. Slow and deliberate. Almost rising from the dead. She was raising her gun hand. By my calculations, she had two shots left. Now, as I climbed to my feet, it was a slow-motion race between two bloody cripples. I let the flashlight roll across the boards. I grabbed hold of the cutting spade, and using it as a cane, I pulled myself together.

I didn't know how Maggie was doing. I didn't care. I only knew what had to be done, like the hero in an old vampire movie. I was blinded by the weather. Blinded by the blood seeping into my eyes. But most of all, I was blinded by my own hatred. I planted my foot firmly in the pit of her stomach. Looked into her eyes. Lifted the cutting spade with both of my arms.

"Good-bye, Maggie."

Then, having said my farewell, I buried the blade deep in her heart.

Maggie Butler sent forth to the winds an appalling scream. An ungodly voice that outshouted the storm. Then all went quiet. Even the gales of the nor'easter seemed to sense it was over. That perhaps the time had come for all of us to move on.

CHAPTER 54

THE DENOUEMENT:
FIRE

I PULLED THE cutting spade from her blood-soaked dress and tossed it over the railing. I picked up the flashlight and staggered to the stairwell. Already, smoke was climbing the steps. Again, I stepped over Maggie's body and peered over the railing of the walk. I could see flames shooting out the first-floor windows. It was obvious that the candles, or maybe the cigarette, had started the house on fire.

Like hell if I was going up in flames. Yet even with the flashlight, it was too dark and snowy to see what lay beneath me. I guessed a yard of some kind. At least when I leaped from Hawk's Bill, I knew what I was jumping into. A raging river. This leap would be totally blind. A leap of faith.

The cut to the back of my head was fast and deep. I felt consciousness slipping away. The smoke had reached the roof. Flames could not be far behind. I wrestled one leg up and over the platform. Then I managed the other leg. I stared straight out to sea, a sight my forefathers must have seen every day of their lives. I crossed myself and asked them to watch over me. With what little strength I had remaining, I pushed myself out as far as possible. And then I jumped.

Apparently, there was some kind of back porch. I caught the railing of that porch with my left leg on the way down. Snapped the wood in two, along with the bone in my thigh. I rolled down a wet, snow-covered lawn in excruciating pain—finally coming to rest on my back, my leg bent into an unimaginable position.

I couldn't say how long it was that I lay there on the ground. Probably just a few minutes, but it seemed like hours. I could hear a siren coming up the hill. I could hear crackling timbers as Captain Monaghan's house began falling from within. The one thing at last I couldn't hear, was the wind. It had all but ceased. The sleet had turned completely to snow—a heavenly white Wisconsin snowfall that had the effect of purifying everything it touched. The last thing I remember, before I passed out, was sticking out my tongue and trying to catch a snowflake. Just as Maggie and I had done when we were kids.

EPILOGUE I

RETURNING HOME

EVERY SMALL TOWN has its share of evil. Kickapoo Falls just got the lion's share. I returned home with my leg in a cast. My head swathed in bandages. In the aftermath of the fire, it's hard to remember how many official investigations there were into my handling of the wheat field murders. There was a federal inquiry by the FBI and the United States Secret Service. Criminal probes were launched by the attorney generals in two states. Massachusetts and Wisconsin. And there were demands for answers from God only knows how many municipalities. I was still fielding questions during the Nixon administration.

But then, much to the chagrin of some, I was still raising questions.

Captain Monaghan's house on Nantucket burned to the ground. Only the sudden cessation of the winds stopped the fire from spreading, averting a major catastrophe. The body of Maggie Butler was pulled from the ruins, burned beyond recognition, my revolver melted to her hand. The film of the wheat field murders was vaporized.

The Friendship Sloop that delivered me to Nantucket vanished at sea—along with the sniper's rifle, the two hundred thousand dollars in blackmail money, and the entire case file on the wheat field murders. No record could be found of any such ship docking at Hyannis Harbor. No fisherman was ever reported missing.

Detective Dickerson was no longer around to back up my story. Webster Sprague never gave a confession. We searched his home, but his collection of pornographic films had disappeared.

It wasn't until we exhumed the two bodies in Oak Hill Cemetery that the tide turned in my direction. There was never a question or doubt about the remains of Michael Butler, but a further examination concluded that the body of the woman found murdered in the wheat field was, in fact, the body of Caren Sprague.

How was it something like that could have happened? I offer no excuses. Only this simple explanation. We weren't Scotland Yard, or the FBI. We were just a county sheriff's department in rural Wisconsin trying to solve a double homicide. We made mistakes. No, correct that, I made mistakes. I was the first cop on the scene. The lead investigator. I was the one who misidentified the body. I never asked the coroner to determine identification. We simply matched the fingerprints of the corpse with the fingerprints on the shotgun, and then assumed those prints were Maggie's. Neither Maggie Butler or Caren Sprague had ever been fingerprinted. Back then, few women were. Maggie wiped the shotgun clean of her own fingerprints, and then placed the murder weapon into the cold, dead hands of Caren Sprague. Squeezed off another shot. Slipped Caren her wedding ring. So we all assumed the murder victim was Maggie Butler. Except, of course, for Sheriff Fats. He knew, standing there, it was Caren Sprague. Maggie held the shotgun. Fats held the camera.

My love for Maggie Butler and my admiration for Sheriff Fats had blinded me in the worst way. I wanted, with all of my heart, for one of them to be innocent. Now, when I think of all that has come to pass since that watershed year, 1960, I think, as criminals, Maggie and Fats were just a few years ahead of their time.

FINAL THOUGHTS

I SERVED AS sheriff of Kickapoo County for thirty-two years. I won eight consecutive elections. The first three elections were close. In the last three elections, I ran unopposed. By the time I retired, I had been wearing a badge and a gun for nearly fifty years. So today, here I sit. In my cabin by the water. Putting to paper the chapters of my life. Trying to tie up all of the loose ends.

A day after his arrest, Webster Sprague, who lost his Senate election, hung himself with his shirt in the Kickapoo County jail. Well, they say he hung himself. I always thought he had some help. Somebody who helped him off with his shirt and lifted him to the noose.

Coincidentally, on that same day, Detective Dickerson departed Kickapoo Falls, leaving behind his written resignation. Said he was returning to Texas. He was never heard from again. State officials in Texas could find no peace officer's license ever issued to a cop named Dickerson. They also couldn't come up with a driver's license, or even a birth certificate. It was as if he never existed. But I knew otherwise. All that time during the wheat field investigation, I thought it was Sheriff Fats and Webster Sprague who were setting me up. But I was wrong. It was Dickerson.

A real conspiracy is many layered. Make sure there is a fall guy. Then make sure there are fall guys for the fall guy. It was Dickerson shooting at me up on Hawk's Bill. Dickerson who let me out of jail. It was Dickerson who killed Fats with no warning. No chance to surrender. It was Dickerson who handed me the money and the plane tickets and sent me off to Hyannisport on election day. He must have figured that being an escapee, I'd make a better fall guy than the sheriff.

They lured me onto a sloop off the Kennedy compound. Equipped it with a high-powered rifle, just like my own. I was probably to die in a hail of gunfire. With my military record, my war wounds, my politics, my obsessions, I'd make the perfect postmortem suspect. Hell, my fingerprints could even be found on the binoculars.

Did I unwittingly become the dupe in a plot to kill John F. Kennedy? And if so, did I sever the cord of that plot—most likely, when I killed the fisherman and hijacked his boat? Or maybe, just maybe, I didn't foil their plot at all. I only delayed it.

Three years later, I came across a newspaper photograph of three tramps in Dallas, Texas, who were arrested after they were found hiding in a railway car several blocks from Dealey Plaza in the hour after the assassination of President Kennedy. The caption referred to the photograph as a roundup of suspects. All of them unidentified. But I swear to this day, one of the three tramps pictured, being led away in handcuffs, was the detective from Texas I knew as Dickerson.

"Sorry, I don't take my politics that seriously."
"We do."

I tried to follow up on the photograph, but as it turned out, the three unidentified men were released shortly after the arrest of Lee Harvey Oswald. They were never seen again. I would spend much of my life searching for a shadow of a man I knew only as Dickerson.

Maggie, for all of her evil ways, wanted no part of a political assassination. However, she may have been the loose thread that unraveled it all. I have to believe that's why she was calling me. She wasn't jerking me around. She was leaving me clues. Pointing me in the right direction. Perhaps, in the end, she did have a redeeming quality, after all. Or maybe, in my mind, I just gave her one.

Russ Hoffmeyer, the state trooper who first told me about the sex games, was nearing retirement when, one night on patrol, a drunk driver swerved across the white lines and took him out. The head-on collision occurred on a dark stretch of highway that snakes through the Baraboo Hills. As a result, the mangled cars were not discovered until the sun came up. The ex-Marine left behind three ex-wives and two grown children.

The Kickapoo Gunn Club filed for bankruptcy in 1974. Ironically, it was the same year Richard Nixon resigned as president of the United States. The few members left, scattered before the wind, to make their mischief in other places. Back taxes were owed, so I seized the property for Kickapoo County. Today the clubhouse and the land serve as a public golf course.

Yes, I did call again on Marilou Stephens at the University of Wisconsin down in Madison, and over the years the luminous psychologist advised me on a number of investigations.

Here the story ends, on a small piece of Wisconsin detached from the rest of the state. An island of my very own. Lake Michigan lapping peacefully at the shores. Down in Kickapoo

Falls, the wheat field murders were talked about for years. And for years the case came up in every sheriff's election. But it wasn't politics that kept me wrestling with the ghost of Maggie Butler. It was love. Or rather, my misunderstanding of love. And so, for the last time, "Good-bye, Maggie."

ACKNOWLEDGMENTS

I WROTE *The Wheat Field* in the summer of 2000. Special thanks are due my friends Celeste Gervais and Al Silverman for their critiques along the way.

To my friend Bruce Kleven, farmer, lawyer, and legislative lobbyist for agriculture at the Minnesota State Capitol, for his advice on wheat fields and all things agricultural.

To Molly Juelich for her advice and information on sailing.

To Louise Burke, Doug Grad, and Phyllis Grann at Penguin Putnam, who made publication possible.

And a very special thank you to my friend and agent, Elaine Koster, who was the driving force behind *The Wheat Field*.

S. T.

If you enjoyed *The Wheat Field* by Steve Thayer and would like to read more about Deputy Pennington of the Kickapoo Falls Sheriff's Department, you're in luck.

Pennington makes his return in *Wolf Pass*, published in hardcover in March 2003 by G. P. Putnam's Sons. Pennington gets caught up in another deadly conspiracy, but this time it's personal. . . .

Eighteen years we spent stalking one another. I was last in his rifle sights on the steps of the cathedral, that bloody October day. I remember it was raining. No thunder. No lightning. Nothing so dramatic. Just a bitter, dispiriting drizzle. In fact, a sickening chill still crawls up my spine when I think about standing on those cold stone steps, the top of my head frozen in the cross-hairs of his rifle. I carried with me the ghosts of that day for over fifty years. Now the time has come to write about it.

He was a handsome man, in a homely sort of way. His face was pocked and scarred. His nose was long and sharp. His eyes were raven black. Lacking a soul. Heartless, but penetrating. As I write this, I have a photograph of him propped up before me. It is the same photograph I carried while hunting him after the war. The official Nazi photograph was taken as he approached forty. He had a receding hairline, his dark hair was cropped short about the ears. The strangest thing about his face, what one noticed first, was his mouth. His lips were so thin he appeared to have no lips. Small menacing scars drop from the lower lip, adding weight to his evil visage. I never knew from where those scars came, but my guess back then was that they were not the scars of war, but rather the scars of disease. He was an immaculate man, posing in his highly decorated SS uniform, a swastika pinned to his tie. I remember him as tall and solid. Even today, if you were to cover up the uniform and just stare at the eyes, you would see staring back at you a frighteningly splendid example of Hitler's superman.

I am retired now. Fifty years of police work in the rearview mirror, almost all of those years spent on the roads of Kickapoo County. Still, it is an island off of a peninsula that I retired to, with my files and my memories. And my rifle. The days are slowed here, and then slowed again. The winds of Lake Michigan blow nightly through my cabin, like the cold winds of time. There is a sailboat tied to the dock, but I'm getting too old to be on the water alone.

For years I had wanted to produce a series of

books that contrasted the beauty of Wisconsin with the state's long history of bizarre crimes. So now I sit at the bay window and write the chapters of my life. And the one chapter that haunts me still is a chapter I simply call "The Wolf." As I look back, it seems I spent a lifetime chasing a conspiracy that forever stayed one step ahead of me. A ghost in the morning mist.

The chain of deadly events I now relate to you actually began high in the Bavarian Alps during the last months of World War II, at a railroad junction the Allies called Wolf Pass. But for the sake of storytelling, let us begin at a later date in my beloved Wisconsin. The year was 1962. The year of the wolf.

In all my life the hills never changed. They were born of glaciers, mountains of ice that reached two miles high. For more than a million years these immense ice packs shifted back and forth, carving out the land below. The last of the predigious glaciers was seen heading north some ten thousand years ago, leaving behind great ridges of dirt and rock, and dark and deep waters that sparkle like stars beneath the summer sun. It is geography with an unusual heft and expanse. Today, enormous boulders are scattered about, and old wooded roads of dirt dip and rise on a dramatic scale. Too rugged for development. Too isolated for big-city tourists.

So the rocks and trees in the heart of Wisconsin roll on for miles, up and down, jutting in and out, acting for a thousand years like a natural protector to all creatures, great and small, who choose to live in the vast green hollows. But too often over the years, unmitigated evil found its way into those beautiful hills. Then violence would shatter this hushed and peaceful world, and spill down into the villages nestled in the valleys. Like my hometown.

I found Frank Prager hanging out of the cab of his steam locomotive, like a sodden rag doll. A swath of blood, dark and red, stained the entire side of the cab, blacking out the white of the locomotive's four-digit number. A semicircle of railroad workers stood before the train station in Kickapoo Falls, like statues in the midmorning sun. Shocked. Silent. Grieving. I stuck a foot into the steel wheel workings of the eighty-two-ton monster, grabbed on to a handrail, and hoisted myself up to the dangling body. The cab was nothing more than a partly enclosed platform on the back of giant, belching boiler that could exceed two thousand degrees Fahrenheit under full steam. The dead engineer smelled of oil and coal. Grease and iron. And blood. Brain bits and skull fragments had splashed around the cab, smearing the gauges on the back of the boiler. His black-and-white-striped overalls were tattered and worn. His cap, equally worn, lay at the track below my feet. Balancing on one foot and clinging to the handrail, I took a fistful of soggy hair and lifted his head with my free hand. He'd been shot between the eyes. One shot. A large caliber. The damage to his face was extensive. Death was instantaneous. I recoiled in horror and unceremoniously let his head drop. What remained of his face made a soft bash against the side of the cab.

I jumped down to the tracks. Wiped my hands with a handkerchief. I slipped on my sunglasses and instinctively searched the high wooded hills, their peaks shered off by ancient ice. White birches lined the lower regions just above the train station. Above that stood some of the oldest rock in North America—quartzite bluffs more than a billion years old, massive boulders that rolled into the spruce and the pine. Behind the pulpwood was a forest of maple, elm, white ash, and black oak that climbed into a steel blue sky, where I was forced to avert my eyes from the glare. Death had found engineer Prager on a near-perfect September morning. The shot that killed him had come out of he sun.

"Tell me what happened."

Walter Beyer, the train's conductor, was standing beside me, visibly shaken. His normally pristine black uniform was askew. His coat was open wide. The tie around his neck had been yanked loose. The cap that was seldom seen off of his head was being wrung between his hands. "We were running two minutes behind," he said. "I checked my watch and called 'all aboard' and . . . I don't know. . . . Frank stuck his head out the cab to look down the train, like he always did. . . . Then his head snapped back, real violent-like, and he dropped over the window there . . . blood running out of him like a faucet. I climbed up there to check on him, and I seen that. . . . Well, you saw it . . . half his face was gone."

The conductor was a good deal older than his friend Frank Prager. The stubble of hair remaining on his balding head had gone to silver and white. The proud age lines of a railroad man creased his eyes. Like the old steam locomotive behind us, he was nearing retirement.

"Did you see anything?" I asked him.

"No, nothing unusual. I thought I might have heard a shot, but you know how noisy train yards can be." He shook his head in amazement. "The thing of it is, Deputy, I was staring up into the hills when it happened. . . . It was such a pretty day. I saw nothing. Had to be some kind of ghost up there. People that live here sometimes, you know, take the hills for granted. But Frank and I never did. We took this old train through these hills near every day. Never tired of the view. Guess I'll never look at them the same."

This was the first I'd ever heard of a ghost in

the hills. In the summertime, the baronial hills were where we went to escape the tourists who flocked to Kickapoo Falls to frolic in the Dells, an enchanting fifteen-mile stretch of the Wisconsin River, where a melting glacier had left behind soaring cliffs and haunted gorges. The region's economy depended on those tourists, who were both a blessing and a scourge.

Walter Beyer nodded at Frank's tattered cap lying on the ground alongside the tracks. "May I?" I asked.

"Yes, go ahead."

The old conductor reached down and picked up the engineer's cap. Held it in his hands, along with his own.

A horde of passengers was strung out along the tracks, standing beside the twenty murky yellow cars that trailed the engine. The Chicago, Milwaukee, St. Paul and Pacific Railway, nicknamed the Milwaukee Road, was a popular train, a lifeline for small towns in Wisconsin. Its importance could not be overstated. Already, word had spread down Main Street. A crowd from town was gathering. Cars and pickup trucks were pulling right up to the tracks. More deputies arrived. I ordered the station sealed off. The sheriff, or rather the acting sheriff, squealed to a halt with lights twirling and a siren screaming. The mayor was with him. I walked their way.

Packy Deitz jumped from the squad. "Frank got shot?"

"Yes. He's dead."

He stared up at the corpse. "Sweet Jesus, here we go again. Do you know who did it, Mr. Pennington?"

"Not yet," I told our cherubic mayor.

In Kickapoo Falls, the office of mayor was largely ceremonial. The real power lay in the sheriff's office. "Dear God," he said, "let's hope this was a hunting accident. The last thing this town needs is another murder. Especially with you two running for sheriff." The mayor moved off toward the body.

Sheriff Zimmer stood beside me now. He surveyed the sight as his deputies tried to clear the murder scene and restore some order to the train station. He was a tall, slender man. Wore a thick mustache at a time when mustaches were not only out of fashion, but they smacked of a sinister character. Still, the thick but neatly trimmed mustache somehow looked right on him. Lent him an air of authority and respect, though I often wondered what he'd look like without it.

Normally at this point I would describe J. D. Zimmer's personality, but he didn't seem to possess one. Some deputies called him "the iceman." I remember him as a reticent man. His steely eyes often made it difficult to discern his thinking. Looking back, I don't think I ever once saw him smile. He came up from Madison to fill the sheriff's position, the governor's appointment after the unfortunate death of our beloved Sheriff Fats. It was a death some still blamed on me. And though he was sent up to our county by the governor, rumor had it Zimmer's appointment came straight out of the Kickapoo Gun Club—a very private and very secretive organization in which Zimmer was said to be a proud member. Perhaps, it was whispered, even some kind of club officer.

Zimmer, too, was hiding behind sunglasses that end-of-summer day. Sometimes he wore them indoors. Claimed bright light bothered his eyes. Maybe it did, but it was an annoying habit. Other than that, at the time of the engineer's murder, I liked the man well enough. He wore the sheriff's uniform as proud as Fats had worn it. On Labor Day we had all switched to our winter grays. Long-sleeved, tapered shirts. Black slacks. Silver Stetsons. Our badges were pinned proudly to our chests. The emblem of the Kickapoo County Sheriff's Department was embroidered on our arms. Fats had kept us looking sharp. He hated the slovenly appearance of rural cops. J. D. Zimmer was continuing that tradition. I vowed, if elected, I too would see that our policy of neat uniforms continued.

Zimmer spoke without glancing my way, focusing his dark glasses instead on the dead engineer dangling from the train. "When is that trip of yours to St. Paul?"

Seemed like a strange question, considering the circumstances. "Next month," I reminded him.

He nodded the victim's way. "Do you think you can wrap this up before then?"

With a homicide, Fats once told me, people want justice, and they want it fast. You want to wrap it up quick. Don't let it linger. For a hundred years, justice in Kickapoo County had been swift and harsh. Zimmer seemed to understand that.

"I can try."

"Frank was a hunter, wasn't he?"

"Yes," I told him, "Frank and Lisa were both hunters."

"Lisa hunts?"

"Yes."

I watched him chewing on a thought. "I know it's out of season, but do you think this might have been some kind of hunting accident?"

"If you were out hunting illegally, Sheriff, would you hunt in the hills above a crowded train station?"

"Kids playing with a rifle?"

"It would have to be one hell of a rifle . . . and one hell of a kid."

"And the shot came from those hills?"

"Yes, it had to."

"Let's get some Boy Scout troops up there. Comb every inch for clues."

"I'm on it, Sheriff."

I was about to turn and go, get back to work, when the sheriff stopped me with a pointed question. "Have you ever seen anything like this before, Deputy Pennington?"

I didn't answer the question, because the truth was, I had. The sheriff noticed my lack of a response. He looked directly at me for the first time. "You are the department's homicide investigator, are you not?"

Despite the upcoming election, we'd had an amicable relationship. Still, I didn't care for the way he'd put that. "Yes, Sheriff, I am."

"Well then, Deputy, it looks like you've got a homicide on your hands."

"Yes, it does. Somebody has to tell his wife. It should probably be me. I have to question her anyway."

"Yes, I understand you two are friends. You should be the one to tell her."

I didn't care for the way he phrased that, either. It would be the first homicide Zimmer and I had worked together. No sheriff likes a murder on his watch, and we were off to a bad start on this one.

The morning sun felt good on my face. We were on the autumn side of summer. Labor Day had come and gone. The tourists had gone back to Chicago, or Milwaukee, or Minneapolis, or wherever the hell it was they had come from. I'd been looking forward to some rest and relaxation before the heat of the election. But as I walked back to my squad, I overheard several snippets of conversation that told me there would be no vacation before November.

"Gonna be a terrible blow for Lisa."

"Lisa's a pretty thing. . . . She'll marry again."

But the remark that troubled me most was the observation our loudmouthed mayor made to the sheriff when he thought I was too far away to hear. "Good Lord, that's no hunting accident, Sheriff. One shot . . . from high in the hills . . . right between the eyes. There's only one man in Kickapoo County who can shoot like that."

Michael McGarrity

THE JUDAS JUDGE

A mass murder in New Mexico lures Deputy State
Police Chief Kevin Kerney into the dark past of
one of the high-profile victims—and dangerously
close to the diabolical killer.

"Highly suspenseful." —*Los Angeles Times*

"Taut and convincing. I read this in one sitting."
—*Chicago Tribune*

20360-7

To order call: 1-800-788-6262